Loving Miranda

TERESA BODWELL

ZEBRA BOOKS
Kensington Publishing Corp.
www.kensingtonbooks.com

ZEBRA BOOKS are published by

Kensington Publishing Corp.
850 Third Avenue
New York, NY 10022

All Kensington titles, imprints, and distributed lines are available at special quantity discounts for bulk purchases for sales promotion, premiums, fund-raising, educational, or institutional use.

Special book excerpts or customized printings can also be created to fit specific needs. For details, write or phone the office of the Kensington Special Sales Manager: Attn. Special Sales Department. Kensington Publishing Corp., 850 Third Avenue, New York, NY 10022. Phone: 1-800-221-2647.

Zebra and the Z logo Reg. U.S. Pat. & TM Off.

ISBN 0-8217-7816-1

First Printing: October 2005
10 9 8 7 6 5 4 3 2 1

Printed in the United States of America

To my father, Leonard Bodwell, who passed away while I was writing this book. Dad was a true gentleman who taught me by example that loving means giving—time, an ear, a smile and a ready hug.

Of many memories that I hold dear, this one perhaps describes him best: In the ICU shortly after his heart surgery, while still on the respirator, he squeezed my hand and mouthed the words, "I love you." He wouldn't rest until he was certain I understood his message.

I know you love me, Dad. I love you too.

Chapter 1

"Three dollars?" Benjamin Lansing laughed. Not for three months' work. Never. "I'm sorry, ma'am. I won't take less than twenty-five." He'd settle for ten, but he wasn't desperate enough to accept three.

Mrs. Wick frowned. "I'd like to help you, Mr. Lansing." She brushed her gloved hands over her gray woolen skirts and leaned forward to heave herself out of the chair.

Damn. He'd offended her. "Since we've been traveling companions, I'll let you have the painting for twenty dollars." Ben had been told his smile could be disarming and he tried for that effect now.

Mrs. Wick returned his smile and settled back into her chair. She studied the canvas he'd spread over the table. The last of his landscapes and a fair imitation of a bright autumn day. She twisted her lips as she contemplated. Before Ben could stop her, she folded the top canvas out of the way and scowled at one of his wartime works.

"That one is not for sale." Ben pulled the two battle

scenes off the table and smoothed the landscape back. "New England in the fall—have you ever been there? The colors are striking."

"It is lovely." Mrs. Wick sighed. "I should think this would brighten my parlor."

"Most certainly." Ben concentrated on breathing slowly, in and out, forcing himself to appear patient. Appearances were one thing that he could control.

He glanced around the busy hotel dining room. As he had found in much of the West, the room was overdecorated. On top of gaudy striped wallpaper hung several immense gilded mirrors and a half-dozen vivid paintings of women carrying baskets of food. His eyes settled on the pretty blonde at the next table. It seemed to him that she was overly intent on watching her spoon dip into her soup bowl. Ben suspected she'd been observing every-thing that transpired between the moody Mrs. Wick and him. Perhaps the young lady was a painter. Or a painter's model.

She was dressed for riding and dusty from the trail, yet she was lovely. Petite and delicate as a porcelain doll. A ribbon tied at the base of her neck barely contained her wild curls. Her slight, feminine body made a perfect match to her dainty features. Ben's left hand twitched with the wild desire to paint her image. He shoved the useless appendage into his pocket and traced his thumb over the stubs of missing fingers his gloves hid so well. His mangled hand made painting this vision impossible.

"I'll give you fifteen dollars and not a penny more." Mrs. Wick's words called his attention back to her.

"You drive a hard bargain, ma'am." Fifteen dollars

was half what the painting was worth, but more than he needed to take him to Fort Victory.

Mrs. Wick gave him a triumphant smirk before digging into her bag for the coins to pay him. "Well, then." She handed Ben the money and stood to leave. "I shall give you a word of advice, young man. Don't imagine anyone would want to have"—she gestured toward his remaining paintings—"death spread across the wall of their parlor." She stood and tilted her nose upward as though his painting had insulted her. "If you want to sell more pictures, I'd suggest you do some flowers. Something pretty that a *lady* would want hangin' in her home."

Benjamin ground his teeth to keep from shouting. "Thank you for your suggestions, Mrs. Wick."

He stood and gave the white-haired lady a stiff nod as she gathered her things and stepped away. Shoving the hard-won coins into his pocket, he turned back to the table and spread his remaining paintings out over the smooth surface.

During the three days of their stagecoach trip Mrs. Wick had talked endlessly about her interest in "fine art." Turned out the woman only wanted pretty colors to complement her furniture. Perhaps she should talk to the man who had purchased the dreadful pictures for this hotel. They obviously had similar taste.

War might not be suitable decoration for a family parlor, but he'd never come closer to creating art than he had with these two scenes from the war. He'd have plenty of money now if his damn foolish pride hadn't kept him from selling the two battle scenes in Boston when he had the chance.

If circumstances forced him to sell them here on the frontier, he'd never get a decent price. No point in worrying about that. If he had any luck at all in Fort Victory, selling these paintings would prove unnecessary.

A pair of small, fair hands rested on the table next to the painting. "May I look?"

Benjamin shrugged and the woman drew closer, touching one corner of the painting. Even without looking at her face, he knew the light voice and graceful fingers belonged to the petite blonde. She leaned in front of him—so close he could smell an intriguing blend of sweet lavender and musky horse. He kept his head down, his gaze fixed on the paintings. He did not need to have another pretty face distract him. His mission was clear, and it didn't include time for dalliances along the way.

"That Mrs. Wick don't know art. This is fine—alive almost." The young woman lifted the top canvas and peered at the painting below. "I think they're both wonderful."

He lifted his head, meaning only to glance, but her eyes captured his. It was the color of the large, round orbs that drew him first—an astonishing cornflower blue. The rich color made a stunning contrast to her skin—pink and cream with freckles sprinkled over her nose and across her cheeks. She was smiling, showing a set of flawless white teeth framed by generous rosy lips. Perfect.

"Your paintings, I mean." She drew her lower lip into her mouth and released it. "They're amazin'."

He forced his eyes from her lips and saw it—a thick scar traced a jagged path from her right ear nearly to her chin. He dropped his gaze back to her hands for fear he'd show some expression of pity in his eyes. It had to be difficult for a beautiful woman to live with that imperfection, and he wouldn't make it worse for her.

"Thank you." Ben had seen enough truly great art in Europe to know that his work wasn't brilliant. Although, he had to admit, it was significantly better than the pictures on the walls around them. "I can't . . . I'm not planning to sell these." Ben spread the canvases over a large leather sheet and made an awkward roll with the leather on the outside to protect the canvases. He pulled a sturdy bit of ribbon around either end of the roll and fumbled as he attempted to tie a knot with what remained of his left hand.

"Damnation," he mumbled. The ribbon slipped from his gloved fingers and he bit back another curse as he picked the ribbon up again. His right boot tapped out an agitated beat while he stared at the loose ends of the ribbons.

The young lady clicked her tongue and mumbled something about careless men as she pushed in front of him to reach for the package. She spread it open, then deftly rerolled and tied the bundle, leaving a tight, compact roll sitting on the table.

"Thank you for your assistance," he said. "I could have tied it myself." He hated the bitterness in his voice.

"You might try taking your gloves off next time." She grinned at him, the bright twinkle in her eyes showing more than her words that she thought him silly for wearing leather gloves in a warm dining room.

He bit his tongue. The gloves served their purpose and he wasn't about to explain it to this girl. Instead, his eyes wandered back to her hands caressing the leather bundle. She traced the length of the roll with one straight, perfect index finger. "I meant what I said. I ain't seen nothin' like your pictures."

"You paint?"

"Me?" She smiled up at him for the briefest moment, then dropped her eyes back to the table. "I draw . . . a little. But I don't have your talent."

"It isn't a matter of talent so much . . . art takes a good deal of work."

She raised her chin. "I know how to work!"

"I only meant that it's not a simple matter of picking up a brush and . . ."

"You don't have to explain, Mister . . ." She glanced over her shoulder toward the door. "I should be goin'."

"It's Lansing. Benjamin Lansing." He made a small bow.

"Lansing?" Ridges formed over her forehead as she studied him.

"And your name . . . ?"

"Miranda Chase." She seemed ready to offer him a hand, then hesitated. Looping her thumb over her gun belt, she cleared her throat.

Ben searched for something else to say to keep her talking for a few more minutes. Why the hell he wanted to waste time discussing art with a frontier woman, he couldn't explain. Merely because she had better taste than old Mrs. Wick didn't mean she understood the first thing about painting. Her tongue swiped over her lips.

A pink glow settled on her cheeks, and she turned her head so that the scar faced away from him. "I just wanted you to know I think these pictures are special."

He laughed at the girl's earnest efforts to convince him of the value of his work.

"No need to laugh at me, Mr. Lansing." She placed her hands on her hips. Though she brushed past the revolver that hung at her side, he could see she meant no threat to him. "I don't have much schoolin', but anyone lookin' at these pictures can see they're special. Even old Mrs. Wick should have noticed. The horses are so close to being alive I thought I could hear them blowin' and snortin'. They're terrified; you can feel it. I reckon that's what makes the difference between real art and a pretty picture."

"You flatter me, Miss." Ben took a step closer and she stepped back away from him like a skittish colt avoiding the bridle. All sense of caution left him. "If you're staying here, perhaps you would join me for supper later and we could continue our discussion." Ben took half a step toward her.

She shook her head but didn't back away from him this time. "I . . . have to go." She spun on her heels and pranced away, her split skirt swishing over her boots. Benjamin stared at the empty door frame for a few moments, until a dusty cowboy filled it.

"What you grinning at, Mister?" the cowboy growled.

"Not a thing." Ben matched the stranger's tone. Surely the fellow was mistaken. Ben was not one to smile without reason.

He hadn't meant to laugh at the girl. *Miranda.* A beautiful name for a young, spirited beauty. She had a good instinct for art, too. A fascinating trait in this wild country. It would be a pleasure to talk to her at length and discover where she had acquired her education.

He scowled. Only a fool lies to himself. It was not the girl's interest in art that had caught his attention, it was the life he saw in those eyes. And the way she'd stood up for herself against him.

Ben puffed out a breath of exasperation. He had

business to attend to, and that girl likely had some cows to chase. He gathered his belongings. If he could reach Fort Victory and find the money his brother owed him, he wouldn't have to sell his paintings.

His first order of business was to find a stagecoach headed to Fort Victory. Once there, he'd collect the money his brother owed him. He'd also have an opportunity to meet his nephew's guardians and assure himself that they were taking proper care of the boy.

No need for him to delay the journey. Denver seemed to hold nothing but trouble for him, including pretty, blue-eyed distractions. He caught his image in the mirror—grinning. *Hell!* Ben's plans did not include innocent blondes. Young women like her wanted husbands and families. His future was in a tropical paradise with long, sunny days spent forgetting everything he'd lost. When the need arose, he'd find willing island women, preferably several of them.

He would never allow himself to depend on the love of one woman.

Chapter 2

Miranda Chase eased her horse, Princess, to a slow walk. She glanced over her shoulder knowing he wasn't behind her. She'd traveled sixty miles since leaving Denver the day before yesterday—the last five alone except for the shadow of Lansing behind her. She knew he was only there in her mind. Why she couldn't forget the pompous city slicker was beyond her.

The last thing she needed was another Lansing in her life. Though surely the man was no relation to Arthur Lansing. A chill shot down her spine at the thought of her former neighbor—the man who had tried to kill her sister a year ago.

The two men could not be related. This Lansing had brown hair, touched with gold, and warm brown eyes. Arthur's eyes had been cold steel gray, and his hair black. She shifted in her saddle, knowing her thinking was flawed. Hell, her own sister was tall with perfectly straight hair and generous curves. Miranda was small, lean, and fair. Her hair was beyond the ability of any earthly being to control. It had a mind of its own and wouldn't surrender to a brush no matter what she tried. You couldn't always judge a family relationship by looking.

Still, it had to be a coincidence. Other than his young son, Arthur had no relations in Colorado Territory. Lansing's family was all back in Boston, so the chances of running into one of them in Denver had to be nil. Though, come to think of it, the man she'd spoken to clearly was not from Denver. Likely he was from somewhere in the East. She should have asked him if he had relatives in Fort Victory. If the man hadn't been so vexing, she might have thought to ask him instead of spending the past two days worrying about it. *Men!*

She rolled her shoulders, trying to relax her stiff back. What she really needed was a nice, hot bath. Once she saw for herself how Mercy was faring, she'd take time for a bath and a good night's sleep. Tomorrow, she'd get to work helping Pa and Mercy and get her mind off Mr. Benjamin Lansing.

It wasn't really the name that troubled her, it was her own foolishness. Why she'd even thought to talk to a fancy-dressed slicker was beyond her. The man's suit, a fine gray wool with a matching satin vest, likely cost more than she'd earned in months of working in Philadelphia. It was strange he'd had trouble making a knot; his black leather gloves looked to be as soft and pliable as a second skin. Could be wearing gloves indoors was fashionable where Lansing was from. Or maybe he was too damn foolish to figure out he should take off the gloves. More likely he was used to having other people do things for him. If that was the case, she was sorry she'd helped him.

If it was a devotion to style, it was a strange one. In all the time she'd been in the city, she hadn't seen a fashionable gentleman with such long hair, nearly down to his shoulders. His face was clean-shaven, except for a thick line of whiskers coming down in front of each ear and tapering to a fine point that seemed to emphasize his strong, masculine jaw. Whether in Denver, Abilene or Philadelphia, Lansing would stand out in a crowd.

She was sixty miles away from him and his appearance was still on her mind. The truth was, it was his paintings that made her curious, but it was his face that had drawn her to him.

And that was the foolish part. A handsome face meant wandering eyes and sure heartbreak, or worse. After what she'd been through, Miranda should have sense enough to run the other way when she spied a fine-looking man.

That arrogant gentleman was no temptation. His image pushed its way back into her mind—tall with a jacket tailored to emphasize his broad shoulders and trim waist, an angular face, and eyes as warm as good, strong coffee. She laughed at herself. Hell, that man could entice her, no doubt. At least she knew it was a temptation that would never find her in Fort Victory.

She stared up at the mountains, a grander and safer sight than the one she'd been contemplating. Nearly home.

Her throat tightened. It wasn't right to think of Fort Victory as home any longer. She didn't belong here. She'd refused to come running home when she needed help, instead choosing to make her life elsewhere. And she would have stayed away, too, if her sister hadn't written. She patted the pocket of her leather split skirt, feeling her sister's letter folded inside. Mercy had never admitted to needing

Miranda's help before. This was Miranda's chance to prove herself to her older sister and Pa too.

Riding in the shadows of the familiar mountains felt comfortable no matter how hard Miranda tried to convince herself that she didn't belong. She'd missed this place. The rugged peaks above her wore their autumn skirts of orange, red and gold as the cottonwoods that covered their lower slopes displayed their fall splendor. Those same peaks also loomed over the Bar Double C ranch, where her sister and father waited. It would be wonderful to find her way once again into the shelter of their home and their arms. But those feelings belonged to the little freckle-faced girl who had always been dependent on her family. The freckles remained, especially after a month of riding under the sun, but the little girl was gone. Miranda was a grown woman who could take care of herself and had for the past year.

She reined her bay mare to a stop at the crest of the hill overlooking Fort Victory. The town bustled under the noontime sun. The settlement had started as a military outpost several years ago, but it had grown considerably since she'd first laid eyes on the place. Between the miners and the ranchers, the military garrison was the smallest part of what folks around these parts thought of as Fort Victory.

She leaned forward and stroked her horse's long, graceful neck, feeling powerful muscles through the buckskin gloves that protected her hands from sun and wind. Straightening, she inhaled cool autumn air. Fort Victory was growing, but she had no trouble picking out Wyatt's Dry Goods Store in the center of town, a few doors down from Rita's saloon. A short respite in town would be nice, but it would take less than two hours to reach the ranch if she pressed on.

She turned Princess toward the ranch, feeling as though a snake were slithering through her stomach. She glanced back at Wyatt's store and made her decision. With a squeeze of her heels and click of her tongue, she urged Princess to trot into town. The small detour would set her mind at ease and make her reunion with Pa and Mercy a bit easier.

The problem with traveling cross-country with a group of strangers was there was too much time to think, to mentally rehearse every possible thing that could go wrong.

"You're a coward, Miranda," she mumbled, shaking her head. All those folks who said she was brave to head West on her own were wrong. Traveling to Colorado from Philadelphia didn't take real courage. She could think of worse fates than dying while trying to help her family. Not that she had any intention of dying, but she was no longer afraid of death. It was the bad choices she'd made that had her wanting to join a prairie dog colony so she could live in a nice, safe hole in the ground.

She lifted her chin. Miranda wasn't about to scurry into any underground den, but she did need to learn some caution—especially when it came to men. Spending time with Mercy and Pa would help. They were always urging her to slow down and be more careful. She'd have time to learn to control her impulses while she took care of Mercy.

The only men living on the ranch probably still thought of her as a child. Even if they didn't, having Pa close by would ensure that the men stayed away from her. It would be almost as safe as that prairie dog colony, after all.

As she secured Princess to the post in front of the store, Miranda braced herself. Clarisse Wyatt was her sister's best friend. She would know how Mercy and Pa were faring. Clarisse also would be curious about Miranda's time away. Hell, Clarisse was nearly as protective of Miranda as Mercy herself. Miranda realized she was chewing on her lower lip and released it. It was going to be damned difficult to keep her secret from Mercy. Another good reason to visit with Clarisse first—Miranda could practice her story before she tried it on her sister.

She shoved her hat back so it dropped behind her, held in place by a leather thong tied around her neck. Her hand smoothed over her hair. *As though that's gonna make a difference.* She avoided her reflection in the glass of the storefront windows, knowing she was dusty and dirty and her hair had no doubt escaped the ribbon she'd used to tie it in place this morning. Cheerful bells sounded as she shoved through the front door of the shop.

"Miranda!" Clarisse set down the tin she'd been arranging on the shelf and had Miranda wrapped in her arms before the younger woman could utter a sound.

Clarisse stepped back, looking Miranda in the eye. "We've been waiting so long for your return."

Her azure eyes scanned back and forth as though taking inventory. Miranda knew the exact moment when Clarisse noticed the scar. She made no dramatic gesture, but her eyes skipped over the spot, then returned for confirmation. She didn't look away as so many people did—as Lansing had yesterday.

Miranda braced herself for the question. She'd rehearsed her answer so well she almost believed the "accident" she'd invented had actually occurred. Lord help her.

People always shook their heads and mumbled things like, "Such a pretty face. What a pity." But it wasn't.

The scar was a blessing so long as it kept men away from her. Her mind flitted again to the artist in Denver. He'd turned away when he noticed the scar. That was fine with her. His kind was the worst— handsome, well dressed, with a smile that could charm a grizzly away from the berry bush. In fact, the female bears would no doubt fight each other for the privilege of feeding those berries to him.

Well, Miranda wasn't going to enter the fight. She was never again going to devote her life to pleasing a man. Nor would she live in fear of the punishment that came when she couldn't please him. Her sister had tried to warn her not to give her heart away, but Miranda hadn't listened.

Maybe keeping clear of men was one of those lessons that had to be learned from experience. Even Mercy hadn't followed her own advice. She'd bound herself to another man after swearing she'd avoid the rascals. Thad Buchanan was exactly the sort Miranda shied away from now. Big, strong, fine-looking men who acted the gentleman so long as they had something to gain from a woman. Once they had her, it was a different story altogether.

Aw, Hell! There were a few true gentlemen in the world. For her sister's sake, Miranda prayed Thad was one of those rare critters. In spite of her hard-earned lessons, Miranda even dared to dream that one day she'd find such a man for herself. Maybe it was foolish, but she refused to give up hoping.

The older woman made no comment about the

scar. She took Miranda's hand, pulling her farther into the shop. "Mercy and Thad must be so happy to have you home."

Miranda opened her mouth to say she was only here to help her sister. She'd stay as long as she was needed, then move on, maybe to San Francisco or New York City. Some busy place where she could fend for herself. Not that she didn't love her family. She did. She missed Pa and her sister, but she couldn't live with them fussing over her all the time. They wouldn't understand why she was determined to be on her own. And if she explained it to them, they'd feel more determined to protect her. Pa was getting on in years, and Mercy had her own family to worry about now. Miranda would take care of herself.

Still, she couldn't refuse help to the sister who had practically raised her. Mercy had sacrificed a great deal for her, and this was Miranda's chance to make a small payment toward that large debt.

"I haven't been . . ." The word *home* stuck in her throat. "Haven't been to Mercy's ranch yet. Thought I'd stop here in case there was mail, or anything to go out." *Tell the truth, Miranda—just ask after them.*

"They picked up the mail yesterday when they came into town for church." Clarisse favored Miranda with a grin. "Now that your sister is married to my brother, we're kin. I'm not sure what the sister of my sister-in-law is to me, but I'm partial to the idea of having another sister." She paused for breath. "Will you have some tea before you press on?"

Miranda nodded. She wanted to hear all the news before she saw Mercy. Her pa and Thad had both written about how ill Mercy had been. Though her sister was the strongest woman Miranda had ever met, she knew darn well it would be hard on Mercy if she lost the baby she was carrying.

The bell rang as a customer entered the shop. "Robert will help you, Mr. Sampson," Clarisse called as she led Miranda to the family living quarters behind the store.

Robert, the oldest Wyatt boy, was bent over the large kitchen table copying something out of a book.

"Look who's here," Clarisse said. "Your Aunt Miranda."

Apparently, Clarisse had settled the matter of their kinship to her own satisfaction. Robert smiled and greeted Miranda.

"You go on out and mind the store while we visit, will you?"

"Yes, ma'am." Robert ducked his head and disappeared into the store, obviously glad to leave his bookwork.

The flat, wooden surface of the chair felt strange after so many days in the saddle. Miranda ran her hand over the smooth pine table. Her pa had made this table and chairs in the shop next to their barn. After years of farming and ranching, he was becoming a fine furniture maker. As Clarisse placed the kettle on the large stove that dominated the kitchen, Miranda wondered whether she would need to ask, or whether Clarisse would volunteer the information she needed.

Clarisse opened the stove and added more wood. Miranda told herself to be patient, but she found it impossible.

"How are Pa and Mercy doin'?" Miranda blurted out the question that had brought her into town.

"I'm sorry, didn't I say?" Clarisse wiped her hands

on her apron and turned to look at Miranda. "I don't know what I was thinkin'. Here I am fussin' over tea when what you're really wantin' is some news!"

Miranda was ready to scream for Clarisse to tell her.

Clarisse smiled. "They're fine. The whole family. No need to worry about your pa. Fenton hasn't had a spell in I don't know how long." Clarisse cleared Robert's books away from the table. "Mercy is . . . well, you know her. Nothing seems to slow her down, although for a few weeks she survived on bread and chicken broth."

"Thad and Pa both wrote me saying how sick she was."

"Your pa knew right off she wasn't sick; he tried to tell your sister that her mama was the same way when she was in a family way. Even so, Mercy was afraid to believe it was a baby for a good long while."

"She was certain she'd never be able to have a child."

"Seems to me good things often happen to us when we least expect 'em."

Seemed to Miranda the same was true of horrible things, but she didn't say so.

"Of course, Thad fusses over Mercy somethin' terrible," Clarisse said. "Men are so protective."

Protective? That didn't seem to describe most men in Miranda's experience. She thought again of the artist in Denver—the way his eyes had burned with interest one moment, then turned away from her when he saw the scar. That was not a man who wanted to protect her. Like most men, he'd been thinking about taking from her, not doing anything for her.

"Haven't seen Mercy so happy in years. You won't

recognize her." Clarisse brought two cups and saucers to the table.

Miranda did a mental calculation. "I thought the baby wasn't coming until winter, January or February?"

"I don't mean that she looks so different. I think it's finally being a mama—has her glowing with happiness."

"I know it means a great deal to her." Miranda's heart squeezed tight as she recalled her own mixture of joy and fear when she had realized she was carrying a child. Of course, Mercy was a married woman, so it was different for her. "She's wanted a baby for so long."

"Yes, you're right. Though I don't think it's the baby coming, it's bein' a mama to Jonathan. If he were the only child Mercy ever had, she'd be happy." Clarisse pulled the teapot from the buffet that displayed her china. The pretty pink rose pattern was one of the small touches of civilization Clarisse had imported to Fort Victory as the Wyatts' business became successful. "Still, having a five-year-old boy to care for when you're newly married, well. . . ." Clarisse poured some hot water to warm the pot. "As difficult as it's been for them, Mercy and Thad have been good for Jonathan. He's lucky to have them."

"It's certain, then? They are keeping him?"

"They've heard nothing from his family in Boston. As far as anyone in Fort Victory is concerned, the boy is their son. Mercy and Thad want to do things right and proper. They've applied to Judge Jensen for a legal adoption. He's supposed to sign the papers when he's in town next week. I've invited everyone here for a celebration afterward."

Mercy's joy over finally becoming a mother was

clear from her letters. After what Arthur Lansing had put Mercy through, some women would find it difficult to show compassion to his son. Miranda wasn't surprised, though; she knew her sister.

"Lansing loved his boy, but he didn't have any idea how to be a father." Clarisse set spoons and napkins on the table. "Thad is teaching the boy a world of things he never knew about."

Miranda touched the rim of the delicate china cup, wondering again about Thad Buchanan. There were good men in the world—her own father was proof enough of that. But she knew now that men like Pa were rare. Most men cared only about themselves.

A great cry from the corner of the kitchen startled Miranda.

"Sorry . . . little Hal never gives any warning, he cries out at full volume."

Miranda hadn't noticed the cradle set where the sun beaming through the window would warm it. She blinked back a tear as she watched Clarisse lift the baby, soothing him with gentle cooing noises. She swallowed the lump in her throat as she reminded herself she had better get used to being around babies if she was going to be of any use to her sister.

"Another boy?"

Clarisse smiled at the tiny bundle in her arms. "I seem to be blessed with a houseful of males. You see why I'm grateful Mercy married my brother: now I have two sisters. Thad has told me he hopes their baby will be a girl. We've enough boys in the family already."

"What does Jonathan think about the new baby comin'?"

"He can't wait to teach his brother to fish and play

marbles. Oh, you ask him—there's a long list. And don't try to tell him the baby might be a girl!"

Miranda took a sip of tea. "I suppose he'll be disappointed when the tiny infant is born."

"My brother has told him that their baby will be small and helpless like our Hal, but Jonathan still believes his baby will be different. Precocious you might say."

"A baby playing marbles would be quite a sight."

Clarisse laughed. "Yes—or puttin' some bait on a fishin' line." She looked down at the infant in her arms. "He'll feel differently when he sees her, or him. I remember how my Robert reacted to being a brother. At first he was disappointed that Tom couldn't play with him, but it wasn't long before he wanted to hold him. He was fascinated with everything from feeding to changing." Clarisse let out a long sigh. "Our family has been truly blessed. And now havin' you back home will make everything even better. I know Mercy will be glad of your help. And I'll be glad to have another woman close. Females are scarce around these parts, and we need each other to help make the town a little more civilized."

Miranda sipped her tea. She liked Clarisse, but she didn't want to make any promises about staying here.

"Good experience for you, too—helpin' your sister with Jonathan and the baby. I reckon you'll be a wife and mama before too long."

Miranda focused on the leaves settling at the bottom of her cup. She'd heard of people with a gift for reading the future in tea leaves—though perhaps knowing what was to come wasn't always a gift. "They're happy together, then." Once the words slipped out she couldn't take them back. She lifted her eyes to Clarisse's face, trying to judge her response.

"Your sister and Thad?" Clarisse rubbed her hand over the golden fuzz on Hal's head, but her eyes were focused in the distance. "If ever two people were meant to be together, it is Mercy and Thad. Of course, I'm a mite biased since I love them both dearly. I'm so grateful they found each other."

Hal turned to face Miranda, milk dribbling from his lips as he cooed at her. "Oh, you." Clarisse lifted him to her shoulder, covering her exposed breast. "I thought you were hungry." She chuckled. "Sorry, he's easily distracted these days." She rubbed his back, then settled him on her lap as she fastened the buttons on her shirt. "Here I've been going on and on. You must tell me how you've been. What was it like living in Philadelphia? After all my years in the West, I can't imagine being in a large Eastern city again—"

"Mama." Robert burst into the room, saving Miranda from answering the questions she wanted so desperately to avoid.

"Excuse yourself, son. You are interrupting."

"I'm sorry, Mama." He appeared to have trouble catching his breath. "I mean, excuse me, Mama, Aunt Miranda." He made a little bow to each of them. "There's a gentleman who wishes to speak to you, Mama. He says his name is Lansing."

"Lansing?" Clarisse hissed.

"Yes, Mama."

Miranda's stomach plummeted to her ankles.

Clarisse glanced at Miranda, then back to Robert. "What . . . What does he want?"

"He has some questions about Aunt Mercy and Uncle Thad."

Clarisse stood, moving as though she were swimming through molasses. "Oh dear."

She held the baby out to Miranda, who pulled the infant tight against her chest as his mother walked out to the store.

"Hello baby . . . Hal." Miranda patted the small bottom as he squirmed and tried to reach for his mother. "You don't suppose this Lansing could be the same one . . . ?" She tiptoed close to the door, trying to hear the conversation in the shop.

Although Clarisse had said he never gave a warning, Hal was making little noises that sounded like he was getting ready for a loud cry. She walked across the kitchen to the window, knelt, set the infant in his cradle, and rocked. "Shh, shh, baby. You don't want to worry your mama now, do you?"

Miranda turned toward the door, wishing she could hear what was going on. It had to be the Lansing she'd met in Denver. *Damn.* She should have asked him a few questions. Found out why he was coming.

Hal turned bright red and let out a yell far larger than his tiny body ought to be able to produce. She snatched him back up and renewed her patting.

"Fine, fine. You wanna be held." She walked around in a little circle, continuing to rub and pat the infant's back. "You'll be thinkin' I've never held a baby. Truth is, I love babies." She pulled him closer, rocking him in her arms as she paced the room.

She frowned. Benjamin Lansing had better not intend to take Jonathan away from Mercy—not months after she'd taken the boy into her home, treating him like her own son. It wasn't fair. Miranda wouldn't allow it.

She looked at the baby in her arms. "He wouldn't be doing that, would he?"

She brushed her nose against Hal's soft, warm cheek and inhaled his sweet baby smell. It had been years since she'd held a baby in her arms. She'd forgotten the wonder of them. "Fine time you picked to remind me of what I'm missing." She sighed.

"I reckon it is time, though, isn't it?" The fist that seemed to be squeezing her heart loosened a little. "I'm gonna help my sister with her baby, and maybe one day . . . Do you suppose I'll find someone like my pa—a good, honest, gentle man who will love me and . . . ?"

And maybe she would have a family of her own. She wasn't ready to make that wish out loud.

Chapter 3

Benjamin Lansing eyed the diverse goods displayed around the cramped mercantile. No doubt the shop had been arranged to be convenient to the proprietor, rather than be aesthetically pleasing to visitors. The result was dizzying.

His eyes rested on the bolts of fabric displayed against one wall. Unlike the rest of the shop, someone had taken care with this arrangement. The simple ginghams and calicoes were displayed by color—dark browns, blues and greens at one end; vivid yellows, pinks, and reds at the other. A small selection of white muslin, silk and lace separated the colored fabric from shelves covered with threads and yarns. After weeks of traveling across the plains, with endless stretches of drab browns and grays, the bright hues were a feast for his eyes.

"Mr. Lansing?"

He turned to face a petite woman with a pretty, heart-shaped face and bright azure eyes.

"Can I help you, sir?" Her voice was polite and calm, with the genteel inflection of the southern regions of the country. But her eyes made it clear that he had better state his business.

"I hope you can, ma'am." He made a polite bow, knowing a southern gentlewoman expected courtesy from a proper gentleman even beyond what the ladies of Boston demanded. "I'm Benjamin Lansing— Arthur Lansing was my brother."

The lady covered a quick spark of surprise with her air of formality. "I'm Mrs. Wyatt. Pleased to make your acquaintance, Mr. Lansing." She gave him a nod and a stiff smile that betrayed her complete lack of pleasure at meeting him. "Now, how can I be of service?"

Ben was astonished that the lady made no expression of condolence for his brother's death, but decided the oversight was attributable to her surprise at seeing him and was not intended to offend.

"I understand my brother left both his ranch and son under the care of Mr. and Mrs. Thaddeus Buchanan. I wonder if you're acquainted with the Buchanans."

Her eyes dropped to his dusty boots and made their way slowly back to his face. "Yes." She locked the fingers of her hands together, as one might do in prayer. "My brother and sister-in-law as it happens."

He wondered why she had hesitated to reveal her relation to the Buchanans. "How fortunate for me." He broadened his smile, hoping to set the lady at ease. "Then you'll be able to tell me how my nephew is faring?"

"He's thriving." This time her smile was genuine. "Mercy and Thad have taken very good care of Jonathan." The smile faded. "And he's grown to love them as they love him." She raised her chin almost as though she dared him to argue.

In fact, he couldn't be more pleased. The last thing he wanted was responsibility for a young child. But the boy was his own blood, and Ben would make certain the lad was in a suitable home before he got the hell away from this dismal settlement. All he wanted to take with him was the money he'd loaned Arthur. He wouldn't even demand the interest. The Buchanans could use that for the boy's care. The original $5,000 would be enough for him to settle down to a simple life in Mexico or one of the Pacific Islands. Some place far from Boston, where he could live out his days in quiet solitude. He almost laughed at that thought. He hadn't yet celebrated his twenty-eighth birthday, and here he was planning his last days like an old man.

A familiar young woman entered from the back carrying a fussing baby. Ben first wondered how the hell the pretty little art critic had followed him to Fort Victory. Then he realized she must have arrived before him.

"I'm sorry," Miranda said before she froze, staring at Ben while the baby continued to cry. She turned to Mrs. Wyatt. "I can't get him to settle down."

The shopkeeper took the baby, who calmed immediately and hungrily latched onto the fabric of her shirt. Ben looked away. For a moment, he had thought the infant belonged to Miranda. Silly. She would not have been in Denver if she were mother to a young infant in Fort Victory. Clearly, the older woman had to be the child's mother. Not that it mattered to Ben in any case.

"Excuse me, Mr. Lansing. My little one wants feeding." She rocked the baby. "Miranda, this is Mr. Benjamin Lansing. Mr. Lansing, Miranda Chase, Mercy

Buchanan's sister." Mrs. Wyatt glanced from Ben to Miranda.

His business would be concluded quickly if the Buchanans were next to come out of the back. But that was apparently too much to hope for.

"Would you mind giving Mr. Lansing some tea while I take care of Hal?"

Miranda nodded, her eyes fixed on Mrs. Wyatt.

"Mr. Lansing is Arthur Lansing's brother."

"Arthur Lansing?" Miranda turned to him, revealing the jagged scar she usually took trouble to hide.

He tried not to look, but he couldn't help studying the rough track of the scar along her jaw. He fixed on her eyes again. The blue color should have been cold, yet the vision reminded him of swimming in a warm spring. Perhaps it was the soft pink of her skin or the freckles the sun had scattered across her nose that made her eyes seem warm. Her tongue peeked out, calling attention to her full lips. He swallowed hard, hit by desire such as he had not experienced in some time.

Damn. This was a fine time for that appetite to rise from the dead. He intended to take care of business and get out. Hell, she was Mercy Buchanan's sister, reason enough to stay away, even if he were the type to violate an innocent. Her eyes narrowed on him and he had the unsettling feeling that she had read his thoughts. Perhaps she wasn't so innocent after all.

He pulled his mind back to the conversation as Mrs. Wyatt left the room. "Yes, Arthur was my brother."

"I . . ." She pushed a stray curl back from her face. "I was sorry about what happened to him."

"Thank you," he said, though her regrets seemed

insincere. Perhaps he was allowing his own anger at his brother to color his observations. Arthur had told him that he was a respected member of this community and Ben had no reason to believe that wasn't true.

"Ain't this a surprise. Here I thought you were just an art peddler." She sashayed ahead, leading him into a large kitchen.

His eyes were drawn to her swaying hips, but he caught himself and focused on the untamed curls bobbing up and down behind her head.

"It is a coincidence, isn't it?" Ben cleared his throat. "That we were both headed to Fort Victory, I mean. We might have ended up in the same stage-coach."

Miranda giggled. "I've had my fill of coaches. They toss a body around 'til you can't tell up from down. My saddle's a good bit more comfortable, I assure you."

"You rode from Denver? Alone?"

Miranda raised an eyebrow, then laughed again. "I ain't been to a fancy city school, but I ain't stupid either. I came from Kansas with a large company. We parted ways just a few miles outside Fort Victory."

"I certainly didn't mean to imply—"

"It's all right. I didn't take offense." The smile vanished. "You haven't come to take your nephew," her voice dropped nearly to a whisper, "have you?"

"I've come to assure myself the Buchanans are providing a good home for him."

She turned to face Lansing. "They are wonderful parents," she said a bit too loudly this time. She stood nearly a foot shorter than he was, chin raised, eyes fixed on his as though daring him to challenge her opinion. He nearly laughed out loud, but she crossed her arms over her chest and glared. "I know what I'm talkin' about. My mother died when I was just a bitty thing and my sister practically raised me."

He cleared his throat and managed to keep from smiling. Fact was he hoped she was right. "I'm certain your sister is taking good care of the boy, but he's my nephew and I'll need to see for myself."

"He's a damn sight better off now than he was—" She spun around and took the last two steps to the table. "Hell, I didn't mean . . . your brother was . . ." She placed a hand on the side of the teapot, perhaps testing the temperature. "Jonathan needs a mother."

"I'm not arguing with you, Miss Chase."

The deep, round pools of her eyes studied him for a moment before she broke into a smile. "Miranda." Her lids dropped, then opened wide again, lighting her face. "If my sister's gonna be mama to your nephew . . ." She shrugged.

"Yes, you're right. We should be less formal. Please call me Ben."

"Ben?" She tilted her head as if she needed to see him from a different angle. "You seem more like a Benjamin."

"How is a Benjamin different from a Ben?"

"Ben is simple, rugged. Benjamin seems more suited to a Boston man."

He laughed. In fact, his father had always called him Benjamin. He'd become Ben during his army days. "Perhaps you shouldn't jump to conclusions about a man based on one short meeting. I think Ben suits me better."

"I'm willing to try it and see how it suits."

"That's all I can ask."

Her eyes locked with his and he thought she'd make another comment. Instead, she walked to the buffet with that little bounce in her step that drew his eyes to her rounded hips. She selected a cup and saucer for him and stepped back to the table.

"Milk? Sugar?" she asked as she poured a cup of tea for him.

"A drop of milk, please," he said, wishing he could shed his coat and gloves. The kitchen was far warmer than the shop had been. He watched her hands as she finished the ritual of preparing his tea. They were small and graceful, perfectly suited to her.

Before his injury he hadn't been so interested in hands—he'd have spent more time observing other parts of a woman's body. And the lady before him did have much to admire about her. She wasn't wearing the bulky jacket and gun belt that had hidden much when he'd seen her in Denver. Her blue shirt complemented the color of her eyes. Even more important—it hugged the curves of her trim body.

He lifted his gaze to her face as he took a sip of tea. One corner of her lips curled up, and he knew she'd caught him admiring her. Ben returned her smile. "Tell me about your sister and her husband."

She stirred her tea, then set the spoon on her saucer. "Likely you know Arthur was our neighbor." She lifted her eyebrows, waiting for confirmation. Ben nodded. "Mercy was there helping the day Jonathan was born. The boy's mama died that day, and Mercy's been looking after him ever since." She ran a finger over the rim of her cup, then looked into Ben's eyes. "Mercy is as close to a mother as Jonathan has ever known."

Better and better. "Sounds like the boy is lucky she was around."

"Damn right he is."

Ben couldn't help grinning at Miranda's defense of her sister. He wondered whether she threw herself with as much enthusiasm into everything she did. A kiss, for example, might be very pleasant with her energy.

Dammit, Ben! She was a girl, perhaps seventeen or eighteen years old. He refrained from asking her age because it didn't matter. He was leaving Fort Victory as soon as possible and he wasn't going to dally with this child.

Pulling his mind away from Miranda, he leaned against the ladder-back chair and looked around the pleasant kitchen. The furnishings were comfortable and simple, made of pine and polished to a fine sheen. He thought it was likely they were locally made, although the workmanship was of high quality. The glass-paned windows were adorned by lace-edged gingham curtains, tied back to allow ample sunlight into the room. Though he was no expert, the large cook stove, which was so efficiently heating the kitchen, seemed very modern. And, he noted, the china was as beautiful as any he'd seen in the finer homes of Boston. The tidy room could hardly have been more different from the shabby storefronts of Fort Victory's unpaved main street.

"It's warm in here." Miranda added hot tea to the remains in her cup. "I'll take your coat and gloves if you like."

"I'm comfortable," he lied, lifting his cup with his right hand as he rested his left on his lap. He wasn't ready to shed the doeskin gloves, which hid his disfigured hand by the simple expedient of cotton stuffed into the empty fingers. Miranda had seen him fumbling with the ribbons in Denver. She'd probably guessed that his hand was crippled, but she didn't have to know the extent of the deformity. All that remained of his left hand was his thumb, a crooked forefinger and three stubs where fingers had been removed. He could have lifted the teacup with his left hand, but he had little strength in the damaged hand and couldn't trust it to hold his cup steady. Pride wouldn't allow him to show Miranda his weakness.

Enough, Lansing. Forget the girl and get the information you came for.

"Mrs. Buchanan's letters indicated that she plans to adopt my nephew."

Her forehead wrinkled in thought for a moment. "I'm not used to calling her Buchanan. She only recently remarried."

"Recently?" He set his cup gently into the saucer. "I was under the impression that the Buchanans were already married a year ago when they took in Jonathan. Did you say remarried?"

"Yes." Miranda set her cup down, and he noticed her hands were trembling before she placed them on her lap, under the table. "Her first husband passed away, three years ago now. She married Thad last fall, shortly after your brother . . . died." She glanced at Ben, then looked away toward the window.

"We weren't close." Ben set his cup down in the saucer. "Arthur and I. He was years older than me. I never had a chance to know him."

Miranda chewed on her lip and stared into her cup. Ben had hoped to set her at ease, but she still seemed uncomfortable.

"Mrs. Wyatt tells me the boy is happy with the Buchanans. Is that your observation as well?"

"Yes." She glanced up at him, then back to her cup,

running her finger back and forth over the rim of the cup. "At least, Mercy's letters say so. I ain't been to see them yet. Just got back to town—from Philadelphia." A quick, nervous smile revealed her white teeth, then quickly dissolved. "Reckon I missed all the excitement."

"The wedding?"

"Yes . . . the wedding."

They sipped in silence. Miranda's eyes remained on the table as she rubbed her finger back and forth over the smooth surface.

"Mercy always wanted a child," she said. "She wasn't able to . . . She didn't have babies with Nate. Of course, now she does have a baby comin', but . . ." Miranda blushed a lovely rose color. "I'm sorry, I shouldn't be talkin' about such things. I only want you to know she does love him. Jonathan. The new baby won't make a difference."

Ben suppressed a grin. Damn, she was cute when she was flustered. So brave and determined to convince him, even though she hadn't a clue what to say to impress him. "As I said, I'd like to see the boy and judge for myself."

"I could take you out to the Bar Double C." She beamed a radiant smile that lit up her eyes like sunshine reflecting off a mirror. "I'm goin' there directly from here."

He was lost in her eyes for several heartbeats before her words worked their way into his mind. "Bar Double C? That's not Arthur's ranch, is it?"

"Arthur's? No. Bar Double C's my sister's ranch. Arthur's ranch is on the way, if you'd like to see it. . . ."

The worried expression replaced her radiant smile and Ben tensed. Something was wrong.

"You did hear about the fire?" she asked.

Ben leaned forward. "Fire?"

"Arthur's house was destroyed." She blinked twice. "Mercy and Thad managed to get Jonathan out, but they couldn't save your brother. You must have known. . . ."

"I didn't know how my brother died, only that it was a terrible accident." Ben wondered why Mrs. Buchanan's letters hadn't been more specific. "She was there? Your sister?"

Miranda nodded. "That's what I heard. Mercy and Thad . . ."

Perhaps Mercy Buchanan had something to hide, after all. "I didn't know anything about a fire. I just assumed that the Buchanans would move into Arthur's home. He said it was the finest house in the area."

"Humph." Miranda poured more tea into his cup. "He was right proud of it," she said in a tone that made it obvious she didn't feel the pride was justified.

Ben realized he was scowling and forced himself to smile instead. "Are the Buchanans not planning to rebuild? It is the boy's home, after all."

Miranda shrugged. "I expect they're more concerned with raisin' cattle than with buildin' a foolish house."

"Foolish? Why is it foolish to give the child a proper home?"

She laughed. "You Lansings. I reckon you think a proper home oughta be made of gold bricks."

"I didn't . . . I only meant the house and the ranch are Jonathan's inheritance."

Miranda shrugged. "In Philadelphia, a dozen families would be livin' in a building the size of your brother's house. The child has no need of such a . . . a . . . mansion."

He bit his tongue rather than argue with her. If the Buchanans intended to merge his brother's ranch with theirs and leave his nephew without his inheritance, there would be hell to pay.

He kept his clenched fist under the table. "I would like to see little Jonathan."

"As I said before, I'm gonna be ridin' out to the ranch. You're welcome to come along." She met his gaze. It was damn hot in this kitchen. "You can stop and see the fire damage on the Lansing spread for yourself, if you like."

"Yes," Benjamin said, "I suppose I should do that." He'd need to evaluate his nephew's inheritance and be certain the Buchanans were taking proper care of the property.

"Fine. Where's your horse?"

"I'll need to rent a horse. I saw a livery stable—"

"No." Mrs. Wyatt rushed into the room cradling the sleeping infant. She spoke so fiercely they both turned to stare at her. "I don't think Mr. Lansing should go out there today, Miranda." Her voice settled back into her accustomed genteel tone. "You haven't been home in a year. Your sister will want to spend some time with you in private. How will she be able to entertain an unexpected guest?"

"But—" Miranda started to protest.

"I understand, Mrs. Wyatt, but I've come a long way and am anxious to get on with my business."

"But surely, Mr. Lansing . . ." She looked out the window, then turned back to him. "It's afternoon. By the time you ride out to the ranch and conduct your business it will be dark. Too late to come back to town for the night. The Buchanans live simply—they have no extra beds for guests. After your long journey, I've no doubt you'd prefer to spend the night in a comfortable featherbed." A smile lit her face as though she'd just been inspired. "My husband will escort you to the Bar Double C in the morning. And you can borrow one of our horses. They are much better than what the livery has to offer, I assure you."

Ben wondered for a moment what Mrs. Wyatt was trying to hide. But perhaps he was too suspicious. It could be simply a desire to prevent him from intruding upon the family reunion. He sighed. It was obvious there was no arguing with the woman.

Besides, he glanced at Miranda sipping her tea. He wasn't sure it was at all a good idea for him to be alone with that temptation.

Chapter 4

Miranda's heart leaped to her throat as she caught sight of the entrance to the ranch where she'd grown up. Her father had used pine logs to fashion an arch over the road. They'd burned their brand—a bar joining two *C*s for Chase and Clarke—into a strip of wood hanging from the arch.

As she approached, she saw the old sign still held the two *C*s, even though Mercy was a Buchanan now. Perhaps the past year hadn't brought as many changes as Miranda had feared. She squared her shoulders and gave a quick click of her tongue to set Princess trotting through the gate toward the house. A movement caught the corner of her eye and she turned. *Cows—dairy cows.*

"Whoa!" Princess stopped short as Miranda pulled back on the reins. In a newly fenced pasture, two cows calmly grazed on the thick prairie grass. In this territory, cows were free-range animals. Seeing them behind a fence was peculiar enough, but these were not the meaty Herefords and longhorns her sister raised for beef. She recognized the animals as

Guernseys from their distinctive white markings and relatively lean build.

Mercy would never allow dairy cows to take the grass that could be used to support a few more head of beef cattle—it went against her principles. Miranda had given up arguing the benefits of having cows for milk and butter. She might as well have tried to persuade the sun to shine all night as convince Mercy to invest in a dairy cow. Her sister had been unshakable on this issue, even ignoring their father's fondness for buttermilk.

Miranda continued on, wondering what strange sight would greet her next. She soon had her answer. Just past the barn, her old home came into view. It was familiar, but not exactly how she'd left it. Two added rooms spread out on either side of the original one-room log cabin. The addition of a large, covered front porch connected old and new so that it all fit together.

Someone, surely not her practical sister, had planted a flowerbed in front of the house. Clarisse had warned Miranda that she might not recognize her sister, but she'd never said she wouldn't recognize the old house. Miranda shook her head, reminding herself that it was no longer her home and her sister could make any changes she wanted.

Miranda dismounted and tied Princess to the railing on the side of the porch where Princess wouldn't be able to trample the lovely flowers. She traced a hand along her mare's neck and glanced around, hoping to see someone, but a little afraid that it would be a stranger that greeted her rather than Pa or Mercy. Blowing out an exasperated breath, she fought a silly urge to knock on the door. Certainly Clarisse would have told her if the family had moved.

Pacing up and down the porch wasn't going to accomplish anything.

The house seemed too quiet to be occupied, so she walked around back where she found a woman on her knees, working in the huge kitchen garden.

The long chestnut braid dangling down the woman's back could have belonged to Mercy, but Miranda knew immediately it was not her sister, for this woman was wearing a blue gingham dress and a straw hat decorated with a bright yellow ribbon. Even if Mercy had decided to take time away from the cattle to grow her own vegetables, Miranda was certain she would never wear a dress to work in the garden, or decorate any hat with a ribbon. Her sister had not worn a dress outside of church since they'd moved West.

Miranda walked to the edge of the garden before she called out, "Excuse me, I'm looking for my sister, Mercy Clarke . . . er, Buchanan."

The woman stood to her full six feet and turned.

"Miranda?" Mercy called out before dropping her trowel and rushing forward.

Miranda covered at least half of the distance and threw her arms around her sister, who pulled Miranda against her with her long, sinewy arms and whispered, "Miranda, oh Miranda. You're home."

It occurred to Miranda that she should pull away, to show Mercy that she could stand up on her own, but she was enjoying the feel of her sister's arms around her too much to worry about showing how strong she'd become. They held each other for a few moments until Mercy finally released her and took a step back.

"Let me look at you," she said with a sigh as she

held her much shorter sister at arm's length for a thorough examination.

Miranda was surprised to see a tear rolling freely down Mercy's cheek. Her stoic sister had been dry eyed at her first husband's funeral, spending the day comforting Miranda instead of allowing herself to grieve.

Mercy's smile faded into a look of worry as she considered her sister's appearance. "Beautiful as ever," she pronounced.

"You always were blind when it came to me." Miranda decided to let her sister get away with the lie, under the circumstances. Her eyes dropped. "Baby doesn't show on you, yet." She smiled up at Mercy.

Mercy blushed, placing a hand over her middle. "Maybe doesn't show yet, but my trousers are too tight for me. I'm forced to wear a dress for working."

"A terrible sacrifice," Miranda teased.

Mercy laughed. "Don't you make fun now, bad enough I have to listen to Pa and Thad."

"I'm happy for you," Miranda said. She was surprised to realize it was true. Maybe with the passage of time she'd be able to see other women carrying babies without aching for her own loss. Feeling joy for her sister was a good place to start.

Mercy pulled her sister close again. "I'm so glad you're home."

"Mama! Mama!"

At the sound of the small boy's shouts, both women turned. Miranda observed that Clarisse had not exaggerated—Mercy was glowing. The joy that caused the light obviously centered on the small boy running toward them, waving a small slate above his head.

"I finished my sums." He handed Mercy the slate

as she squatted down to look him in the eye. "Can I help you in the garden now?"

Miranda watched the corner of Mercy's lips twitch as she attempted a stern look. "Have you forgotten how to make a proper greeting?"

Jonathan looked up at Miranda. It had been over a year since the boy had seen her. After a brief hesitation, he broke into a wide grin, revealing a missing tooth.

"Miranda?"

"Aunt Miranda." Mercy brushed a stray lock of hair back from her son's face.

Miranda squatted next to the boy. "Can you call me Aunt Miranda?"

"Auntie Mirandy," Jonathan chanted, then launched himself into her arms, nearly knocking her over.

She drew his small, warm body against her. His baby-fine hair felt like silk against her cheek, and he smelled of mud and straw. Feeling a strange sensation against her ribs, she drew back. Sure enough, the lump in the boy's pocket was moving. Mercy saw it too, inserted her hand into his pocket, sighed, then pulled out the small toad.

"How did that toad get into my pocket?" Jonathan asked, his eyes on the toad.

"I wonder." This time Mercy's stern look seemed to come more naturally. "I told you he can't live in our house. It's too dry for him. Take him back to the creek. Now!"

He wrapped his hands around the toad and nodded reluctantly. "Yes, Mama."

"Then come right back and we'll check your sums."

The boy brightened. "Can we save them for Papa to see?"

Mercy nodded. "I'm certain Papa's looking forward to seeing them."

The boy beamed a smile at Mercy, then took off running in the direction of the creek.

"He's grown in the past year," Miranda said.

Her sister favored her with a bright smile, maternal pride gleaming in her eyes. Mercy turned toward the house where Miranda's horse stood patiently waiting.

"I thought you'd sold Princess before you went to Philadelphia."

"To Uncle Will and Aunt Emily. They were happy to sell her back." Will had offered to give her back the horse, but Miranda insisted on paying. "I took the train as far as Abilene and stopped to see them. They sent you a letter and two books."

"Books?"

"They're safe in my bag." Miranda grinned. "I was careful with them, I promise."

"You didn't ride here alone, did you?" Mercy scowled.

"Do you suppose Uncle Will would have allowed that?"

Mercy turned so that she could keep one eye on the trees where Jonathan had disappeared. "I wasn't sure you'd listen to Uncle Will's advice."

Miranda sighed. "I'm always willin' to listen to advice. But I have to make my own decisions."

Instead of arguing with her, Mercy asked after Will, Emily, and their children. In a minute, Jonathan emerged from the trees and trotted back to them.

"I found him a nice place in the mud," the boy said.

Mercy pulled out her handkerchief and wiped his hands. "Are you sure you left some mud for him?" She brushed at Jonathan's britches.

Jonathan scowled. "Are you teasing me?"

"Yes." Mercy winked, then handed the slate back to Jonathan. "You take this up to the house and wait while Miranda and I see to her horse."

"Can I swing while I'm waiting?"

"I reckon. Put the slate on the kitchen table first."

"Yes, Mama."

"And scrape that mud off your shoes before you go inside the house!" Mercy shook her head as Jonathan sprinted ahead of them. "Sometimes I wonder if that boy even knows how to walk." She wrapped an arm around Miranda's shoulders and pulled her toward the house. "You must be exhausted after your journey."

Miranda was tired, but too full of nervous energy to imagine herself relaxing. "Princess deserves a long rest after all she's been through."

"Was it a difficult journey?"

There was no mistaking the note of anxiety in Mercy's voice. She had been shot by thieves a year ago when she made the same 500-mile journey from Uncle Will's place in Kansas to Fort Victory. Mercy might have died if Thad had not managed to get her to the doctor in Fort Victory. Whatever else Miranda might think of her brother-in-law, she would be grateful to him for saving her sister's life.

"No." They stood on either side of the horse, removing Miranda's bags and bedroll from the saddle. "We had mostly fine weather and no serious trouble."

"Thank the Lord." Mercy dropped one of the bags onto the porch.

Miranda peered at her sister over the saddle, then turned to loosen the cinch on the final bag. Church on Sunday was as much a social event as a religious one. But mentioning God on Monday was an entirely different matter. Something had changed her sister in the past year and it wasn't just that she was wearing dresses and frivolous ribbons. Miranda caught her sister's clear green eyes, then looked away. She wasn't about to give Mercy a chance to study her. Once her sister guessed she had something to hide, she'd be relentless in going after the truth. Then she'd probably strap her Colt over her pregnant belly and head East to seek justice. Only it wouldn't be possible for her sister or anyone else to set things right this time. Miranda had to live with her mistake alone.

"Were you traveling with a large group?"

"About thirty people, not counting the younguns." Uncle Will had found a large extended family that was bound for Oregon. They were a close-knit group. All of them had known each other their whole lives. It was easy for Miranda to keep to herself, which suited her fine. But she didn't mention that part to Mercy. "Three of the men served in the Union Army during the war. How Uncle Will managed to find me such a protective group, I'll never know."

"Well, I'm grateful he did." Mercy pushed the brim of her hat back and examined Miranda again. "We wanted you home, but we worried about you making the journey."

She turned away from her sister's piercing green eyes. "Lovely flowers." Miranda pointed to the fresh beds on either side of the porch. "Are they marigolds?"

"You know I couldn't tell a petunia from a posy. Clarisse planted them. Said it would make our house look more like a home."

Miranda laughed. "I suppose she put the ribbon on your hat, too."

Mercy smiled and shook her head. "No." Removing her hat, she ran a finger along the bright satin strip. "This was a gift from Jonathan. I was going to wear it in my hair, but Thad suggested the hat. This way, even when I'm not wearing it, Jonathan's gift is always hanging where he can see it." She plopped her hat back on her head. "We want Jonathan to understand that he's important to us."

Perhaps her sister hadn't changed so much, after all—she'd always loved her family. They led Princess into the barn, leaving the door open to let light in as they worked together to settle the horse comfortably.

"Jonathan seems at home here."

Mercy nodded. "It hasn't been easy for him. At first he tried so hard to please us . . . I'm almost glad when I see him getting into mischief."

As Miranda stored the saddle and tack, her sister checked the mare's legs with skilled fingers. Mercy seemed radiantly healthy and quite capable of keeping up with the demands of the ranch. Perhaps Miranda wasn't needed, after all.

"When Pa wrote, you were feeling sick."

"Sick?" Mercy stood up and ran her fingers through Princess's dark mane. "I suppose I was. Now that I know the cause, it doesn't seem so bad."

If Pa and Mercy were well and healthy and Thad was truly as protective as Clarisse said he was, maybe Miranda could make her excuses and be gone before winter set in. She'd miss the birth of her niece or nephew, but Mercy didn't need her for that.

Miranda chewed on her lower lip. She'd just arrived and already she was looking for an excuse to leave—to go off on her own and hide. *No!* She was done with cowering. No matter how hard it was, she wouldn't leave here until she was certain Mercy didn't need her.

Suddenly, Mercy turned toward the door, as though some force had drawn her. Miranda followed her sister's gaze and saw a giant shadow that could only be her brother-in-law.

"Mercy, you in here?" Thad moved into the barn. "I saw some things on the porch and I wondered—" He caught sight of Miranda and smiled. "Miss Miranda, it is so good to have you home."

He was even bigger than she remembered. Huge, in fact. Not just tall, but so broad she feared he could crush her with a single blow. Her first instinct was to escape. Before she could move, he wrapped his arms around her, lifting her off her feet and forcing the air out of her lungs. She went stiff, pushing against his chest with all her might until he put her down.

Thad looked down at her, his face unreadable in the shadow. "I . . . I'm sorry, ma'am. I was carried away."

Mercy moved to his side, wove her arm around his waist, tilted her head up and kissed his cheek. Miranda felt herself relax as Thad turned and brushed a kiss to Mercy's forehead, then turned back to Miranda. "Mighty fine having you home, Miss Miranda."

Miranda nodded, her mouth too dry to speak.

"Where's Pa?" Mercy asked.

"He's still with the men, bringin' the last of the cattle down from the summer range. Buck will make sure he gets home safe. I came on ahead to see about supper."

"Is it too late to make a pot roast for dinner, do you think?" Mercy asked.

Thad extracted himself from his wife's hold. "Not if I start it right now."

"How long will it take?" Mercy asked. "I'm starving."

Thad chuckled, his deep bass voice sounding like a steam engine rumbling down the tracks. "I thought you were wantin' to kill the fatted calf in honor of your sister's homecoming." He placed a hand over Mercy's middle. "Didn't know it was this fella wantin' his dinner."

"Well, I do want to celebrate Miranda's arrival." She placed a hand over his. "But, I expect it is this little one who has my mind on food in the middle of the afternoon."

"I'd best start supper then." Thad looked at Miranda and winked. "For all three of you." He chuckled. "If you'll see to my horse, I'll go straight to the kitchen."

"And Jonathan has something to show you!" Mercy called after her husband.

"I already checked his sums. He ambushed me when I arrived." Thad took a few steps toward the door, then turned. "There's some biscuits left from breakfast, if you're truly starvin'."

"I didn't see any biscuits left," Mercy said.

"Good. I guess my hiding place worked."

"Thad Buchanan, you are a cruel man!"

He laughed as he walked out the door. The light streaming through the window fell on Mercy as she watched her husband stride away. The expression on her face made Miranda wonder whether Clarisse was wrong, after all. Maybe it wasn't only Jonathan that made Mercy radiant.

It was a worrisome thought. A year ago, Miranda had hoped her sister would fall in love with Thad. At that time, Mercy had dubbed Miranda a "hopeless romantic." Now, she was more realistic. True, her father and her Uncle Will were as dependable as the cycles of the moon, but that wasn't the way of most men. Mercy turned to look at her sister, still smiling like a child on Christmas morning.

"Pa and Thad alternate fixing dinner," Mercy said as she prepared a bucket with grain for Princess. "They claim it is downright dangerous to let me loose in the kitchen. Can you imagine?"

"Unless your cooking has improved in the last year, I'd say they're very wise."

Mercy grinned. "You were right when you told me to open my heart again." She squeezed Miranda's shoulder. "I'm a very lucky woman."

Miranda forced herself to return her sister's smile, hoping that Mercy was right. It was obvious that her sister wasn't thinking clearly enough to look out for her own best interest. But Miranda would be watching. If Thad ever did anything to harm Mercy or their children, Miranda would make certain that he regretted it.

Both sisters turned to the barn door as a tall, thin man entered with two dogs at his heels.

"Miranda?" Pa called.

"Pa!" Miranda was in her father's arms instantly, breathing in the scent of horses and cattle. She could feel his ribs as she wrapped her arms around his lean body. He held her so tight she could scarcely breathe. It was wonderful.

Mercy sat facing out the window as she ran a brush through her hair. Clouds had rolled in to cover the moon, so the yard was dark. A gentle breeze brought the smell of coming rain and she pulled her shawl tight over her cotton nightgown to ward off the chill. It would soon be time to sleep in her woolen gown. She smiled; she was going to need a larger one.

Thad's soft footfalls drew her attention to the porch. She pictured him following his evening ritual of filling the kettle at the well, so that they could warm water quickly in the morning. While he was outside, she knew he would also check the barn, then walk around the house making sure everything was secure, his family safe for the night. She could take care of herself and had for many years, but it was comforting to know that he was protecting her and Jonathan, too.

The moon peeked through the clouds, briefly illuminating the apple trees that Miranda had started from seeds when they had moved here eight years ago. The trees had grown and matured enough to produce small apples. Miranda was no longer the little girl she had been either.

The fluttering movement inside Mercy drew her attention away from the window, and she placed her hand over the baby. "Do you feel your papa coming close, Little One?"

The door clicked closed behind her. "Talking to yourself, Mercy?"

She felt a rush of pleasure when he spoke her name. The baby seemed to react, too, flitting against the walls of her womb.

"I was chatting with your little one."

He bent over her, brushing a kiss against her temple as he wrapped his arms around her, one hand covering her belly, while the other captured a breast.

"How is the little cub?"

"Very active. I think he knows your voice."

"Really?"

She put her hand over his and squeezed. "Well, he seems to react to you, or maybe he can sense my pleasure at having you near."

He rubbed his hand over her belly. "I wish I could feel him moving."

Mercy leaned back against her husband, his clothes still cool from the evening air. She rubbed her cheek against the rough stubble on his face. "It won't be long now and you will."

He took the brush from her hand and gently gathered a handful of her hair, pulling the brush through.

"It's good to have Miss Miranda home."

"Mmm." Mercy let her eyes drift shut.

"I was wonderin' . . . Did she say anything to you about how she came to have that scar?"

"She said a buggy she was riding in overturned when a wagon loaded with fruit ran into them. She said such accidents are common in big cities."

Thad continued brushing in silence for a few minutes. The rain began and he stepped to the window, pulling it nearly shut, leaving a small gap for fresh air. They listened for a moment to the rain pattering gently against the glass.

"You don't believe her." His voice was barely audible.

"No, she would have written about that accident, or Lydia would have. Thad . . . she was in the hospital for a week." Mercy shivered, thinking of her sister hurt and suffering so far from home. "Lydia certainly would have written."

"Unless your sister asked her not to write us about it."

"Exactly." Mercy nodded. It hurt to think of Miranda wanting to hide something so serious from her. And it frightened her to think what it might be that she was hiding. "Whatever happened, it was something she doesn't want me and Pa to know about."

Thad pulled Mercy from her stool, sat, and gathered her onto his lap. She rested her head on his shoulder, shivering a bit from the damp cold that was now blowing in through the window. He pulled her shawl tight around her.

"Even though I haven't laid eyes on Miranda since we've been married, I've come to think of her as a sister."

"The same as I feel about Clarisse." She drew a hand along his jaw, brushing her thumb against his thick mustache.

"I'm afraid Miranda wasn't prepared for me greeting her with a hug, not even a brotherly one."

"You surprised her, is all." She lifted her head to look into his eyes. "There was nothing wrong with you embracing her."

"It wasn't only surprise." His finger caressed her cheek, his hand bringing her head to rest back against his shoulder. "She was frightened."

Mercy's stomach felt as though it were careening down a mountain in a wagon with no brake. "You think . . . ?" She couldn't bring herself to complete the thought.

"I think it is likely that a man has hurt her. Hurt her badly."

Mercy shut her eyes, seeing again the dark circles under her sister's eyes, the prominent cheekbones that showed she had lost weight in the past year. "I never should have left her alone. I should have—"

"Shh." Thad placed his finger over her lips. "There's no point blaming yourself. She's a grown woman with a right to make her own decisions. You couldn't have stopped her. Besides, whatever happened is in the past, and you can't change it. You won't be any use to her if you're busy punishin' yourself for what you think you should have done differently."

They sat quietly for a few moments. In spite of her worry, Mercy began to drift to sleep in the shelter of her husband's warm body.

"You tired?" he whispered.

"Exhausted," she said through a yawn.

"Best get you in bed, then." There was a note of resignation in his voice.

Mercy lifted her head, but she couldn't see his face in the dark room.

"I don't think it would take too much effort to revive me," she whispered.

He stood with her in his arms, settling her gently on the bed before pulling his clothes off and sliding under the blankets next to her. They cuddled together in the nest at the center of the featherbed, shutting out worries about Miranda. Thad drew his wife into his arms and slowly, skillfully revived her.

Chapter 5

A loud cry brought Miranda out of a deep sleep. She sat up, disoriented, her heart pounding like the bass drum in the Fourth of July parade. By the time she heard the second cry, she knew where she was. Home. And it was her sister's voice she heard. She was standing next to her bed, ready to run to Mercy's aid, when she realized it was not pain or fear that she heard.

Heat rushed to her face and she dropped back to the edge of her bed, acutely aware of every sound now coming from her sister's bedroom. The soft rumble of Thad's voice, the shifting of the bed. She put her hands over her cheeks, trying to cool them. *She had nearly run into their room.*

Miranda tried not to listen, tried to focus her mind on anything else, but it was impossible. Surely Thad was careful not to hurt the baby. Even if Thad wasn't cautious, Mercy would be. From the sound of things Thad was . . . enthusiastic to say the least. She thought of Lawrence—he'd told her that men needed to be rough in order to find their pleasure.

The house was quiet again, and Miranda slipped

back under the covers. She stared up at the ceiling, which also formed the floor of the loft above, where Jonathan was sleeping. The whole idea of joining with a man had seemed strange to Miranda when she was growing up. Living in this small house with Mercy and her first husband, Miranda had some idea that a husband and wife could both enjoy coming together. Mercy had told her it was nothing to be afraid of and could be downright nice. Though come to think of it, in all those years she had never heard Mercy cry out in pleasure as she had done tonight.

Miranda had awakened more than once to quiet rustling from Mercy's bed, and her adolescent mind had imagined something gentle and loving. It had been like that at first with Lawrence—gentle and tender. Until he lured her into his bed with words of love and promises of marriage.

"A real man takes what he wants from a woman," he had told her. "And a real woman is satisfied with that."

Satisfied? As if a pot was satisfied to hold the soup.

Lawrence said there was something wrong with her if she didn't enjoy what he did to her. Dammit, she had tried, had even felt a few times as though she was near to discovering something, but she was always disappointed. Maybe there was something wrong with her.

She wouldn't cry. She was done bemoaning her foolish mistakes. That wasn't going to do her any good. What she knew for certain was that Lawrence was a cruel man who didn't care one lick about her. She had no reason to believe anything he'd ever told her. All she could do was hope that someday she'd find a man who really cared about her. Maybe then everything would be different. She closed her eyes as a tear rolled down her temple and into her ear.

Miranda finally began to drift back into a troubled sleep. Whether it was hours or moments later she could not say, but another cry brought her fully awake again. Her eyes sprang open, but she didn't move until she recognized Jonathan crying for his mama. Miranda sat up, thinking to go to him, when she heard Mercy's bedroom door fly open.

"It's Jonathan. I'll see to him," Mercy spoke quietly to Thad. "Go back to sleep, dear."

Miranda peeked through the opening at the edge of the curtain, which separated her bed from the main room of the cabin. In the darkness, Mercy's white gown seemed to float across the room until she reached the ladder to the loft.

"I'm here, sweetheart," she crooned, and the boy's sobs quieted. Miranda imagined the boy burying his face in Mercy's chest as his sobs grew muffled. "What is it, son?"

"I saw him . . . I saw Fa . . . Father." The little voice choked on a sob. "He was black and gray, like the coals and ashes of my old house after the fire."

"Shh, shh. Let me climb into bed with you, it's too cold to be standing here with bare feet and a thin nightgown." The boards squeaked as Mercy moved onto the bed. "There, that's better."

The boy's muffled voice was difficult to make out.

"It was a terrible accident, sweetheart. I told you all about it, remember?"

"You said he was trying to get upstairs—to make sure I was safe." The boy sniffled.

"That's right. Here, blow your nose." Mercy's quiet voice carried down to Miranda. "There now, that's better. Your father loved you, Jonathan. I want you to always remember that."

"And his last thought was about me."

"He loved you so much he wasn't thinking about himself even though he was badly hurt. . . . Do you remember Thad told us when he came into the house your father was crawling—he couldn't even stand up, but he was looking for you. He begged Thad to find you and get you out of the house. And Thad did."

"Mama?"

"Hmm?"

"Do you think Father is in heaven?"

Mercy hesitated, perhaps wondering whether she should lie to the boy. It would be impossible for her sister to imagine Arthur Lansing—the man who had nearly succeeded in killing her and stealing her ranch—in heaven.

"I . . . I don't know, for certain."

"You always say that." Jonathan sounded angry. "Why don't you know? Grandpa told me your mama and Miranda's mama are both in heaven. How come he knows that, but you don't know about my father?"

"Jonathan, only God knows—"

"Some other boys said my father was in hell and I'm going there, too, because he was a liar and a cheat and blood will tell."

"Who?" Mercy's voice was suddenly much louder. "Who told you such a thing?"

"George Meier."

The blacksmith's son. He was years older than Jonathan and should have known better than to tease the boy. Miranda felt her own pulse increase as anger surged through her.

"He had no right to say those things to you."

Mercy was obviously fighting to keep her voice quiet now. "Next time I'm in town, I'll speak with that boy's father."

"But . . ." Jonathan's voice became even smaller and higher. "Is it true about my father?"

There was no response for so long that Miranda wondered if Mercy would say anything. When she finally spoke, her whisper was difficult to hear. "Everyone makes mistakes, Jonathan, your father included."

"Was he a liar and a cheat?"

There was another long silence.

"Your father did a lot of things, Jonathan. Good and bad. No different from any of the rest of us. But the best thing he ever did in his life was to have you for a son. You're a good boy, and you're going to make a fine man. Don't let anyone tell you different." Mercy sighed. "You'll make mistakes, too, I'm certain. But, use your head for thinking and your heart for caring about others and you'll make mostly right choices."

Miranda could picture the scene in the loft above as Jonathan sniffled and Mercy spoke affectionate nonsense words to him, urging him to go to sleep.

"Sing to me, Mama?" Jonathan asked, his little voice fighting through a yawn.

Mercy sang, her alto voice so gentle and sweet Miranda found herself crying. She blinked once, then again, and pulled the pillow into her arms, squeezing tight as she rubbed her damp cheek against the smooth surface. In the solitude of the darkness, she allowed the tears to flow as she cried for herself, for the child she'd lost, and for the lullabies she would never sing to him. Tomorrow would be soon enough to begin forgetting.

* * *

Miranda added another pancake to the stack on Thad's plate, then turned to see her sister pour herself a cup of tea while Thad poured out coffee for all the other adults.

"You're not drinking coffee?" Miranda was beyond surprised. Mercy's fondness for coffee was legendary.

Thad chuckled. "She only just started letting us brew it in the house again."

Mercy wrinkled her nose in disgust. "The smell's tolerable now, but I'm not going to drink that muck."

"It makes the baby sick," Jonathan declared.

"We thought about diggin' Mercy her own privy, she was sick so often."

"That's not funny." Mercy placed her hands on her hips and glared at her husband.

"Then we figured it might be easier to live without coffee for a while." Thad pulled Mercy's hands off her hips and dragged her to him for a kiss.

"You get used to all that kissing," Jonathan whispered to Miranda as she bent to fill his glass with buttermilk.

He pointed to Mercy and Thad. Mercy's cheeks flamed red as she broke away from Thad and turned to the boy. Pa cleared his throat, apparently covering a chuckle.

"I reckon we'd better say grace before this fine breakfast goes cold."

Once everyone was seated, Miranda closed her eyes, listening to her pa's quiet, steady voice as he asked a blessing over their food and their day. She'd missed Pa. If ever there was a man who should be called "gentleman," it was her quiet, thoughtful father. Why was that word so often reserved for fancy, educated men with polished manners and no real tenderness? Ben's fierce eyes came to her, making her stomach churn.

"You've been quiet this mornin', Miranda." Thad refilled his own coffee cup, then reached across the table to fill hers.

Miranda nodded her thanks, then reached for the cup. "I guess I'm still tired from the journey." It was the truth—she was tired. Not to mention confused and unsure how she was going to fit into this household.

Thad grinned. "Well, we all appreciate the delicious breakfast you've made, Miranda."

"Mmm." Pa chewed on his pancakes. "I'd forgotten what a fine cook you are, sweetheart."

"I'm glad you like it." She smiled at her father. "I hope it will be a help. Having me here for cookin'." The kitchen was one place Miranda had always felt useful.

"I know it will," Mercy said. "And don't you worry about finding work around here. There's plenty needs doing. I reckon we'll let you have a few days' rest before we give you the full brunt of it."

"I'm ready now."

"Your sister's right." Pa winked at her. "We don't want to see you jump back on Princess and hightail it out of here before we've had a chance for a good visit."

"I'm not going anywhere so long as you need me here."

"Good." Mercy buttered a second slice of bread. "Then you'll be staying a long while."

Don't count on it. Miranda shoveled a forkful of eggs into her mouth to hold back the retort. She wanted to stay; she was already feeling comfortable in many ways. Except that she didn't belong. She'd do what she came for, then move on.

While Miranda and Mercy finished the breakfast cleanup, Thad announced he would climb up on the roof to check for loose shingles. Mercy explained her husband was dedicated to making the cabin warm and safe for the winter.

"I think it's a natural protective instinct that men have." She took a wet plate from Miranda and wiped it dry, but her eyes focused out the window to where Thad was gathering his equipment.

Miranda held her tongue, wondering how her independent sister had so willingly allowed herself to fall under the illusion of a man's protection.

"Come on, Grandpa." Jonathan pulled on Pa's arm. "Let's go."

"Hold on, son." Pa extracted himself from Jonathan's grip. "I want to put on my sweater. Seems a bit chilly this mornin'."

"Okay, but hurry, Grandpa."

"You should wear a sweater, too," Mercy said.

"I'm not cold," Jonathan protested.

"You're not cold in the kitchen where the stove is warm, but there's no fire started in the workshop. It'll be cold out there."

Jonathan let out a dramatic sigh before climbing the ladder to retrieve his sweater. He was down in a moment, trying to wriggle into his sweater as he danced impatiently from one foot to the other. Mercy bent to help him pull the woolen garment over his head, then smoothed the hair that was sticking straight up on the lad's head. Miranda recognized Mercy's handiwork. Playing the piano and knitting were Mercy's favorite pastimes during the long winter months. No doubt Pa and Thad had similar sweaters.

"Come on, Grandpa, I want to get started."

Pa emerged from his room, wearing, as Miranda expected, a sweater made of the same dark blue wool that Jonathan was wearing. His thin white hair was also standing at attention. Miranda couldn't help but giggle at her father's hair, which caused him to comb his fingers through it.

"I ain't gonna slick my hair down, if that's what you're expectin'."

"Me neither." Jonathan glared up at his mama. "Come on, Grandpa, let's hurry. We have to make that cradle before the baby comes."

"Well, I think we might manage it, if we get started right away." Pa winked at Mercy. "What do you think, Mama?"

Mercy laughed and pecked a kiss on Pa's cheek, then another on Jonathan's. "I think even with the help you're going to get from Jonathan, you'll still be able to build a cradle in the next four months."

Miranda laughed, too, as Jonathan dragged Pa out the door and across the yard to the workshop Pa had built in the old bunkhouse. Ever since the accident that had left him with a bad leg, Pa spent more time making furniture than he did with the cattle.

"All the hired hands bunk at the Lansing place now, so Pa's workshop now fills the whole bunkhouse," Mercy said. "Just as well. I worry all day when he rides out with the men."

"Clarisse said he hasn't had a spell in months."

"No, he hasn't. Naturally, Pa figures that means he's cured."

"He isn't?"

Mercy shook her head. "Doc says there's no tellin' what's going on inside his head."

Miranda scrubbed the last dish and handed it to

her sister. "Having Jonathan in the house sure changes things."

Mercy smiled. "The boy has enough energy to keep all of us busy 'round the clock. I'm glad Pa enjoys spending time with him, too." She yawned.

Miranda watched her sister putting the dishes up on their shelf. The morning light revealed dark circles under her eyes that had not been apparent yesterday.

"Does he get you up at night often?"

"No, but he does have an occasional nightmare." Mercy looked at Miranda. "Did he wake you last night?"

"I was already awake," Miranda blurted out.

"Oh." In spite of her golden complexion, Mercy had always blushed easily and she did so now, likely guessing what had awakened her sister.

"I'm sorry if the house . . . um . . . wasn't quiet enough for you."

She turned away, placing the cups in a straight line on the shelf.

"I didn't notice any particular noise," Miranda lied. "You know how sometimes it's harder to sleep when you're overtired? I reckon I was too exhausted to sleep proper, is all. Or maybe Jonathan was stirring in his bed because of his nightmare and that noise woke me. I'm not sure. I'd have gone up to him, but you were too fast for me."

"Don't feel you need to do that," Mercy said. "I mean, it's my job. Comes with being a mother."

Miranda turned to work on the skillet so her sister wouldn't see the tears pooling in her eyes. The pain of losing her baby was raw now, but Miranda knew she would heal. In the meantime, she didn't want Mercy to know how foolish her younger sister had been.

Mercy wet a rag in the dishwater, then turned to wipe the table. When she faced the sink again, she peered out the window where Thad was carrying a ladder from the barn. "I can't imagine my life without Jonathan and Thad."

Miranda didn't think Mercy was aware that she had placed her hand over her middle as though caressing the baby there.

"I only pray that you'll find this kind of happiness one day." Mercy favored Miranda with a full smile. "Soon."

Miranda studied the skillet in her hand, making certain she'd greased it completely so that it wouldn't rust. "You warned me once that giving your heart away is a sure way to see it broken."

"I was wrong." Mercy gripped her sister's elbow and Miranda met her eyes. "Giving your heart away is the only way to find happiness. Nothing sure about it. It might lead to heartbreak, but there's no way to protect yourself against that—not even hiding away."

Miranda pulled away to rinse her hands in the warm dishwater. Mercy turned back to wiping the table. "I know things went badly between you and Harold."

Harold. Miranda had nearly forgotten her crush on the auburn-haired boy who'd been the first to kiss her, the first to awaken her womanly desires. But she had not been woman enough to hold her first beau as it turned out. He had turned away from her directly into the arms of another woman when Miranda had refused to share his bed before marrying him.

The two dogs, Boon and Daisy, started barking to wake the dead. Mercy pulled back the pretty yellow curtains from the window. "Looks like we have company." Her brows creased together. "A city fella, judging by his dress."

Miranda peered around her sister's shoulder. *Benjamin Lansing.*

"Oh, I'm sorry." Miranda dried her hands on the dishtowel. "I should have told you yesterday, but with all the excitement of seeing you, it went clean out of my mind."

Mercy turned and gave her a puzzled look.

"I met him . . ." She didn't have time for the whole story. "He was in Clarisse's store yesterday, asking for directions to the Lansing place."

Mercy turned to look out the window again, then back to Miranda.

"It's Benjamin Lansing," Miranda said, "Arthur's brother."

"Why is he here now? What does he want?"

Miranda squeezed her sister's hand. "He only wants to be sure Jonathan is well cared for. Don't worry."

Her older sister pulled in a deep breath as though to steady herself before she turned and marched out the door with Miranda right behind her. Ben Lansing was taller than she remembered, his shoulders broader. He stood next to his horse, erect, confident, the polished gentleman. As Miranda introduced Mercy and Thad, he made a polite bow to Mercy and shook Thad's hand. Both men maintained eye contact in the way she expected pugilists would do before a fight. When they finally let go, Miranda sensed that neither of them had won their first match.

"Would you like to come inside?" Mercy offered, interrupting the men's ritual.

Ben seemed to notice the house for the first time.

He stared a moment too long, seemed to realize it, and turned to face Mercy again, wearing a disarming smile, which Miranda suspected he kept in his pocket for important occasions.

"I'd be pleased to, Mrs. Buchanan. Is my nephew in there?" The word *there* was spoken with disdain.

At the mention of Jonathan, the color faded from Mercy's face. Thad stepped up beside her and took her elbow. "He's with his grandfather at the moment. I'll fetch him—" Thad kept his gaze steadily on Benjamin. "After we've had a chance to visit."

Miranda watched Thad holding his wife possessively. He was marking his territory as surely as any wolf might do. His wife. His house. His son.

Benjamin smiled at Thad—a fierce smile that made it clear he accepted the challenge from the bigger man. Miranda found herself grinning, too. There was something about Ben's confident posture that made him seem as big as Thad. In fact, Ben must have been two inches shorter, and he was not nearly as broad. Miranda reminded herself she should be loyal to her brother-in-law, but she hated seeing any man use his size to intimidate.

Thad was the first to turn away. He pulled Mercy close and guided her into their small house.

"Reckon I could fix some coffee," Miranda said as she followed the others into the kitchen.

"That would be nice." Lansing caught her eyes, and it was a moment before Miranda remembered to move. She reached for the coffee pot and set to work as the others settled into chairs around the table.

"I'll come right to the point," Benjamin started. "I'm here to see to my nephew and to get the money my brother owed me."

"Arthur owed you money?" Thad turned to his wife.

"You're meaning to visit Jonathan?" Mercy's voice was hoarse and she cleared her throat. "You don't mean to . . . take him?" Miranda noticed her sister was clutching her husband's hand.

"Of course, I want to see my nephew . . . to make certain he's healthy and well cared for—"

"You have no need for concern, sir," Thad said. "We love him as we would our own son. I promise you we'll do everything in our power to keep him safe and well."

"I'm glad to hear it." Benjamin leaned over the table, holding one gloved hand with the other. Miranda had yet to see the man without his gloves on. "As to the money, I lent my brother five thousand dollars some years ago. He was to pay that with interest by the end of last year."

"That's impossible." Mercy's voice was quiet, but it held a note of authority that caused Lansing to turn to her. "A loan that size would have been in the books somewhere."

"It is not only possible, but quite true." Ben pulled some papers out of his jacket pocket. "I have some of my brother's letters here. Arthur wrote that his ranch was prospering. He'd invested the money I'd loaned him in a special breeding program, and he expected to earn a handsome profit once the cattle were ready for sale." He turned to Thad. "I take it he was able to sell the cattle last fall, before his unfortunate accident."

Again, Thad looked to Mercy.

"Arthur didn't do any breeding." She stared at Thad.

"I don't suppose . . ." Thad said. "Did he mention the breed?"

"Something about Herefords imported from England, I believe."

Thad muttered something that might have been "hell."

Mercy sighed. "It was us. Our ranch. We imported the Herefords with money Arthur loaned us."

Ben shrugged. "He only said he was investing. I assumed he was doing the breeding himself, but he might well have invested in your ranch." He turned to Thad. "Now, I understand, sir, that you are the trustee of my nephew's property."

Thad nodded. "My wife and I are both acting as trustees for Jonathan."

"Then you no doubt have had access to my brother's accounts. You will know the extent of his assets—"

"There's no money," Mercy interrupted. "None."

"That can't be!" Lansing growled.

Thad leaned across the table. "I'll thank you to use a civil tone in my house, sir!" Thad's voice had the edge of a steel blade.

"I apologize for my sharpness." Ben glared at Thad, then turned to Mercy. "But I find your wife's words difficult to believe."

"It's a fact, Mr. Lansing." Mercy held his gaze, her chin raised in challenge. Lansing turned to Thad.

"My wife has spent a good deal of time in Arthur Lansing's books. What we could salvage from the fire and what we could ascertain from his banker. We've been able to pay every creditor who has come to us—"

"I can show you the journal I made to keep track of it all. There were many debts," Mercy added.

"We have struggled this past year to keep the ranch running," Thad continued. "Our men have

had to run both herds together; there was no money
to keep his cattle separate—"

"Ah, ha!" Lansing jumped to his feet. "You've
been profiting from my brother's estate without
regard to my nephew's inheritance!"

Thad stood more slowly, raising his hands as
though trying to push down Ben's fury. "Please, sit
yourself down, Mr. Lansing." His deep voice was
soothing. "If we can't discuss this in a civilized
manner . . ."

Lansing dropped back into the chair, his hands
resting on the table.

"The coffee is ready," Miranda announced, hoping
to break the tension.

Mercy rose to fetch the cups.

"Mama! Mama!" Jonathan's voice carried across
the yard. Mercy opened the door as the little boy arrived, panting from the exertion of his run.

"What is it?" Mercy squatted in front of the boy.

"It's Grandpa!" Jonathan said between heaving
breaths. "I think he's dead."

Chapter 6

Ben stood back as Thad raced out the door, followed by Miranda. Mercy lagged behind with Jonathan. She kept one arm around the child and waved at her sister and husband to go on without them. Ben felt rather helpless as he watched Mercy sit on one of a pair of rocking chairs on the porch. She pulled the crying child onto her lap, brushed the hair back from his face, wiped an errant tear from his cheek, then gasped.

"Good Lord," Ben said as he saw the blood. "What happened?" he asked as Mercy wrapped the boy's hand in her apron, stood, and pulled him into the kitchen.

"It's just a cut finger," she said.

Ben followed them inside. "How bad is it?" he asked, unable to keep the edge of fear out of his voice. "What do you mean, just a finger?"

The boy sniffed, staring up at Ben. "Grandpa was showing me . . ." He sniffled. "He was showing me how to use the plane. Then it slipped and the plane cut me, and Grandpa fell."

While Mercy washed and dressed the finger, Benjamin bent for a closer look. He swallowed. With so much blood, he'd imagined a severed finger hanging from the boy's hand. The wound was not bad at all, now that it was cleaned and Mercy had the bleeding under control.

"Don't you worry." Mercy looked into Jonathan's face. "We'll wrap it tight and it will be better soon."

"Unless it gets infected." Ben had not intended to speak the words aloud.

Mercy stared at him. "Sit down, Mr. Lansing!" She growled through clenched teeth, then turned back to Jonathan, her voice once again soft and melodic. "It will be fine, Jonathan."

"It hurts," he said through his sobs.

"I know it does, sweetheart. You're a very brave boy." She wrapped the finger, and then kissed the wrapping. "I want you to stay quiet in my room for a while. Will you do that for me?"

Before the boy could respond, she had lifted him up to her shoulder. When she stood, Benjamin was struck for the first time by how tall she was, very nearly as tall as he was. Jonathan seemed tiny and fragile in her arms.

"What about Grandpa?"

Grandpa. The boy had used the term before, but Ben hadn't grasped the importance. Only now he wondered what his father would think of his descendent, growing up here in this wilderness. Forgetting his heritage.

Mercy looked out the open door toward the workshop. There was still no sign of Miranda or Thad.

"I'm going out to check on Grandpa. I'll come right back and tell you what I find out. All right?"

"I want to come."

"It'll be better if you stay here. Walking around will make your finger hurt more."

The boy rubbed his face against her shoulder. Ben watched as she opened the door and walked into a small bedroom. She placed the boy in the center of a huge bed and removed his boots. Good, quality boots that appeared to be new, Ben noted.

"But, Mama, I'm not tired."

She sighed, then knelt and pulled a box out from under the bed.

"Will you sit here and look at some pictures?"

Opening the box, she removed a stereoscopic viewer, inserting a picture in it before handing it to Jonathan.

"Who's that man?" Jonathan was looking through the door directly at Ben.

She turned and squinted at Ben as though seeing him for the first time. "That is your Uncle Benjamin— your father's brother. You will have a chance to know him later."

"I didn't know I had any uncles, except Uncle Wendell." Jonathan scowled. "And Uncle Will in Kansas; he's my great-uncle." He glanced from Ben up to Mercy. "Is Uncle Benjamin a great one, too?"

"No, sweetheart, he's just a plain uncle. He came a long way to visit you."

A wave of guilt swept over Ben. He had come a long way, but he doubted he'd have made the trip if he hadn't come looking for his money.

"Do you want to see my pictures, Uncle Benjamin?"

Uncle Benjamin. His oldest brother had two children, yet Ben had never been an uncle to them. Nor would he stay in Fort Victory long enough to become an uncle to Jonathan.

Mercy and Jonathan both focused on Ben, waiting for his response. He nodded and walked over to the bed.

"You rest here for a while." She brushed a kiss upon Jonathan's cheek.

"Yes, Mama," Jonathan said in a tone that made it clear he was suffering a great indignity.

She bent for another kiss and turned to Ben. "I'll be right back."

"We'll be fine," Ben said, though he had no idea whether it was true.

As Mercy walked away, Jonathan's eyes fixed on her. And Ben saw clearly that Mercy Buchanan was Jonathan's mother. That was exactly what Ben had hoped for. A good home for his nephew without any effort on his part. Much to his surprise, watching the fondness in the child's eyes left an empty ache in Ben's chest.

Ben pulled a chair next to the bed and sat down. "Let me know if you need help changing the picture."

"No," Jonathan said. "I can do it myself." He lifted the viewer up to his eyes.

Ben glanced at the window, but the curtain was drawn and he couldn't see out. "Do you have enough light to see?"

The boy shrugged, but didn't look at Ben. Ben walked to the window and opened the curtain.

"Can you see my Mama?" Jonathan asked.

"Yes," Ben said. "And your Aunt Miranda, too."

Jonathan sat on the edge of the bed and Ben placed a hand on his shoulder. "Your mama said for you to stay here."

"But—"

Ben guided the boy back onto the pillow. "I'll tell

you what. If you promise to stay here, I'll go outside and check on your mother."

Jonathan scowled, but he nodded and settled back into the pillow.

"Pa?" Thad helped his father-in-law to a sitting position. "How do you feel? Are you hurt?"

Pa looked at Thad, then at Miranda. Her heart pounded as she watched her father lift a trembling hand to his head. "Nothin' more than a dizzy spell, I expect. Where's Jonathan?"

Miranda knelt beside her father. "Jonathan is with Mercy. He came to tell us you . . . you collapsed."

Pa stared at her for so long she wondered whether he recognized her. She took his hand in hers, feeling it icy cold. "You'd best come inside and rest a while, Pa."

He nodded. She gripped Pa's hand as Thad helped him to his feet. "Ain't had a spell in months," he mumbled as he shuffled toward the door, leaning on Thad's arm.

"You've been working too hard, Pa." Thad pulled the door open for them to exit. "Doc warned us—"

"Fact is, Doc don't really know much about it." Pa's voice rose in a rare burst of anger. "When that bull knocked me senseless, something happened inside my head. Sometimes I get dizzy, sometimes I forget things. Don't know when it's gonna happen. Don't know when I'm gonna die either. No point in coddling me."

Thad grinned. "You're too stubborn to go before your grandchild is born. I'm certain of that."

"There's nothing wrong with a little good, hon-

est . . . persistence." Pa threw a challenging look at
Thad.

"Not so long as it is laced with a bit of good sense,"
Miranda spoke up. "Thad's right, Pa. You need to be
more careful."

"Land's sakes, child." Pa stopped halfway across the
yard and cast a tense look at his younger daughter.
"I was only trying to build a cradle, not as if I was
chasin' down a bull."

Mercy walked up to them, wearing a worried look.
"Pa"—she glanced at Thad—"we were scared half to
death."

"How's my grandson?"

"He cut his finger."

"You mean I did."

Miranda noticed Mercy hesitated before respond-
ing. "Jonathan said the plane slipped when you fell."

Pa sighed. "I'd best not work with the boy—"

"Nonsense," Mercy interrupted. "It was an accident
that could have happened to anyone."

"You're the one speaking nonsense, Mrs.
Buchanan," Ben nearly shouted. "The old man is
right. He's a danger to the boy."

Miranda stepped between Ben and the others.
"My pa is no danger to Jonathan. He loves the boy.
He wouldn't hurt him—"

"If he could help it." Ben glared at her. "But it's
obvious that—"

Miranda stepped up to him, laying a hand on his
chest and tilting her head up to look him in the eye.
"This is family business. You don't have any right—"

"He's my blood, not yours."

"And where the hell were you and the rest of the
Lansings for the past year, when Jonathan needed

you?" Miranda shouted. "You and your whole damn family were—"

"I can't speak for them." Ben's voice came from deep in his throat. "*I* came here as soon as I heard."

"We're not going to solve anything standing in the yard shouting." At the sound of Thad's quiet drawl, Miranda jerked her hand away from Ben's chest. "Let's get Pa inside so he can rest," Thad continued, "then we'll *talk*."

Ben backed away to let the others pass. Miranda's face flamed as she watched her sister and brother-in-law take Pa into the house. She rubbed her palm against her skirt, trying to smother the memory of her hand pressing against Ben's solid chest. *Aw, hell.* If this was her reaction to a self-important meddler like Benjamin Lansing, heaven help her if she actually liked the man. She had to get better sense. Somehow, she would.

As her family stepped onto the porch, Miranda turned to Ben. "I'm sorry if I was sharp with you."

His eyebrows rose. "*If* you were sharp?" He grinned, the first genuine smile she'd seen him wear. "I don't think there's any question about it."

His smile brought a light to his eyes that threatened to melt her resolve. She refused to allow her lips to curve upward. "You have to understand, I'll do what I must to protect my family."

"I do understand." Ben schooled his features to match Miranda's serious expression. "I feel the same way about mine. Jonathan is my responsibility far more than he is yours."

The words spilled out of their own accord, but Ben couldn't regret them. Up until that moment he had assumed that he'd lost the only family he'd ever be willing to fight for on the day his mother died. Now, he felt a surprising urge to protect an innocent little boy, even if it meant delaying his planned exile.

He might even consider taking the boy with him. Lord help him, he was even willing to suffer the temptation of fiery blue eyes that invited exploring, a freckled nose that demanded to be kissed, and a proud, straight jaw that he wanted to caress all the more because of the ragged scar that marred its perfect surface.

"You can see that Jonathan is a part of this family. Mercy and Thad have given him all their love."

"It's obvious the boy cares for them."

"But you ain't sure their affection is sincere? Why do you suppose they took him in?"

"Why, indeed?"

She blew an exasperated breath out of her nostrils. "For pity's sake, they have treated the boy as their own son and they plan to legally adopt him."

"Which will put them in complete and final control of his inheritance."

Her eyebrows went up. She shook her head, which set some of the curls that had strayed out of her hair ribbon bouncing. "Is that the only thing a Lansing can think about—money?" Her hands went to her hips. "It ain't the boy you're considerin' at all."

He took a step toward her and stared into her eyes. "You have no right to speak of my family in that tone."

She stepped back, wrapping her arms around herself as though warding off a chill. "Then prove me wrong." She stepped back toward him, challenging him again. "Show me you have some . . . feeling for something other than wealth."

He reached for one of the golden curls and she flinched. He let his hand drop to his side.

"I'm not the one who has anything to prove." He kept his voice quiet. "If the Buchanans can show me what they've done with the money—"

"Money again. You see—"

"Yes, money!" The woman would try the patience of a monk. If it weren't for little Jonathan, he might surrender now. "So we understand each other, I will state my position in the simplest possible terms."

"I am not a simple—"

He raised his hand to cut her off. "Don't put words in my mouth, Miranda. I'm not accusing you of being dim-witted." *Mule-headed would be more accurate.* "Just hear me out. I won't leave here until I'm certain that his inheritance is safe—for Jonathan's sake. It is not to be used to enrich the Buchanans or the other children they will have. My nephew has nothing left of his father except his name and his fortune. I will make certain the lad keeps both of those things. And I'm quite sure any judge will agree with me."

"You'd go to the judge to stop this adoption?"

"Damn right I will."

He pivoted and marched over to his horse, Miranda following on his heels. She reached up and grabbed his shoulder.

"Please, you can't do that."

"I must do what I feel is right."

"It'll break my sister's heart."

"Frankly, your sister doesn't matter to me." Ben nodded toward the house. "That little boy is all I care about."

He swung a leg over the horse the Wyatts had lent him and headed toward the muddy road. He'd come to Fort Victory with a clear mission—to get his money and get the hell out. Sometime in the last hour, his duty had changed.

Miranda watched Benjamin ride away, his horse splashing in the mud left by last night's rainfall. The sky darkened as a cloud covered the sun. She wrapped her arms around herself, guarding against the chill. *Just the damp air. It has nothing to do with that man.* Miranda bit her lip. He hadn't done anything to threaten her, still she'd backed away from him in fear. She lifted her head. At least she'd kept her wits and stood up to him. She wouldn't let her fears keep her from defending her family.

"Mr. Lansing left?"

Miranda turned to see her sister looking after the horse that was only a speck against the horizon now.

"He'll be back," Miranda said, lifting her leaden feet to carry her back to the house.

"What did he say?"

She looked at her sister, then away. She couldn't bring herself to look into Mercy's piercing green eyes. But her sister's gentle touch on her shoulder kept her from moving away.

"He wants Jonathan." Mercy's fearful whisper forced Miranda to turn and face her sister.

She captured both of Mercy's hands. "No." Miranda shook her head. "He doesn't want Jonathan."

Mercy closed her eyes and pulled in a deep breath. "I was afraid he'd come to take him away." She blinked to clear the tears from her eyes, but she didn't release Miranda's hands. "I was prepared to send Jonathan away a year ago. I thought it was right for him to be with his kin. But now . . ."

"But now you're his mother." Miranda completed the thought that seemed to have caught in Mercy's throat.

Her sister smiled. "We love him."

"Anyone can see that."

"Mercy?"

Miranda startled at the sound of Thad's voice. For a big man, he walked quietly.

"Sweetheart, are you all right?" He took Mercy's elbow and guided her to the porch.

Miranda hadn't noticed the color was gone from Mercy's face. She protested, but allowed Thad to help her into one of the rocking chairs on the porch. Thad knelt before her, caressing a cheek. "What is it, honey?"

"I'll be fine in a minute." She took a deep breath. "I was afraid. . . . I thought Mr. Lansing wanted to take our Jonathan away from us."

Thad turned to Miranda. "Did he say something to you?"

Miranda watched Thad's eyes. The look of tenderness was unmistakable. Nothing like the fierce expression Benjamin had cast upon her. She sat on the second rocking chair, next to Mercy, and tried to find the words to tell them.

"No." Miranda took a deep breath. "He doesn't want the child. He's interested in the inheritance."

"There's nothing left but the land," Thad said.

Mercy nodded. "If he wants the things from the house . . ."

"No." Thad stood. Miranda shivered at the savage look on his face. "The few things we were able to salvage belong to Jon. I won't see anything taken from him."

Miranda held up her hand. "What Ben said was

that he wanted to be certain Jonathan keeps his inheritance. If you can find a way to assure him of that, he will leave you be."

"And if we can't?" Mercy jumped to her feet.

"Then . . . he said he will fight the adoption."

Mercy stepped off the porch, looking down the road Lansing had taken. "If it's a fight he wants—"

Thad wrapped an arm around her and pulled her against his chest. "Don't fret, honey. We have taken nothing from the boy. If that is honestly Mr. Lansing's concern, then our interest is the same as his. In a week, the judge will sign those papers and no one will take Jonathan from us ever."

Miranda came up to stand next to her sister. "Jonathan is your son now, Mercy. Judge Jensen will see that and do the right thing." If Ben Lansing thought he could stop the judge from granting the adoption, he was wrong. Miranda had no idea what she could do to prevent him, but she would find a way. Of that, she was certain.

Mercy nodded, blinking back tears. "What about the five thousand he says we owe him?"

Her sister didn't need to finish the thought. The ranch was solvent now, barely. But they couldn't possibly have five thousand dollars in cash. If Ben Lansing demanded payment, they had no way of paying him.

Chapter 7

Fort Victory had no real hotel, but the saloon did have rooms to let. Benjamin had been tempted to ask the lovely Spanish proprietress whether an extra fee could lure her up to his room. Fortunately, his good sense intervened. Rita probably would have thrown him out on the street at such a suggestion. A pity. He needed something to distract him from the pretty little lady with the bright blue eyes and sunshine smile.

Ben spun around at the light rap on the door. For an instant he imagined it was Miranda coming to see him. He opened the door to find Rita's young servant with the hot water he'd requested. She set the pitcher and towels down, made a quick curtsy, and left the room without a word, being careful not to come within arm's length of Ben.

He glanced in the small mirror that hung over the table, trying to see what it was about him that might frighten the girl. Hell, his lust didn't extend to children. Maybe working in a boardinghouse with strange men passing through had taught the youngster to be cautious. He pulled his boots off and kicked them under the bed, then bent to wash his face and hands. He wiped the crisp, clean towel over his face, too damn tired to shave.

Leaving his left hand to soak in the water, he walked over to the bed and sat with the bowl on his lap. He fisted his hand under the water, stretching the web of scars. Slowly, he pulled his thumb out, bent it back and forth, then unfolded his pointer finger until it was nearly straight. As the warmth of the water penetrated, his stiff fingers began to relax. He regarded his good hand, agile and complete. The surgeon had explained the complexity of hands to Ben. Bones, sinew, and vessels for carrying blood, all working together to make possible the simple movements he had taken for granted for the first twenty-four years of his life.

When his left hand was smashed, all of that had been disrupted—bones shattered, muscles torn. The flow of blood was interrupted. That was the most difficult part for the surgeons to repair. Without a supply of blood to the fingers, they couldn't live. He touched the tip of his index finger to his thumb, opened the circle, then closed it again. His index finger had survived almost intact. Perhaps, if he could get enough strength back in that finger one day, he could hold a brush again. He pulled his hand out of the cooling water and dried it.

He'd promised himself to exercise his hand every day. It was easy to forget, though, especially when he saw little progress. He always seemed to have more pressing matters to attend to. And now he'd found himself with a mystery to solve. The judge wasn't due in town for a few days. In the meantime, Ben hoped to discover what he could about his brother's estate, as well as the Buchanan and Chase families and their relationship to Arthur.

His brother had never mentioned any particular friendships, yet Miranda had said that Mercy had taken care of the boy since he was an infant. It seemed odd. Much of what Ben had learned in the past few days seemed inconsistent with what his brother had written.

Arthur's letters indicated that he was an important man in this town. No doubt his affairs were popular topics for the local gossips. That didn't mean it would be easy to separate truth from fiction, but at least information should be abundant. Since the saloon was quiet this afternoon, he would start with Rita. And if the time he spent with the Spanish woman helped him to forget a certain blond beauty, so much the better.

Miranda bumped along in the old wagon beside her father. It was the slow way to get to town, but without the wagon, they couldn't carry all the things they were bringing for trade. Besides, Pa wasn't much for talking, and riding with him gave Miranda a chance to think.

Too bad the subject of her thoughts was Benjamin Lansing. She'd just as soon be nose to nose with a rattler as contemplate dealing with that suspicious, irritating lout. That was just the right word for him, too. He might appear to have refined manners, but that didn't make him a gentleman any more than nibbling on grass would make her a cow.

The man could sell creek water for whiskey with his genteel ways and that charming smile. He wasn't fooling her. Miranda was not going to stand by and allow Ben to sweep in from Boston and steal Jonathan away from Mercy.

Money was the key to everything. He'd come looking for money and money he would have. If she could figure a way to raise enough. Miranda chewed on her lip. She'd never raise five thousand, but she had a feeling he'd settle for far less. With Lansing gone, Mercy and Thad would keep Jonathan.

Her brother-in-law was good with the boy. He was good for Mercy, too. Thad would die to protect his family; Miranda was now certain of that. He would never use his strength against them.

Her brother-in-law had not had any trouble tackling Miranda and pinning her to the ground when thieves had attacked their camp a year ago. She well remembered the way he'd held her down with his powerful legs, while she struggled beneath him. Even as she used all her force to push him away. He'd probably saved her life that day. If she'd run out in the open, she'd have been an easy target. As strong as he was, she'd never been afraid of Thad before. Now she was skittish as a rabbit around any man and she hated it when she let her fright show.

She'd never been afraid of any man before meeting Lawrence. And now that she'd escaped his torturing, she refused to spend her life fearing every man who was bigger and stronger than she was. Most men weren't worth fearing and sometimes they could be downright useful.

Miranda liked the idea of a strong man protecting her sister and little Jonathan. The idea that she might also find a man who would look after her appealed to her more than she was ready to admit. Ben Lansing's gentle grin appeared in her mind's eye and Miranda blinked it away, like a speck of soot. True, he was a fine, strong man, but she couldn't see him playing the role of protector. It was impossible to imagine him in her life at all. Everything she'd seen of him in the last few days confused the hell out of her. At least he didn't scare her. Not really. She pulled her jacket closer around her.

There were acres and acres between not being afraid and trusting. Ben claimed he wanted to take care of Jonathan, and maybe he did. At first, she was certain the only reason he'd come to Colorado was to demand his money. But his anger yesterday wasn't about the claimed debt. He'd been worried for Jonathan's sake, and that made it more difficult to judge the man.

Hell, she admired the way he was willing to stand up for his nephew, even if his concern was misplaced. Miranda sighed. Ben Lansing. She ignored the way her stomach lurched when she pictured him studying her with those deep brown eyes. The sensation was no doubt caused by the old wagon pitching up the rutted mountain road. At least that was the safe explanation.

It would take more than a handsome face and a pair of broad shoulders to make her give in to a man. In fact, she didn't care if the man looked like a grizzly bear, just so long as he cared about her and treated her right.

She leaned against her pa and wrapped her arm in his.

"What is it, child?"

"I'm so glad to have you for my pa." Miranda looked up at her father's scruffy, lean face. "You're a true gentleman."

"Ain't no need to insult me now, daughter. I always worked for my livin'."

Miranda laughed. It was good to be home. The thought stabbed at her heart. Now that she was here, she wasn't sure she'd be able to leave again. Pa was getting older and likely didn't have many years left. Until yesterday, it hadn't occurred to her that if she left, she might never see her pa again. It would be horrid to get a letter from Mercy telling her of their father's passing.

"A gentleman doesn't have to be a fancy city slicker, Pa. I don't believe any city has a man as fine as you."

He gave her hand a squeeze but didn't speak for a long while. "Miranda." He squeezed her hand again. "I worried about you every day when you were gone, off in Philadelphia. Crowds of people everywhere, but no one lookin' out for you."

"I . . . Lydia was nearby." She couldn't bring herself to lie, to tell him everything had been fine. He most likely would never believe it anyway. "Besides, I'm a grown woman, Pa. I can take care of myself."

"I keep forgettin' you're not my little girl anymore."

"Sometimes I wish I were, Pa." Life had been much simpler when she depended on her father and sister for everything.

"Ain't no turnin' back, I suppose."

"No, I don't reckon so."

"Seems likely you encountered a rascal or two back East."

"I was workin' in a ladies' dress shop, Pa, not taking up with . . . men." There'd been only one man, and she would spend the rest of her life trying to forget him.

"Men have a way of finding pretty girls like you."

Miranda closed her eyes, trying hard not to picture

the sweet-talking man who had made all the girls in the dress shop blush and giggle when he visited them by day. The man who never seemed to be happy when they were alone together.

"There's all kinds of men in the world, Miranda. Ain't who he is or how he makes his livin' that makes a man. Oh, I reckon I'd have turned out different if I'd been a city boy, but scraping a livin' from the land wasn't near the most important thing that happened in my life." He looked down at Miranda. "Having daughters to raise up likely changed me more. The two of you were my biggest challenge by far."

"Were we very hard on you, Pa?"

"No, child—being without you would have been harder. I reckon I'd have died of loneliness long ago if it weren't for you and your sister."

"And now you'll have your chance to help Mercy raise her children."

"Oh, no." Pa tugged on the reins to steer the horses around a large hole in the road. "That'll be up to Thad."

"He loves her, doesn't he, Pa?"

"That fella's the best thing could have happened to your sister. He's exactly what she needed." He clucked at the horses to pick up the pace. "I hope to see you wed before I leave this earth."

"Pa!" Miranda sat up and glared at him. "Don't you be talkin' like that. I expect you have a good many years left."

"I don't mean to rush you, sweetheart, but you are twenty years old."

"An old maid, am I?"

Pa chuckled. "Not an old maid. But, as you said yourself, you're a full-grown woman."

Miranda kissed her father's weathered cheek.

"I was afeared you'd settle down in Philadelphia—raise up a passel of grandchildren I would never get to know."

Miranda felt a pang in her chest thinking of the child she would never mention to her father. If that baby had been born alive and well, she likely would have stayed away. "I'm here, now, Pa, and I ain't plannin' on heading back East."

"Promise?"

"I promise." Miranda leaned back against her father's shoulder. "I don't know about finding a man here, though."

"This territory's full of good men. A pretty girl like you will have your pick."

No point in correcting her father. He would always believe she was beautiful. "A fine welcome home— I arrive one day and you want to see me married off the next."

Pa laughed. "I did say not to rush, didn't I?"

"That's good, because I intend to take my time and choose right." *Leastwise, I hope I'll make a good choice this time.*

"You're so much like your sister." Pa reached his arm around her and squeezed. "Mark what I say now. The right fella's gonna come when you ain't lookin', and likely you'll both end up surprised."

Miranda hoped her father was right in predicting that there was a man for her somewhere, and that he would find her. So far, she'd shown little ability to find the man herself. The best thing for her to do was to put the whole thing out of her mind. She didn't have time for such foolishness now in any case. Her first task must be to send Lansing packing.

That brought her back to the problem of raising money. Five thousand dollars. A hell of a lot of money. It would have taken her a lifetime to earn that much at the rate she'd been paid for sewing dresses in Philadelphia. Miranda didn't have many skills, and she didn't have much money to start with. The only way to turn a small amount of money into thousands of dollars was to gamble.

There were always men looking for someone to invest in a new gold mine. Or there was the big poker game at Rita's. When Judge Jensen was in town, it wasn't unusual for thousands of dollars to be on the table. Miranda sighed. She wasn't sure how to invest her money, but she did have an idea of how to earn a small stake.

She had to try for Mercy's sake. It wasn't possible for her sister to raise the kind of money Ben claimed he was owed. Not and have anything to eat this winter. Her sister wouldn't fail to pay the hands. Or perhaps she would let the men go, if she couldn't pay them. That would be a fine situation. Miranda could picture her pregnant sister out chasing the cattle, risking her health and the baby's, too. That wasn't going to happen if Miranda could help it.

She'd sell the only thing she had to offer. As the town came into view, Miranda sat taller in the seat. She was going to need an ally for this venture. The best person for the job was Clarisse Wyatt. While Pa went in to talk to Doc Calvert, Miranda would have a private chat with Clarisse.

It was only a few doors up the boarded walkway from Doc Calvert's office to Wyatt's store. Miranda marched past the assay office. Sheriff Bradford waved at Miranda from across the street; Miranda saluted him with the rolled papers she was carrying.

When the weather was pleasant, the sheriff often sat out in front of his office, figuring he could prevent a lot of mischief by making himself as visible as possible. Whether it was due to the lawman's presence or not, the street was quiet now.

Wyatt's Dry Goods Store was the second busiest place in Fort Victory. Rita's saloon was the most visited place in town. Seemed as though more people would need the food and other goods that Wyatt's had to offer, yet Rita's drew the biggest crowds. Maybe it was just that the folks who frequented Rita's were a bit noisier and more boisterous.

The bells on the inside of the door chimed as Miranda pushed her way into the store. "Hello?" she called out, though she knew someone—Wendell, Clarisse, or one of the boys—would appear when they heard the bells. As she'd hoped, it was Clarisse who stepped into the store with a welcoming smile on her face. Miranda's chest tightened at the sight of the baby on her hip, but she returned her friend's smile.

"Miranda!" Clarisse walked around the counter to greet her. "Look who's here, Hal. It's your Aunt Miranda." The baby gurgled at his mother and she beamed at Miranda. "How are you settlin' in? Everything the way you remember it?"

"As you warned me, there are plenty of changes at the ranch."

"Everyone well?"

"Mostly." She took a deep breath. "Pa had one of his spells."

"No!" Clarisse looked worried. "He's been doing so well."

Miranda shrugged. "Mercy said he has been fine except for the one spell. He's over visiting with Doc Calvert now. Pa says it's a waste of good money, but he figured seein' the doc would be easier than arguing with Mercy."

"Your father is a wise man."

Miranda grinned. "You're right about that." Both women knew from experience that there was no point arguing with Mercy when she set her mind to something.

"Let's hope it's just the one spell. I'd hate to see him like he was just after the accident." Clarisse shifted the baby to her other side.

Miranda nodded, remembering how easily confused Pa had been. They didn't dare leave him alone for more than a few minutes at a time.

"What can I do for you?" Clarisse's question brought Miranda's mind back to their conversation.

"Oh." Miranda swallowed. She had no idea why she was suddenly so nervous. "I won't take a lot of your time." Miranda walked over to the counter. "I wondered . . ." She sucked in a deep breath. "I have a business proposition for you."

As Miranda's mouth was too dry to speak, she spread the papers over the counter and turned them so that Clarisse could see her drawings. It had been months since she'd worked on them. She had put this whole scheme out of her mind when she left Philadelphia.

"Well!" Clarisse pressed one corner back with the index finger and thumb of one hand while Miranda helped her hold the other end of the papers flat. "It's beautiful." Clarisse lifted the top paper and the next, carefully examining each of the four sketches Miranda had brought her.

"Is this what women are wearing in Philadelphia?"

"Something like." Miranda chewed on her lower

lip. "I got some of my ideas there. Mostly it's, well, the sort of dresses I would like to wear."

"You did these?"

Miranda nodded. "I was beginning to make some of my own designs at the shop when . . . the accident—"

"Accident?"

"I was . . . there was an accident with a buggy I was riding." She touched the scar on her face. "I was injured." She looked away. It was much more difficult to tell the story to someone she knew. She wondered whether she'd told it this badly to Mercy, and if so, whether her sister believed any of it.

"Oh, honey. I'm sorry you went through that." Clarisse placed a hand over Miranda's. "You seem fine now—no lasting injuries?"

"No, I was lucky." Except for a scar that would mark her for the rest of her life.

Clarisse smiled. "I suppose it could have been worse."

Miranda nodded. She could hardly imagine anything more difficult than what she'd been through. Dying would have put an end to everything. Instead, her heart kept beating, and here she was pretending to be alive. No—determined to find a new life. That was a better way of thinking of it.

"You want to sell the sketches?"

"No," Miranda answered quickly. "No, I mean to sell the dresses. If you'll help me with the fabric and the customers."

"I see." Clarisse smiled, her eyes twinkling with delight. "An interestin' idea." She took the sleeping baby over to his cradle and set him down. "I sell some ready-made dresses, but this—"

"I worked in a dress shop in Philadelphia. Learned

to make dresses that were right fine for the city ladies. We'd make the same dress in different sizes, so it would take only minor alterations for a good fit when a lady came into the shop. Others were sold through mail order and women did their own fitting."

"Hmm." Clarisse walked over to set the kettle on the stove. Miranda expected she was trying to find the words to explain why the arrangement wouldn't be suitable. After all, there was no good reason for her to believe Miranda's dresses would sell, or make any money at all for the store.

Miranda opened her mouth to relieve Clarisse of the responsibility. "It's all right—"

"Yes," Clarisse said at the same time. "Yes, a wonderful idea. It is high time the women of Fort Victory had a source of fashionable clothing. As it is, a woman either makes her own simple clothing from the cloth I sell here, or she must send away for a ready-made in her size. And we both know those never really fit properly."

"They aren't made very well either."

"No, they're not." Clarisse nodded. "This is an excitin' idea. Lots of possibilities. Imagine if we could find a shop in Denver that would carry them."

"Denver?"

"It's the nearest city. I'll wager women there have nearly as much trouble keeping up with fashion as we do right here in Fort Victory."

Miranda felt her stomach relax for the first time all day. "Do you really think they'll sell?"

Clarisse grinned. "Honey, we are going to make some money on this venture."

Miranda smiled until she remembered her sister needed five thousand dollars. She wasn't going to make that by selling dresses. All she could hope was that the money she earned would help somehow.

The door chime rang and Clarisse called out, "Mr. Lansing! Good afternoon."

Miranda's stomach flipped as she turned to see Ben Lansing striding toward her.

"Good afternoon, ma'am." He nodded at Clarisse, then turned to Miranda. "Afternoon."

He looked over her shoulder, and she realized he could see her sketches laid out on the counter. She spun around to snatch them up, but his hand covered hers, wedging the piece of paper to the counter. And sending her heart racing like a wild horse running from the lasso.

"Fine drawings." He glanced at Clarisse. "Yours?"

"No, indeed. You're looking at a new dress design by my partner—Miranda Chase."

Miranda stared at Ben's hand, resting over hers. He wasn't applying pressure. She could move her hand if she wanted. Could have snatched up her sketches and walked away. Instead, she gazed at his poor fingers. It was the first time she'd seen him without gloves. Initially, she assumed his fingers were bent into an awkward fist. Then she realized they weren't so much bent as missing. Three of them were short stubs cut off at the first knuckle. His forefinger and thumb were present, though they were oddly crooked.

She thought back to the way he'd acted when she saw him attempting to tie a knot in Denver. She'd laughed at him for not taking off his gloves. He must have thought her terribly cruel.

He pulled his mangled hand away and shoved it into his pocket. She thought he might say something. Instead, he reached around her other side with his

right hand, gripping the opposite corner of the
sheet and lifting it to look at the other pages. She
could feel his warm breath against her shoulder.

"Very nice work, Miranda. You have a gift." He
looked into her eyes—so close she could see his
eyes weren't the pure dark pools she'd thought
them to be—there were tiny flecks, as though someone had sprinkled gold dust into a cup of coffee.

"I'm no artist, Mister . . ." She swallowed. "Ben."
She turned to look at the picture she'd drawn; the
simple lines were nothing special. "Not like bringing horses and men to life the way you did." She still
had a vivid memory of his battle scenes. "These are
only pencil sketches."

"They show a good eye, though." Ben leaned
closer as he examined the pictures again, and she
could feel heat radiating from him. A day's growth
of beard darkened his jaw and made him look even
more dangerous than usual. "And a steady hand."

"Nothing like your work."

"Better than I could do now."

He stepped away from her and it was all she could
do to keep herself from reaching out to him. She
wanted to tell him she knew exactly how he felt about
his hand. She wished she could hide her face as easily
as he shoved his hand into his pocket, or covered it
with a glove. The thought made her feel guilty and
selfish. Her scar was ugly, but it didn't keep her from
doing simple tasks. She fisted her hand and wondered what it would be like to do without her fingers.

"Miranda and I are going to make them, Mr. Lansing. You're a city man—what do you think? How do
they compare to the fashion women are wearing in
Boston these days?"

Ben looked back through the pictures. "I'm no

expert on fashion, but I imagine Boston ladies would be pleased to wear these."

"I think so, too." Clarisse picked up the papers and walked over to the fabric lined up against the wall. "Don't know if I have any cloth here that suits. We may have to order something nicer if we want to start a new fashion in Denver."

Miranda was relieved to have an excuse to step away from Ben. She ran her hand over the many colors of cloth, then thought of Mrs. Wick. "I expect we'll do better if we can sell them for a good price."

"Yes, you're right." Clarisse pulled a red wool off the shelf, then set it back. "One thing about having money, it tends to make people appreciate a good bargain."

"That is why the rich always grow richer." Ben's voice came from right beside her and Miranda jumped, causing her arm to brush against his. Instead of moving back as any decent man would do, he edged closer to her. "I think the blue there is very nice." Ben reached for a sky blue gingham and pulled the end in front of her face. "It would bring out the color in your eyes."

Miranda's foolish heart was now thumping so violently in her throat she couldn't speak. Even more vexing was the fact that nothing remotely clever came to mind.

"Oh, Mr. Lansing," Clarisse said. "I'm sorry, I've forgotten to ask what you need."

"That's quite all right, Mrs. Wyatt. You have good reason to be distracted."

Again, his eyes met Miranda's and she felt the same warmth as when his hand had touched her. It was time to escape. "I . . . I should go to Doc's and find Pa." Miranda hastened toward the door. "I'll stop in later, Clarisse." *After Ben has gone and I've regained my ability to think clearly.*

Once out in the bright sunlight, she stared up at the mountains. *Dammit, Miranda, get some sense. May as well put the silver in a bag and hand it to the thief as fall for that man's charm.* She stood tall and marched down the street and right past the doctor's office. She stopped when she reached Rita's and looked up and down the street, hoping no one was watching as she turned and headed back to her destination.

That evening Ben was ready to do just about anything to take his mind off Miranda Chase. Hell, he'd even ordered a whiskey to try and rid his memory of the scent of lavender that filled his nostrils as he leaned over her—much too close for propriety. Damn it, he knew better.

He gazed across the table at the lovely lady he'd invited to join him. "Rita Diaz." Benjamin toyed with the glass, swirling the amber liquid around. "You're Spanish, then?"

"Yes." She laughed. "Does this surprise you?"

"No, although I am surprised to see a Spanish lady running a saloon."

She laughed again. "I'm a widow. This"—she spread her arms, indicating the saloon—"was the only thing my husband left me."

He set his full glass down again, then looked into Rita's dark brown eyes. "I'm sorry, ma'am, for your loss."

She acknowledged his words with a tilt of her head. "It has been many years."

He had persuaded Rita to join him for a few moments, but he hadn't yet found the words to ask his question. He wanted to have a sense of Rita's position in the town first. After a few moments of conversation, he had found her open and charming. No doubt she knew as much as anyone about everything that went on in Fort Victory. This saloon, perhaps even more than Wyatt's store or the church, provided a central meeting place for the community. Everyone in the area—ranchers, townspeople, miners, and soldiers—came to Rita's occasionally. Even Thad Buchanan. According to Rita, he was a regular at her poker table.

"My mother was Italian," he said. "I spent some time living in Italy and France. I visited Barcelona once."

"I have heard that Barcelona is beautiful."

"Yes, it's very impressive. My father has always been so proud of the traditions we have in Boston, all of our history. Barcelona had a university and great cathedrals before Boston was even discovered."

Rita laughed. "You do not agree that God created the world, starting with Boston first?"

"Certainly not."

"That is very strange. I was told that you are a brother of Arthur Lansing."

Ben laughed. He liked Rita. The small glass in his hand seemed far heavier than it should. He set it down. The last thing he needed was to journey back to those months of darkness he had experienced last year in Europe, when he marked time by the number of wine bottles that accumulated in his rooms. When he'd finally run out of money and sobered, six months had passed. That was a lot of time to waste, even for someone who had nothing better to do with his life. If his prudent father hadn't insisted Ben buy a return ticket when he left Boston, he might still be in Paris.

He'd come home intending to write Arthur and insist his brother pay the money he owed. It was a shock to learn that his brother was dead and no one had bothered to inform Ben. He lifted the cup and swirled the whiskey around again. Liquid courage— but he was afraid to drink it.

"I'm keeping you from your drink, *Señor* Lansing." Rita started to rise.

"No." Ben lifted his hand indicating she should stay, then swallowed the whiskey in one gulp, feeling it burn down his throat. Liquid courage. He used his maimed left hand to wave to the bartender for more whiskey, then let the hand remain on the table where Rita could see it. Hell, the whole town may as well see it now. Miranda had managed to hide her repugnance, but he could see she had been shocked when she set her eyes on his mangled fingers.

Rita glanced at his hand, then back up to his face. "Perhaps you will tell me what you wish to discuss?"

Her accent was dark and exotic, like her eyes. There was no pity in those eyes, just the same friendly light he had seen when he first met her.

"May I call you Rita?"

"Of course. Everyone calls me Rita." She rolled the "*r*" delicately.

"What brought you to Colorado, Rita?"

"I was born in what you call Colorado Territory."

A tall gentleman suddenly appeared at her side. "Rita's people were here long before your people, Mr. Lansing. Rita's family came here with a grant of land from the Spanish government—"

"Our land was far to the south of Fort Victory," Rita

interrupted. "Mr. Lansing, may I present my defender, Dr. Calvert. Cal, this is Benjamin Lansing."

Ben shoved his left hand into his pocket and stood to shake the doctor's hand.

"Mr. Lansing." The doctor peered into Ben's eyes.

"Arthur's brother," Rita said.

"Ah." The doctor nodded. "Most folks hereabouts call me Doc, or Cal. I answer to pretty much anything."

"Please, join us." Benjamin indicated a chair. He sat when the doctor did.

Almost before they could be seated, the bartender arrived with another glass and a bottle.

"Real Scotch whiskey," Doc said, pouring a healthy shot into his glass, then holding the bottle over Ben's empty cup. "Would you care for some?"

"Thank you," Ben said, against his better judgment. As the doctor poured, Benjamin noticed the man's coat was worn, the cuff of his sleeve beginning to fray. He turned back to the saloon owner.

"How well did you know my brother, Rita?"

The light in her eyes dimmed, but she didn't turn away from him. She wasn't one to avoid an unpleasant topic, but he had no doubt that the subject of his brother was distasteful to her.

"Everyone knew Arthur Lansing. He made certain of that."

"Did he?"

"He wore only the finest clothing and built the grandest house this side of Golden and Denver." She glanced at the doctor seated beside her, then turned back to Benjamin, raising her chin to look directly into his eyes. "Everyone knew him."

There was something she was holding back. What, and why?

"What is it you want to know?" Doc spoke slowly, before tilting his cup for a sip.

Ben lifted his cup with his left hand, just to prove he could. He trembled slightly but didn't spill a drop. He tasted the whiskey, then set the cup back on the table, dropping his hand onto his lap.

"I'd like to know more about how he died, to start with."

Rita had been leaning an elbow on the table, but at Benjamin's question she sat upright, straight and stiff.

"I reckon you heard about the fire, Mr. Lansing." The doctor's eyes narrowed on him.

"Ben, please." He hoped to return the conversation to the friendly tone they'd enjoyed a moment ago. "I've heard there was a house fire, but I haven't heard any details." Ben curled his fingers around his glass, bringing it halfway to his lips. "How'd it happen? Who was there?" He took a swallow, feeling heat clear to the pit of his stomach.

"You should speak with Mercy and Thad Buchanan. They can tell you the entire story. You know they saved young Jonathan's life."

Ben couldn't help wondering whether the Buchanans would tell him everything. If they had something to hide, listening to their version of the facts would be unlikely to help him find the truth. "Yet they weren't able to save my brother."

"What are you suggesting, Mr. Lansing?" Rita drew herself up as though she'd been personally offended.

Hell, he wasn't suggesting anything, just inquiring. "It seems to be quite a coincidence that Mr. and Mrs. Buchanan were the only witnesses to the fire. Where were the hired men? I understood that my brother employed a large number of men, yet they were all gone that day. It might be a coincidence, but it still means that the two people who most stand to benefit from my brother's death were the only witnesses when he died."

"Benefit?" Doc asked. "You mean because of the boy?"

"Yes." Ben slammed his glass down, splashing whiskey over his fingers. "They adopt my nephew and have control over Arthur's entire fortune. It could be a coincidence. Or it could have been planned."

"If you are looking for someone to confirm your suspicions, you have not asked the right woman, *Señor* Lansing." Rita glanced at Doc, then back to Ben. "Mercy Buchanan has honor. Enough that she will raise the son of the man who tried to—"

"Rita!" Cal placed his hand over Rita's.

"He must hear it, Cal."

Cal held Rita's gaze for a moment, then relaxed, withdrawing his hand from hers. He nodded.

"*Señor* Lansing, I am sorry to be the one to tell you. Your brother was not an honest man. He sent men to kill my friend—Mercy—"

"No!" Ben would not believe his brother was a killer.

"She owed him a great deal of money."

"More reason for him to want her alive. Why would he—"

"He wanted her ranch."

Ben stared at the Spanish beauty. She was either lying, or she had lost her mind.

"It is true, *Señor*, when Mercy went to your brother's house, she found him trying to burn the evidence that he was behind the theft—"

"Theft?"

"Mr. Lansing," Doc said, "it's all rather complicated. As I said before—talk with Thad and Mercy."

"They'll tell me that my brother intentionally burned his own house?"

"No, most likely that was an accident," Doc said. "He used too much kerosene, apparently."

"According to Mercy."

"*Sí, sí!*" Rita clucked impatiently. "Kerosene everywhere and soon the house went up in flames."

"Kerosene?"

Rita raised an eyebrow. Hell. Someone had set the fire intentionally then. *Damn!* He thought again about his young nephew. Ben determined to find out exactly what had happened.

"Thank you for the information," Ben said.

"I hope we've set your mind at ease, Mr. Lansing."

At ease? Hardly. He was more suspicious than ever.

"I think you'll agree in the end that your brother made his own problems," Doc said. "A shame really, for the boy's sake. Have you seen your nephew?"

Ben nodded, breaking away from Rita's gaze to study the doctor. "Yes, I met him yesterday."

"I'm glad. Then you saw for yourself how well he's doin' with the Buchanans. He's a fine boy."

Ben nodded again. He'd seen how the boy cared for the Buchanans, but he had mixed feelings about how well they took care of him. *Hellfire and damnation. Why does everything have to be so damn complicated?*

"*Señora?*"

Rita turned to a young girl who was calling to her from the kitchen. "You gentlemen will excuse me?"

Ben stood as Rita walked away. He was definitely feeling the effects of the whiskey.

"Tell me, Mr. Lansing"—Doc leaned toward him

and refilled his glass—"did you injure your hand in the war?"

Ben flexed his maimed appendage. He lifted the whiskey glass and swallowed the contents. "Stupid accident. War was nearly over." He chuckled, though he knew it wasn't in the least bit funny. "We were loading the cannons onto a train and one broke loose, slipped down the ramp."

The doctor bent to examine the hand more carefully. "It was crushed? I'm surprised they were able to save your fingers at all."

"One doctor wanted to cut off the whole damn hand, but another surgeon said he could fix it. You know the funny thing?" He didn't wait for the doctor to respond. "It doesn't make any difference. Might as well have cut it off."

"I'm sure you'll find as time passes that you can do quite a lot with your thumb and index finger intact."

Ben chuckled. "You doctors. I'll wager you've never tried to paint with a hand that can barely grip a brush." He nodded to the doctor and made his way toward the stairs. What he needed was some time alone to decide what he would do next. Near the foot of the stairs a clumsy cowboy stumbled into him.

"Sorry," the man mumbled, clinging to Ben for a moment until he regained his balance.

Ben shrugged out of the man's grip and started up the stairs. A few steps up, Ben turned and watched the drunken oaf swagger out of the saloon. He slipped his left hand into his coat pocket and felt a piece of paper that hadn't been there before.

Ben raced out the door, hoping to get a better look at the cowboy. Peering up and down the street, Ben found no sign of the man. Pulling out the sheet of paper, he stared at the sentence that had been scrawled across the surface:

If you want to know who kilt your brother, follow the road to the Lansing ranch tomorrow at sunrise.

Chapter 8

Benjamin Lansing was no fool. Although he was not in the habit of wearing a gun, he strapped on his old Colt Army before leaving his room. He'd arranged to borrow a horse for the day, and now sauntered over to the livery to pick up the nag and be on his way.

He walked warily down the quiet street as the sky turned from deep blue to indigo. Daylight was perhaps a half hour away. In spite of the whiskey he'd drunk last night, he'd slept poorly. He did not want to believe Thad and Mercy Buchanan were murderers. And he couldn't bear the thought that Miranda was lying for them. No. It wasn't possible.

He caught himself smiling at the thought of her. In spite of his better judgment, he was fond of the petite young lady with the grace of an antelope and the heart of a lioness.

His instinct to trust Miranda might be based on all the wrong reasons. The spark in her eyes that had intrigued him from the moment they met, the way her smile burned so easily through the layers of reserve it had taken him years to build up. Or the sway of her hips as she walked. Just looking at Miranda drove every bit of his good sense far beyond his reach. And yet he knew he was right to trust her.

He drew a breath and released it slowly—a trick he'd learned to help him keep his wits about him in every situation. He must concentrate on the facts. Miranda Chase was beautiful and he was drawn to her, true. As to her character, he admired the way she defended herself and her family. Her carriage and the determination in her voice conveyed as much as her words that she believed in her cause. He'd wager that she was convinced of her sister's innocence beyond the natural loyalty of a sibling. If she was fooling him, then he could never again rely on his ability to judge honesty in a beautiful woman.

In the end, it didn't really matter whether he trusted Miranda or not. He couldn't let his feelings for her cause him to ignore the evidence against her sister and brother-in-law. Ben glanced around the sleeping town. He didn't have evidence, yet. Suspicion and allegations in abundance, but no way to prove anything. And he couldn't be certain that his meeting this morning would lead him to proof of anything. It could as easily be a trap.

If someone had killed his brother, that same person might also want to be rid of him. The most likely suspects seemed to be Thad and Mercy Buchanan, but he hadn't ruled out the possibility that there was someone else behind his brother's death. Rita was convinced that Mercy was a victim of Arthur's plot. A small doubt entered Ben's mind. As he'd traveled across the country, Ben had considered the possibility that his brother had cheated him, that he'd never intended to repay his debt. The possibility that Arthur was dishonest was one thing.

But accepting that he was a murderer? Ben shook his head. He did not know Arthur well, but he couldn't believe his brother was a killer.

What if Arthur and Mercy were both victims of another plot? It was a possibility Ben needed to rule out.

He gripped his Colt with his right hand, slipping it out of the holster and letting it drop back in. He'd spent years in his youth training himself to shoot as well with his right hand as his left. He'd taken money from foolish gamblers on more than one occasion, challenging them to a game with pistols and targets and goading them into doubling the bet when he switched to his "bad hand."

Little did he suspect how important that skill would become to him one day. Now he could barely grip the gun with his left hand, let alone pull the trigger. Ready for anything, Ben walked into the small livery that was attached to Jock Meier's blacksmith shop.

"Morning, Mr. Lansing." Young George Meier stifled a yawn as he greeted him.

"Morning, George," Ben said. "Have my horse ready?"

"Yes, sir." The boy led a dappled gray gelding out of a stall. The animal looked as though an afternoon of grazing in the pasture might do him in. Ben wondered if he could carry a full-grown man any distance.

"Does he have a name?"

"We call him Lightning."

Ben studied the docile creature. Either the beast had been very different in his youth, or the name was intended to be ironic. He led the horse out into the pink light of dawn. The animal didn't protest, but Ben doubted he could achieve a gallop.

He thought about exchanging the horse for one with more spirit, but then remembered he was lucky to have any ride for the price he could afford to pay.

He mounted Lightning and set off toward his brother's ranch at a modest pace that would allow him to keep a sharp lookout for danger.

The first rays of dawn reflected off the rugged peaks, creating a spectacular scene. Ben was impressed anew with the grandeur of the Rocky Mountains as they reached for the crystal-blue sky. The snow-covered crests shone like diamonds in the morning sun, sparkling above the purple granite and bright fall colors of the slopes below. The entire scene sent a shiver up Ben's spine. Beauty and majesty such as this would be a real challenge to capture on canvas. The knowledge that he would be forced to leave that joy to another artist did not diminish the wonder of the view.

The morning quiet was broken only by birdsong and some small critter, perhaps a squirrel, chirping excitedly up in one of the trees that forced themselves miraculously out of the rocks above the trail. As he rode away from town, Ben breathed deeply of the clean mountain air. An unaccustomed serenity settled over his shoulders as he rode up and away from town. He shook off the feeling, reminding himself that he must remain vigilant.

He refused to be fooled into thinking there was real peace available to him here. This place, these mountains, contained no magical cures for his troubles. Just the opposite—this town embodied trouble. His brother had been killed here; his money had disappeared here as well. The loss of the money and his brother's death could be an unfortunate coincidence, or they could point to a plot of theft and murder. To solve the mystery, Ben must keep a clear and objective mind. He mustn't allow the beauty of his surroundings to lull him into complacency. That way was for fools—he knew better. No one alive would look out for his interests. That was entirely up to him.

After thirty minutes of traveling at a steady pace, Ben spotted a group of men, about a hundred yards ahead, knotted together at the side of the trail. He transferred the reins to his left hand, letting his right hand drift close to his revolver. The men glanced up as he approached but paid little attention to him. It was either a very clumsy ambush, or a coincidence that they were gathered in this spot. He slowed the horse to a walk, waiting for some sign of the group's intentions.

When they made no move, he took the initiative, reining Lightning to a stop a few yards from the cluster of men. "Morning," he said, searching the faces to see whether he recognized any of them.

A stout man tossed his black hat at one of his colleagues and approached Ben. "Mornin', Mr. Lansing." The man walked with a slight limp, his hands hovering near the pair of revolvers that hung from his hips.

Ben sat taller and gave the man a slight nod to acknowledge the greeting. He kept one eye on the stout fellow, while remaining on guard for any threatening move from the others. There was no point in pulling his revolver against a half-dozen armed men. On the other hand, if any of them pulled a gun, Ben's only chance would be to see whether Lightning had it in him to live up to his name.

"And you are?"

The man favored him with a broad grin. "Name's

O'Reilly, Mr. Lansing. I'm an old friend of your brother's."

"You'll forgive my skepticism, Mr. O'Reilly, but my brother never mentioned you." Nor could Ben imagine his brother would befriend an Irishman, unless the man happened to be wealthy. If O'Reilly had money, his clothing and appearance didn't show it. Arthur was very conscious of class and social standing. Few sat lower on society's ladder than the Irish.

O'Reilly laughed. "Very good, Mr. Lansing. You're a smart one, you are." He crossed his hands over his large belly and continued laughing for so long that Ben wondered if the man had consumed whiskey for breakfast. "Sadly, I didn't have a chance to know your brother well before he passed on. But some of my men here worked fer him. They told me the full story of how he was killed and his son cheated out of his rightful inheritance."

"What's your interest in this, O'Reilly?"

Impossibly, the man's grin widened. "I hope you'll be willin' to pay for my services in setting things to rights. Besides, I have me own reasons for seeing justice is done to the bitch who killed him."

"Killed?" Ben's stomach knotted at the thought of his brother being murdered. "I heard it was an accident."

"Come," O'Reilly said. "Have some breakfast with us and hear the whole story. Decide fer yerself if it were accident, or murder."

Ben swallowed. That was exactly what he wanted to do. He nodded and waited for the men to mount their horses and lead the way up into the mountains.

Even the bright sunshine did not diminish the chill in the air as they climbed up a steep trail that seemed to lead to oblivion. An excellent location if these men intended to kill him and leave his body for the wild animals to consume in the wilderness. Just as Ben was considering how best to escape, the trail widened and he caught sight of a bustling encampment.

It didn't take long for Ben to conclude the tent city was a mining settlement. He'd heard of such outposts springing up at the mere rumor of gold. Both sides of the muddy road were lined with canvas tents and lopsided wooden shacks, quick shelters erected with no thought for the future. The group brought the horses to a stop after passing through most of the makeshift village.

Inside one of the larger tents, O'Reilly introduced Ben to several men who used to work for Arthur. All were dressed in filthy rags. It was hard to say which man was more desperate until he met a skinny little fellow named Jed, who barely looked up as O'Reilly spoke his name.

"Mr. *Lansing* here"—O'Reilly raised his voice to get Jed's attention—"is interested in finding evidence that Mercy Buchanan killed his brother."

That comment brought Jed to his feet. "Lansing?" He squinted up at Ben.

"That's right. Arthur Lansing was my brother."

"Well, then." Jed combed his fingers through his greasy hair. "Evidence you want, you come with me."

Jed led them outside, behind the row of tents and up a rutted path to a small graveyard.

"That's where we laid Luther to rest." Jed pointed to a wooden marker that sat next to a large chunk of granite. There was no name on the marker, only a primitive cross cut into the wood.

"Who's Luther?" Ben was growing impatient. None of the men had said a word that would help him understand his brother's death.

Jed sniffled and wiped his shirtsleeve over his nose. "He was workin' with me and O'Reilly to get the money rightfully belonging to Mr. Lansing, your brother, when Mercy shot him dead."

"Mercy Buchanan killed this man?"

"Damned right, she did," O'Reilly said. "Folks in Fort Victory say we was tryin' to rob her. But that ain't it. As Jed says, the money was rightfully Lansing money. All we was doin' was tryin' to make certain that cash made it to your brother."

Ben stared at O'Reilly. "I heard another story. That my brother tried to kill her—Mercy."

"That's the rumor *she* started in town. It's why none of us can show our faces there. They all believe the bitch." O'Reilly punctuated his remark by spitting on the ground.

"If you're truly innocent, why don't you go to the sheriff?"

"The bitch is clever and she has friends in that town. Even the judge and the sheriff are friendly with her, if you take my meanin'." He winked at Ben and shot him a disgusting grin.

"Look at us, Mr. Lansing," Jed said. "You think anyone's gonna listen to our side of the story after she tells 'em we come after her and shot her and all?"

"Who did shoot her?"

"I admit I shot the bitch," O'Reilly said. "Wouldn't you, in self-defense? You seen what she done to Luther." He pointed at the grave. "He died slow, too; it took three days. I ended up with a piece of lead in my leg from that cheat Thad Buchanan. He was with her, you see. We didn't have a chance—with Luther dyin' and me wounded. By the time we made it to Fort Victory, she had 'em convinced we were the thieves. We couldn't even get near the town to talk to the sheriff, not with a price on our heads." He glanced up, but didn't hold Ben's gaze. "Then after she gets your brother's money and ranch, she marries Buchanan. I say the two of 'em were plottin' together all along."

Ben turned away. A man buried in the ground wasn't proof of anything. And he wasn't inclined to take the word of this bunch without some real evidence; but he couldn't just ignore these men, either. Their story was consistent with what his brother had written him.

Arthur had mentioned an unreasonable neighbor standing in the way of expanding his ranch. Although the letters hadn't mentioned a name, Ben had no doubt his brother was referring to Mercy. Too bad he hadn't kept the letters so that he could see the precise words Arthur had used. Ben hadn't really cared at the time. He'd skimmed the letters for news of when Arthur would repay the loan. Arthur always worded his letters carefully, bragging about how well his ranch was doing and all the money he would be making in the near future. He never mentioned a definite date. There was always one more investment opportunity that Arthur couldn't miss. Ben considered the men gathered around O'Reilly. If his brother had hired this lot, he was a poor judge of character.

"I thank you gentlemen for your candor, but I'm afraid it doesn't help me." He turned and headed down the hill, his head spinning with possibilities. With all these conflicting stories, he was never going to be able to prove anything.

"I've an idea of how we can set things right, Mr. Lansing." O'Reilly favored him with a wide grin as they reached the bottom of the hill. "The cattle."

"What do you mean?"

"They'll be roundin' up the cattle next week. You mark my words—all the new calves will get the Bar Double C brand. Not a one will be left for that poor nephew of yours. They aim to take it all."

"You have a plan to prevent it?"

"With your permission, the men and I will make certain that doesn't happen. We'll see the boy gets his fair share and the Buchanans don't cheat him."

"How can you do that?"

"These boys are the best cattlemen around these parts. You leave everything to us."

"Your plan sounds illegal."

O'Reilly grinned. "Certainly not. That cattle belongs to the boy, doesn't it?"

"Yes."

"We're preventing an injustice then. That's all we're about. Setting things to rights again after those Buchanans have tried to steal from an innocent child."

Ben tried to look O'Reilly in the eye, but the man's eyes never settled long enough. He always seemed to be planning an escape. Ben chose his words carefully. "You're talking about stealing the cattle."

"'Tisn't theft when it's the boy's property, now is it?"

"I'll go to the judge and seek an order—"

"Based on what? The judge'll believe Mercy as to how much of the cattle is hers and how much is Lansing cattle. She's had the past year to mix them until no one will be able to tell."

"Weren't the cattle branded?"

"Not the calves. They're the real value."

Without knowing the cattle business, Ben couldn't

be sure whether O'Reilly's accusations made sense. "I'll go to the Buchanans, they have been willing to talk—"

"And you think it likely they'll admit they've stolen the boy's cattle." O'Reilly laughed. "You're a trusting soul, Mr. Lansing."

Ben glared at the man. His instinct was not to trust anyone—not the Buchanans, and certainly not O'Reilly. "What exactly do you propose, then?"

"We find the herd and take out those with the Lansing brand and half of the unbranded calves."

"You'll want a share of any cattle you salvage, naturally."

"Yes, I should think half—"

"Half?" Ben nearly shouted it.

"We're taking all the risks. And if we don't act, the boy will have nothing."

He clamped his teeth together and forced himself to appear calm. "I can't agree to half."

"You drive a hard bargain, Mr. Lansing. Same as your brother." O'Reilly smirked. "The boy will have two head for every one we take. And we'll be wantin' some cash for our trouble."

"Cash?"

"I assume you will want to remunerate us for lookin' out for your nephew's interest."

"One third of the cattle would be compensation enough for returning Jonathan's own cattle to him." Ben shook his head. "No, I'm not interested in recovering the cattle. What interests me is the question of whether or not the Buchanans have treated the boy fairly. I'll pay fifty dollars for real proof that the Buchanans stole from him. And I want a promise that you won't violate the law. No theft."

"Goes without sayin', Mr. Lansing. We're law-abiding men." O'Reilly shoved a cigar between his teeth. "You count on us, sir." He pulled the cigar out and showed his crooked teeth again. "We'll get you your evidence."

Ben nodded and shook hands with O'Reilly. He had a peculiar sensation deep in his gut that he'd made a pact with the devil, but it was getting very difficult to tell who was right and who was wrong in this matter. All he wanted was to get to the root of it, sort it all out and find his money. If there was any money left to find.

He reminded himself that his money was the most important thing. Without cash he wouldn't be able to move on to the new life he had planned far away from a certain pair of blue eyes—sweet innocence attached to temptation. He had to get out of Colorado Territory and soon. If that meant taking the boy with him, so be it.

He'd take Jonathan to Boston. Surely one of his married brothers would take responsibility for their nephew. They weren't entirely heartless. The image of Jonathan looking up at Mercy gave Ben a slight twinge of doubt, but he couldn't rely on the judgment of a six-year-old boy. Children became attached to any adult who looked after them. His own childhood was proof enough of that. Ben had adored his father, even though his father had always treated him like a bad investment—the son who was destined to be a failure. Ironically, his father's prediction had come true.

Ben would make his own determination of what was best for his nephew, then he could get on with his life. Greece, the Caribbean or perhaps the Sandwich Islands. Somewhere warm, tropical, and far away.

He mounted Lightning, wondering briefly whether the animal could run downhill, but then thought better of trying. He allowed the horse to meander down the mountain while Ben sorted through the alleged plots of theft and murder. Mercy Buchanan did not seem capable of murder. She'd been far too gentle with Jonathan. Miranda had said her sister had raised her. Ben could believe that, seeing the natural way she had with his nephew. It seemed unlikely that such a woman would plot to kill an innocent man, not even for the substantial fortune that Arthur had. Her husband might well be the real culprit.

He decided to turn toward the Lansing ranch. It was time he looked at the rubble himself, to see whether there was anything left that could point to what had happened the day of the fire. There was little chance that anything remained there after a year, but he needed to see for himself.

He glanced back over his shoulder at the mining camp. He'd forgotten to ask the men gathered there whether any of them had been present the day of the fire. If not, where had all the hired hands been? Now he knew where to find them, he'd be back. There were many questions he needed answered. They might be more likely to talk if he could get them away from O'Reilly. Today, he'd look around his brother's property before he headed over to the Bar Double C ranch to check on his nephew.

It was his nephew that drew him, not Miranda. *Damn!* It was a sad thing when a man lied to himself. And worse when he couldn't succeed.

Chapter 9

Miranda stood up in the stirrups and let Princess run. It felt wonderful to be out in the open with the wind blowing through her hair. She'd regret it later when she tried to brush out the knots, but sometimes she had to let go no matter the consequences.

She watched ahead for holes or other obstacles as Princess flew over the gray-green autumn grass. She felt the pounding hooves from her knees to her hips as she leaned into the wind. Back home, Mercy was working on lessons with Jonathan. Thad and Mercy had both talked about wanting a real school for the children, but Miranda couldn't help feeling Jonathan enjoyed having his mother to himself, whether it was for lessons, chores, singing, or playing games. Her heart ached seeing the two of them together and knowing that Ben Lansing might try to take the boy away.

She refused to dwell on that thought. Instead, she urged Princess into a faster gallop, building up speed as she approached the creek and leaped over it. They raced across the open field a hundred yards from a group of cows, and Miranda laughed at their startled bellowing. This ride was exactly what she needed. A bit of time alone with her thoughts, away from the family and their watchful eyes.

She eased Princess slower until they were trotting and then walking toward the old Lansing place. She sighed. Mercy and Pa were in the habit of watching out for her; they couldn't get used to the idea that she was here to help them. But Miranda knew something they couldn't understand: what she wanted most was to feel useful and needed.

She leaned forward to stroke Princess's neck, wondering whether to head home. The ride had cleared her head as she'd hoped it would, and there were plenty of chores waiting for her. Curiosity kept her riding toward Lansing's barn. She wanted to see how badly the house had been damaged by the fire. Besides, she might see Buck, or one of the other hired men. It would be nice to talk to a plain man for a change instead of a fancy-talking city slicker who set her heart racing and her mind crawling, or stopping altogether.

Buck was a gentle soul. He might not be as handsome as Ben, but he was a good, honest, hard worker. And he kept himself pretty clean, for a cowboy. It was bad luck that looking into Buck's eyes never made her heart thump against her chest like a wild beast. Maybe she'd try flirting with Buck anyway. Maybe if she showed a little interest, it would change the way he looked at her.

The remains of the house finally came into view beyond the barn. Little more than a foundation with a stone fireplace in the center. Near the barn, Miranda spotted a man and a horse. Perhaps she would see one of the hired men, after all. She clucked her tongue, prodding her horse to trot.

Too late, she saw it was not Buck mounting the dappled gray. It was Ben Lansing.

Ben thought for a moment he was imagining her—the small, wild-haired blonde on the dark mare. "Miranda?"

She hesitated before bringing her horse closer.

"What brings you here?" he asked.

"Went out for a ride and ended up here." She glanced down at his steed and grinned. "I hope you didn't buy him."

Ben shrugged. "He's not so bad. Goes where I want and works hard."

"So long as you aren't in a hurry." She chortled. "Old man Meier can't seem to get rid of the critter."

"I'm in no hurry. Been enjoying the views." And none as lovely as the one he had now—Miranda smiling and looking as though she were holding back a laugh.

She turned away toward the remains of the house. "You wouldn't know to look at that pile of rubble that it had been a fine house." Miranda dismounted. "Do you mind if I look around?"

Ben watched her take in the sight. "There's not much left to see." He swung down from Lightning. "I'll join you."

They tethered the horses near the barn and walked over to the charred remains of the house. "Do you know whether they salvaged anything?" Ben asked.

She shrugged. "Mercy told me there wasn't much. Some silver, I think. A few trinkets they put aside for Jonathan."

Half of the back wall stood—several large logs that

Lansing had brought down from the mountains. Miranda stepped over what she thought had once been the threshold. "It's hard to picture it. There were steps going up here." She swept a hand up. "This stone fireplace was in a parlor near as big as our whole cabin, least before Thad added on the bedrooms. I never saw nothin' like it in this territory. Furniture come all the way from Boston. Fancy lace curtains and oil paintings on the wall." She looked at Ben. "Nice pictures. Were they . . . did you paint them?"

Ben nodded. "I did give them a painting I'd done of a foxhunt and a pencil drawing of our father."

"Yes, I remember those. The foxhunt hung right here in the entrance, next to the stairs. And your father, he . . . Arthur didn't look a bit like him, but you do."

"Funny you should say that. Father always said I was the only son who didn't look anything like him. I think it was because I have my mother's dark brown eyes."

"But Arthur's face was so round and your face has strong lines . . ." She blushed bright red and turned away from him so quickly she nearly fell over a large rock.

He caught her arm and she looked up at him, surprise making her eyes even larger than usual. She blinked and righted herself, pulling gently away from him. "Sorry, I was going to point out the dining room over there. Do you see where those broken bricks are? That was another large fireplace, only I reckon someone took the good bricks. Back there, where the one wall is still standing, that was Arthur's study." She walked toward it. "There was a heavy oak desk that didn't completely burn. Mercy found some ledgers in the desk."

"Ledgers?" That could help him find his money. "I'd like to see them."

"I don't know if she still has them. She told me they were pretty badly damaged."

Ben scowled.

"It's nicer when you smile."

He glared at her. "Not much to smile about here."

"I'm sorry." Her eyes dropped. "You're right. I wasn't thinkin'."

He touched her shoulder. "Don't apologize."

She looked up at him. His heart skipped a beat. The uneven rhythm pounding against his chest was the only evidence that time continued moving as they stood, his hand resting on her shoulder. Her eyes gazing into his.

"I'm sorry, Ben." Her eyes dropped to his chest, and she wondered if he, too, was struggling to breathe. She forced herself to smile back up at him. To appear calm, although her pulse was racing. She swallowed. "I'm sure seeing your brother's house like this is difficult for you. I should go."

Ben leaned forward until his nose nearly brushed hers. The heat from his palm against her shoulder had radiated on down through her body, causing pulses in strange places. She managed to draw in half a breath before his left hand settled on her hip and the world suddenly spun upside down.

She tilted her face up to meet the kiss she was certain was coming. He jerked his head back and seemed to notice his hands on her for the first time. He stuffed them into his pockets as he stepped back, nearly stumbling over a pile of debris.

"I'll come out to the ranch another day and check on those ledgers," he said. "You might ask your sister to save them for me, if she still has them."

When Miranda's heart started beating again, she nodded. "Of course." She looked around, focusing on anything other than Ben. *Dammit, Miranda, you'll have him thinking you wanted him to kiss you.* She pulled herself up taller and threw him a smile she hoped conveyed her indifference. "I'll be sure and give Mercy your message."

She led the way back toward the barn. When they were a few feet from the horses, they both started to speak at once, then grew silent. She took Princess's reins and met Ben's eyes over the horse's back. When no witty phrases came to mind, she turned and made a show of checking Princess's bridle. The silence extended for at least a minute until she mounted her horse.

"Tell your sister I'll come see her in the next day or two."

"I'll tell her," Miranda called over her shoulder as she pulled away.

"I'll see you then." Ben's voice faded behind her as she urged Princess away from him.

Later that afternoon, Miranda sat on the porch steps, shucking corn. The sunshine wasn't half as warm as the feeling of family that Miranda sensed around her. What a difference a few days had made. She could no more picture herself leaving Pa and Mercy than she could imagine trading Princess for a zebra.

Everything would be perfect here as soon as Ben Lansing left town. Surely, that would be soon. The man wouldn't want to be stuck here for the winter. Her chest ached as she thought about him. Only because he was causing her sister so much anguish.

It had nothing to do with the way he'd nearly kissed her. Hell, that made it sound as though he wanted her. The man was discussing business—it was Miranda who had crazy ideas about kisses and touches that made her tremble and want more.

"You found the last of the corn." Mercy lifted an ear from the pile on the top step.

Miranda felt her cheeks heat, though surely Mercy couldn't read her thoughts. "I'll take care of that."

Mercy kept the corn away from her sister and sat down next to her. "I can be trusted with corn husking. I've even been known to boil water without ruining it."

"All right." Miranda dropped the cleaned ear into the pot. "I'll get started on the biscuits." Miranda made to stand up.

"Wait." Mercy pulled her sister back down to the step. "Stay a minute, I'd like to talk."

Miranda retrieved another ear of corn, peeling the husk away as she waited for her sister to announce the topic of conversation.

"Seems longer than a year ago when we first met Thad," Mercy said.

Miranda thought back to her first encounter with Thad Buchanan on the street in Abilene, Kansas.

"It was more than a year, more like thirteen months."

Her sister smiled at Miranda's weak attempt at humor, then smoothed her fingers over the corn she held, removing the clinging corn silk. "You liked him immediately."

"And you hated him." Miranda grinned, remembering how hard Mercy had worked at avoiding the big man. Strange how things had worked out.

Mercy dropped the cleaned corn into the pot

and took another ear off the step. "No, I didn't hate him. I was scared."

"He is very big."

Mercy laughed. "Big men don't frighten me." She ripped the husk from the ear in her hands. "It wasn't his size—it was his eyes." She turned to look at her sister. "I felt as though he could see . . . my soul." She worried her lower lip. "That probably sounds silly. I . . . can't describe it any other way. I hated feeling so exposed." She sighed. "That and . . ." Mercy looked away, then seemed, for a moment, to be examining her boots. Finally, she looked at Miranda. "We're speaking woman to woman now, you understand?"

Miranda didn't know how to respond to that, so she nodded.

"Just between us, what frightened me most was that looking at him made me wish he was touching me"—she looked away again—"in the most intimate ways." Mercy turned back to Miranda. "I had thought those feelings were buried with Nate; then I met Thad and it . . . I didn't know how to react when all those feelings came back stronger than I had remembered them."

Miranda's mind rushed to Ben and she bent to pick at a stubborn bit of husk, hoping her sister wouldn't detect the heat glowing in her cheeks. If her sister had noticed the way she looked at Ben, perhaps he'd seen it as well. *Aw, hell, he could hardly have missed the way I made a fool of myself.*

"But . . ." Mercy put her hand over Miranda's, drawing her sister's eyes to her face. "I don't think that is what scares you about Thad."

Miranda blinked. "I'm not afraid of Thad." She

swallowed, relieved her sister hadn't mentioned Ben. "What makes you think he frightens me?"

Mercy raised one eyebrow.

"I am not." She smiled and held her sister's gaze. "I'd forgotten how big and strong he was, at first. . . . But I'm used to him now, and I reckon he wouldn't so much as smash a flea, unless the critter dared try and hurt you, or Jonathan."

Mercy favored Miranda with a half-smile and nodded. "You can count on him to look after you, too. Thad thinks of you as a sister, and he wants you to feel safe here."

"Are you truly happy with him?" Miranda asked.

"Do you really need to ask?"

Miranda looked at her sister. Glowing, Clarisse had said, and it was a good description. Still, she knew from experience a woman could fool herself into believing she was happy.

"You do seem happy. But . . ." She pushed a curl behind her ear. "A year ago you were so certain that loving a man could only lead to pain."

"I was wrong." Mercy leaned back against one of the posts that held the porch roof, her eyes far off again. "Pain comes, with or without loving. It's the loving that makes joy, though. We all need joy, little sister."

Miranda still had trouble believing that she was seeing tears glistening in Mercy's eyes. Something had changed her sister in the past year. Clarisse, Mercy, and even Pa seemed to think it was a good change. Miranda didn't know what to think. There was a part of her that figured the independent life Mercy had as a widow was ideal. But deep in her heart, where her good sense held no sway, Miranda wanted exactly what Mercy had. A man who loved her, and the chance to raise a family with that man.

"I'm glad for you. I am really. . . . Only I worry that he could hurt you."

"Hurt me?" Mercy tilted her head, her eyebrows coming together in a puzzled expression. "He loves me. Of course that means hurting me sometimes. The ones we love have the ability to really hurt us, much more than a stranger ever could." Mercy stretched a hand toward her, and Miranda thought perhaps she meant to touch her scarred face, but she squeezed her shoulder instead. "That is no reason to avoid love. Trust me on this." She pushed herself to her feet. "I'll leave you to fix supper now, I've got to bring the cows in for milking." She took a few steps and turned. "You were right about the cows, too. It's nice to have milk and butter."

Miranda brushed the last strands of white silk off the ear in her hand as she watched Mercy walk away. Her sister had been given a second chance at happiness. Miranda closed her eyes and sent up a quick prayer for her own second chance. "I'll be careful this time, Lord. If you give me another chance— I won't waste it."

Chapter 10

It had been a long while since Miranda had done hard work. It felt good. She stepped out of the small cabin her family called home, pulling the wet mop behind her. She'd cleaned everything from top to bottom. Now, some work in the garden, while the floor dried, then she could start supper. The water in the bucket was filthy, so she carried it out back to dump.

All day long she'd wanted to find a moment alone with Mercy, but Thad had managed to find chores that kept him underfoot. Now he seemed to be gone and Miranda couldn't find Mercy, either. She wiped her hands over her apron before carrying the bucket and mop out to the shed. There she considered the tools she would need for digging potatoes and onions. She sighed. Perhaps this would be a good day to work on putting up the beets.

She'd have to do something with the apples, too. The trees had never given so much fruit before. Mercy would enjoy some apple butter, and that could be preserved. She glanced up at the sun, high in the sky. Too late to start all that today. Time enough for an apple pie for dinner. Pa's favorite. She was going to need a lot more sugar next time they went into town.

"Better make a shopping list," she mumbled.

She'd pick some apples after digging potatoes. First, she should check on Pa. Maybe Jonathan was bored and would want to work with her for a while. He seemed to enjoy anything that involved digging in the dirt. She hurried past the barn in the direction of Pa's workshop.

"No!" Mercy cried out.

"Yes, I think so." Thad's voice sounded menacing.

A loud crash followed by Mercy groaning sent Miranda rushing into the barn. She grabbed the shovel they used for cleaning out the stalls.

"What the hell are you doing to my sister?"

Miranda cursed herself for not wearing her gun. She raised the shovel, ready to use it over Thad's skull if need be. He was on top of Mercy in a pile of straw.

"Stop!" Mercy yelled.

Miranda managed to hold back, to keep from bringing the shovel crashing over Thad. He rolled away from Mercy, who quickly pulled her dress over her naked body.

Miranda stood gaping at them, holding the shovel up in midair, still ready to strike.

"What the hell are you doing?" she managed to say, though the answer to her question was obvious.

Thad kept his back to her and she realized he was buttoning his pants. Miranda lowered the shovel. "Hell," she muttered, looking down at the dirt under her feet. Maybe she could take the shovel and dig herself a deep hole to crawl into.

"I thought you were busy in the kitchen." Mercy's voice was higher than usual.

"I finished cleaning and came out to check on Pa." Miranda cleared her throat. Out of the corner of her eye she saw Thad reach down to help his wife to her feet.

"I reckon I should make sure Jonathan isn't giving Pa too much trouble." He caressed Mercy's cheek. "I'll bet the boy would like to pick some apples."

Miranda looked up in time to see Mercy nod and Thad stalk out of the barn. Mercy watched her husband walk away, then turned, her face flushed a red so bright it shone through her sun-bronzed skin. "Miranda!" Mercy growled. "What possessed you to . . ." Her sister took in a deep breath and released it. "We thought we were alone here," she said more calmly.

"I'm sorry, I just . . . I heard a noise in here and I thought . . . Hell, with the baby coming and all, I'd have thought you'd be more careful."

Mercy closed her eyes and Miranda could almost hear her sister counting to try and calm herself. "Miranda, is that what you . . . Are you worried about the baby?"

Mercy pulled at the shovel and Miranda realized she'd been gripping it so tightly her hand was tingling. She released it and Mercy took the handle and leaned it against the wall. "Let's go for a walk. We need to talk about this."

Her older sister pulled an arm through Miranda's and they walked out into the sunshine together, feeling the warming rays against their backs as they made their way toward the aspens that screened Jake's Creek from the house. It wasn't until they were close enough to hear the murmuring of the stream that Mercy spoke.

"I appreciate you lookin' out for me and the baby,

but there's truly no need for you to be concerned."
Mercy squeezed Miranda's arm tight against her
side. "I think maybe I need to explain . . . about
Thad."

"I know . . . I know you're married and he's entitled to—"

Mercy giggled. It was a deep, throaty sound, but
still held a bit of the girl Miranda remembered
from her childhood. Mercy tugged Miranda to a stop
and turned to face her sister. "You make it sound like
it's his right and my obligation."

Miranda nodded. That was how she understood
it. Exactly.

Mercy flushed again, glowing in the sunlight,
even more beautiful than Miranda remembered
her. She'd always been so proud of her older sister
and felt so embarrassed that Mercy chose to hide her
beauty behind her rough men's clothing and bossy
ways. Now Miranda wanted to hide.

"It isn't like that." She sighed and looked across
the creek up to the mountains that stood sentinel
over their ranch. "What Thad and I share is special
for both of us." She favored her sister with a smile.
"I don't expect you to understand; you've not experienced it for yourself."

Miranda blushed and walked away so that her
back was to her older sister. Lord, it was hard to lie
to her. Not that she had experienced anything she'd
call pleasurable, but she was hardly the innocent
Mercy assumed her to be.

"I . . . I know it's difficult, but it's time we talk about
this. I tried before, but . . ." Mercy walked up behind
her and touched her shoulder. "At Fort Kearny,
when it seemed you were going to marry Harold
Pearson. We talked some about this, didn't we?"

"You said I shouldn't be afraid." Miranda managed almost to sound normal. "That it hurt a little at first, but it wasn't a bad hurt and it gets better."

"Is that what I said?"

Miranda thought back to the hurried advice her sister had given her before they parted. Most of it had been about money and protecting herself from the soldiers. There had been a brief talk about what to expect in the marriage bed. "That's all I remember."

"Well, I reckon I left out a good bit." Mercy walked over to the creek and sat on a rock. She pulled off her boots and stockings and wriggled her toes in the water.

Miranda pulled off her own boots and waded in, glad the uncomfortable conversation was over. She lifted her skirt and walked out to the middle of the stream where the water was halfway to her knees. The creek was so cold her feet went numb almost at once.

"Must have been a wet summer," she said. The creek would usually be much lower by October.

Mercy smiled up at her. "Yes, we were due one after five drought years." She reached into the water, pulled out a stone, and studied it.

Miranda watched her sister turn the rock in her hand. She rubbed at the mud, then bent to swish the rock in the water and study it some more. "Jonathan likes rocks with shiny bits in them. Of course, he likes them better when he finds them himself." She studied the rock for another moment, then dropped it back into the water. "Do you remember when we were girls and we wondered what it would be like to ride on a shooting star?"

Miranda smiled. Her sister had finally recognized that Miranda had grown up. They had been girls together, and now they were women together.

"We talked about how it would be to fly so fast through the black sky, remember?" Mercy continued.

"I remember you talking endlessly about the stars." Miranda kicked water at her sister.

Mercy laughed. "You've never been curious about them?"

"I reckoned you'd be the one to fly up there, not me."

Her older sister's face grew somber as she looked up at Miranda. To escape her sister's inspection, Miranda kicked water up at her.

"Hey!" Mercy scooped up a giant wave with her hands and Miranda was forced to retreat to the other side of the narrow creek.

Mercy's laugh floated over the water and Miranda couldn't help but join in. They faced each other, laughing. Mercy stopped first, gasping for breath and holding her side. Miranda splashed across the stream, feeling her gut twist.

"Are you all right?" Miranda put a hand on each of Mercy's shoulders.

Her older sister nodded and smiled. "Got to laughing so hard I couldn't breathe." She brushed a damp lock of hair back from her face. "Don't you start treating me like a china doll; bad enough I have Thad fussing over me all the time." She used a thumb to wipe water off of Miranda's cheek. "Look at the two of us acting like a couple of little girls."

Miranda smiled, glad to have her sister distracted. "We should change into dry clothes."

They collected their boots and turned back to the house, walking arm in arm, bare feet padding against the sun-warmed earth.

"What I've been trying so damn hard to say is this," Mercy said. "I know now what it feels like to ride a shooting star. At least as close as I'm ever likely to come to it. It's what Thad does to me when he touches me; I feel like I'm flying across the night sky. It isn't only Thad who gets pleasure from our loving. And you don't need to worry about the baby—"

"I heard you tell him 'no.'"

"Did I?" Mercy squeezed her brows together, then smiled. "Oh, yes, I did say that." She glanced at Miranda, then back up to the mountains. "He suggested we wait until tonight and I said 'no.' He likes to tease me, but it didn't last long. I have ways of getting what I want from him." She cleared her throat. "We really did think we were alone."

"You need to take care of yourself."

She reached for Miranda's hand and squeezed it. "You know how much it means to me to be carrying a baby after all those years of believing I couldn't."

Miranda nodded.

"I wouldn't do anything to risk harming our little miracle."

Miranda knew her sister spoke the truth. "I know that, only"—she drew in a long breath—"I reckon a baby growing inside you must be a fragile little thing."

"Fragile, yes, but not like a window pane. We . . . Thad and I are careful. He cares as much as I do about our baby. He's always been tender with me, but since we found out I was pregnant, he is so gentle."

Miranda chewed on her lower lip.

"Miranda." Mercy sighed.

The pity Miranda saw in her sister's eyes made her want to cry.

Mercy sat on the porch step and pulled her sister

down beside her. "Did someone hurt you? . . . When you were away?"

Miranda shook her head. "Why do you ask?"

"I don't mean to pry into your business, Miranda. But if you want to tell me anything . . ." Miranda turned away from Mercy's probing eyes. "I know you've seen a lot more of the world in the last year, and I can only imagine . . . Hell, even here in Fort Victory there's plenty of ugliness. But please trust me about Thad. He's a good man."

Miranda blinked back a tear. "I can see he is. He loves you."

"I hope one day you'll be lucky enough to find someone who loves you as much."

"I don't know . . ." Miranda swiped at the tear that rolled down her cheek. "How will I know when I've found him?"

"When it's right you'll know."

"Easy for you to say, you've chosen two men and been right both times. I've chosen two and look what happened."

"Two? So there was someone besides Harold?"

Miranda stared across the yard at the barn. "It was a silly mistake I made in Philadelphia. Luckily, you sent for me before it could go too far."

When her sister didn't respond, Miranda turned to see her staring. She waited for Mercy to accuse her of lying. Instead, she reached over and took Miranda's hand, giving it a warm squeeze. "Don't let a mistake or two in your past keep you from listening to your heart. You gave me that advice, remember?"

Miranda looked into her sister's eyes. "I don't think I understood how much it might hurt, opening up your heart to the wrong man."

"I won't promise you it'll be painless. But I can tell

you loneliness hurts just as much, and love is the only cure."

"I won't be lonely, Mercy. Not while I have you and Pa."

"I'm glad to have you here, but for your sake I hope when you're ready you find your own home. If I'm lucky it will be nearby. I want my children to know their Aunt Miranda."

"I want to know them, too." Miranda smiled at her sister. At least she could be certain she would find love here at home.

Miranda walked out to the pasture where the two milk cows spent their days grazing contentedly. "That's a nice simple life," she muttered as she opened the gate and walked in.

She'd left the supper cooking and offered to bring the cows in for milking while Mercy helped Jonathan with his lessons. Pa would keep an eye on the stove, making certain that Mercy didn't do anything that could ruin the stew. How her sister had managed to grow up without learning how to cook was beyond Miranda's understanding. She'd always thought her sister was smarter, stronger, and just better at everything. Only in the past few days had Miranda realized how important her own skills were to the family. It was good to feel needed.

At the sound of hoof beats, Miranda turned to the road in time to see a lone rider trotting toward the house. "Ben?" she whispered. It shouldn't have been a surprise; he had said he was coming. Still, her pulse started a wild jig at the sight of him. She was hopeless.

Slapping Gertie's rump, Miranda got the cows to

head toward the barn. Rosie followed the first cow at a pace that would make a snail impatient.

"I suppose you two will give plenty of cream tonight," Miranda said. This pair didn't waste energy on anything other than making milk. Just as well, maybe she could avoid seeing Ben altogether. He'd come to inquire about the books, not to see her. That was for the best, because she didn't need the likes of Ben Lansing troubling her.

After settling the cows into their stalls, Miranda fetched the stool and bucket to prepare for milking. The pad of footfalls near the door startled her, and she dropped the bucket. The outline of a large man appeared in the door with the evening sun behind him so that it was impossible to see the man's face.

"Thad?" Miranda's voice faltered.

"It's me." Ben walked toward her.

Miranda pulled herself taller. She sucked in a breath. "Are you looking for my sister, or my brother-in-law?"

"I've already spoken with your sister. You were right—she didn't keep my brother's ledgers." Ben stepped into the light from one of the open windows. "She's going to let me look through the copies she made." He kept walking toward her. "I came in here looking for you."

His eyes slid down and crept upward until she felt he was studying every inch of her. She lifted her chin in an effort to appear calm and certain of herself.

"Why are you afraid of me?"

"I'm not afraid." She glared at him, or at least she tried to glare.

He took another step forward and she stepped back before she could stop herself. *Damn the man!*

She set her hands on her hips. "What business do you have with me?"

"Unfinished business." His eyes held hers, and for a moment she couldn't breathe.

"It wasn't me who stepped away." The words slipped out and she realized that his rejection, which should have been a relief, still hurt.

"I know." Ben smiled and she could almost feel his lips on hers. "I want to apologize."

"Don't be silly. Why would you apologize?"

"Because I think I misled you."

"What do you mean?"

"I may have given you the impression I wasn't interested in kissing you."

"Who said anything about . . . kissing?"

He stepped forward again and she took another step back, finding her back against the solid wood of the barn wall.

"I did." Ben caressed her cheek, smooth as satin, but warm against his fingertips. "Stayed awake all night thinking about it."

She smiled and her eyes seemed to reflect the sunlight itself. Ben's heart skipped a beat. He skimmed his thumb under her chin and tilted her face up to his. Somewhere in the back of his mind a small voice warned him to stop. He didn't listen.

Her lips tasted good, felt wonderful. Soft, moist, and warm. He teased them open with his tongue and found his way inside, touching and tasting her tongue in a dance of sweet yearning that echoed the need he felt. For a moment, the pleasure of holding her was enough. Her small body tight against him—her scent sweeter than honey. Curse his weakness, he couldn't help wanting more. Reaching down, he cupped her bottom, feeling the round, supple shape even through the wool skirt she wore. He pressed her solidly against him, which only increased the agony of his desire. A quiet moan of pleasure came from deep in Miranda's throat, and the sound brought him a joy nearly as intense as the need he felt. He lifted his head and looked into her face—her eyes closed, a sweet smile upon her lips. Her lids slid open and she stared at him, the only movement the tip of her tongue touching her lips.

A tear trickled down her cheek. He dipped his head, kissing and licking the salty tear away. "Well, that was better than I dreamed it," he murmured against her cheek.

"Mr. Lansing?" Mercy's voice came from outside the barn.

Ben spun around and walked toward the door. "Yes, ma'am, I'm coming." He didn't dare look back at Miranda as he stepped quickly out into the sunshine, cursing himself for the fool he was.

What mad impulse caused her sister to invite Ben Lansing for supper Miranda couldn't imagine. Out of the corner of her eye she could see him sipping his coffee. He set the cup down and scraped the last of his pie onto his fork before lifting it slowly up to his lips.

He wiped a napkin over his lips and turned to face Mercy. "I've had no complaints about the food at Rita's, but this is the finest meal I've had in recent memory."

"I'm pleased that you enjoyed it, Ben. My sister is a fine cook."

Miranda's cheeks flamed as he turned his gaze to her. "My compliments to you, then, Miranda."

"Thank you."

"I hope you young folks will excuse me. I've had a long day."

"Are you feelin' all right, Pa?" Miranda studied her father as he shoved to his feet.

He smiled and bent to kiss her cheek. "Just tired, my girl." He pecked Mercy's cheek, too. "Good night."

"Good night, Pa." Mercy stood and began gathering the dishes, but Thad stopped her. "You and Ben can take some time reviewing the books. I'll help Miranda." He retrieved the two thick ledger books from the shelves and set an extra tallow candle on the table.

"Thank you, dear." Mercy wiped off a corner of the table and opened one of the books. "I'm afraid you won't get too much information here, Ben. Your brother's ledgers were damaged in the fire. I copied what I could into a new ledger, but some of it is outright guessing."

"Hmm." Ben bent over the page and studied it.

Miranda scraped the plates, while Thad took the kettle off the stove and filled a pan with hot water.

"I can wash," Miranda said.

"After that fine supper? Least I can do is wash the dishes." Thad took a wet rag and commenced scrubbing. "Here, Jonathan. Leave your mother be. Aunt Miranda and I can use your help."

They worked together in silence for a time. Finally, Thad started whistling the "Blue Tail Fly." Jonathan puckered his lips and tried to imitate Thad with little success. Miranda chuckled and Thad winked at her. She smiled at her brother-in-law, hoping he had forgiven her for her foolishness earlier.

"What's this page?" Ben asked.

Miranda noticed Thad tense, though he continued whistling. He fished out a rag for Jonathan and handed the boy a tin cup to wash.

"Cattle." Mercy leaned forward and pointed to the page. "Couldn't find a record of what Arthur had, so I took Buck out to the herd and counted."

"Buck?"

"One of our hired men. Been with us almost as long as we've been in Colorado."

"So, he works for you."

Miranda cringed.

"That's right, he works for me." Mercy's voice sounded strained now. She hated being questioned. "And he's an honest man. You're welcome to talk to him."

"I'd like to do that."

"I'll arrange it tomorrow," Mercy snapped.

"This shows the count, then. And this?"

"Those are the animals we sold for meat." Mercy brushed her hand over the page. "And these we kept for breeding."

"You have the bulls marked separately."

"That's right. Generally we'd put aside some bulls for breeding."

"It looks like you sold them all."

"We had to. I told you there were a good many debts."

"Without breeding bulls, Jonathan's herd will die."

"That would be true, except that we're running our bulls with both herds; there were plenty of new calves born to Jonathan's herd. Now the advantage—"

"The advantage is you run the herds together and soon Jonathan's herd becomes a part of your—"

Mercy's chair scraped against the floor as she leaped to her feet. "Now you lis—"

Ben caught Mercy as she nearly toppled over. Thad was there an instant later and helped his wife back onto her chair.

"I'm fine." Mercy's voice trembled as she spoke. She smiled at Thad. "I stood up too fast." She touched his cheek. "Don't fret."

Thad captured her hand and turned to Ben. "I'm sorry, Mr. Lansing. I'm going to insist my wife gets some rest."

"Don't be sil—" Mercy started.

"Rest." Thad's voice was quiet, but firm. He glared at his wife for several seconds before turning back to Ben. "You're welcome to look over the ledgers all you want. I'll get you some paper so you can write down any questions to ask my wife in the mornin'."

"Of course." Ben stood as Thad helped Mercy to her feet and led her toward the bedroom.

"It was a little dizzy spell, no need to make a fuss," Mercy muttered.

"Mama?" Jonathan tugged on Mercy's skirt.

"Come on, then." Mercy ran her fingers through Jonathan's hair. "If your father is going to insist I lie down at this hour, I'm going to have to read. What would you like to hear?"

They couldn't hear Jonathan's response as Thad pulled the heavy door closed behind him. Ben looked at Miranda.

"I'm sorry if I said anything to cause . . ."

She set her hands on her hips and stared at him. "It didn't occur to you, I suppose, that some people take offense at being called thieves."

"I never said—"

"You're impossible! You think because you and all your Lansing kin worship money that the rest of the world feels the same way. Well, let me tell you something, Ben Lansing, Mercy and Thad took your nephew into their home because they care about him." She stomped her foot against the rough pine floor. "Love is more important to them than money ever will be."

"I hope you're right," Ben snapped. "I'm not the evil man you insist on making me. All I want is to be certain my nephew has his due."

"And you get your five thousand dollars!"

"Yes, I made a large loan to my brother, and I would like to be repaid. Thad and Mercy can keep the interest, but I need the money. I have plans."

Miranda raised both eyebrows. "Must be very important plans to need five thousand dollars."

"I'm staking my whole future on this." Ben glanced at the door to Mercy's bedroom. "If the money is gone, so be it. I'll leave without causing any further grief here. But I will be certain Jonathan has not been cheated."

Miranda pulled a chair away from the table and sat down. "What do you know about cattle?"

"Very close to nothing."

"Ever heard of longhorns and Herefords?"

"Those are breeds, aren't they?"

"Very good. You ain't so ignorant, after all." She grinned at him. "Sit down and let me explain something about my sister and her cows."

Ben sat next to Miranda. She studied the way his collar fit against his sinewy neck and raised her eyes to the shadow of beard on his cheek. *Think, Miranda. Concentrate.*

"I reckon Mercy could explain this better, but there is a simple explanation for why they sold off those bulls."

Ben crossed his arms in front of his chest, waiting for her explanation.

"If you're not going to listen . . ."

"I'm listening!"

She shrugged. "Longhorns are known to be rugged; that's why you'll see them all over the West. They're a good choice for raising in wild country." She looked at Ben. "Now Herefords are meatier, plenty of fat on 'em to make the meat more tender."

"I'm certain you're going to explain why this lesson is relevant."

She tapped two fingers on the table and sighed. *The man is being dense intentionally!* "There was no point in keepin' the longhorn bulls for breedin' when they could use the Herefords instead. Jonathan's herd will be more valuable now that he has a mix of Hereford and longhorns. That's why Mercy imported those Hereford bulls—to make a breed that would be rugged like longhorns, only meatier."

"I think my brother wrote something about a new breeding program he was involved in."

"That's right. He loaned Mercy some of the money to import the bulls. I don't think he expected her plan to work."

"Why would he loan her money if he didn't expect to earn a profit?"

"So he could grow his ranch. He wanted our land. His land was near dry. Arthur wanted the water from Jake's Creek that runs through our property."

Ben thought about that for a moment. Arthur had mentioned a plan to acquire his neighbor's ranch. "But your sister's plan did work."

"Yes."

"And she never repaid Arthur."

"Well, she did and she didn't."

"She either did, or she didn't."

Miranda laced her fingers together on the table. Forcing herself to remain calm wasn't easy. "What she told me was that the money was lost in the fire. Most of the greenbacks burned. Mercy didn't have time to save the cash. Instead, she chose to risk her life to save your nephew."

Ben stared at her. "So she paid Arthur, but the money was lost when the house burned."

Miranda looked at Ben, the light from the tallow candle dancing in his dark eyes. "I reckon you deserve to hear the whole story." She worried her lip for a minute before plunging ahead. "We can only guess how that money came to be in Arthur's house. It was stolen from Mercy."

"You're saying she saw money in Arthur's house and assumed that was the cash that was stolen from her."

"She didn't assume, she knew."

"It had her name on it, I suppose?"

"Something like that." Miranda rubbed one hand over the other, trying to find the right words to tell him. "She was carrying the money in the lining of her jacket when she was shot. The money was stained with her blood."

"That could be a coincidence," Ben said, though he knew that was an unlikely explanation.

"Might be, except that before he died, Arthur admitted he'd hired the men who attacked her." Miranda locked eyes with Ben, knowing how it must hurt for him to hear these things about his brother. "He tried to get the land legally, but when he knew she had the money to pay the loan, he sent those men to rob her. Luther and Jed were his hired hands."

Ben watched Miranda ball her hands into a fist. She looked ready to fight someone, maybe him. "I don't know what to say. He was my brother . . ." The wonderful supper he'd eaten suddenly felt like lead in his stomach as he considered his brother's role in this. If it came to a choice of believing O'Reilly or Miranda . . . "O'Reilly is a liar," he muttered.

"How do you know that name?"

"I . . . I heard he was involved, too."

Miranda nodded. "Yes, the three of them got away—lucky for them. They show their face around here again, Thad'll likely kill 'em with his bare hands."

Ben's head was beginning to throb. "There was no money left, then? That's why Thad and Mercy sold the cattle, including his bulls."

Miranda nodded.

"Can you prove any of this?"

"The cows you can see for yourself. Other than that, you'll have to take our word. You should be able to see by now that Mercy wants Jonathan to have his legacy when he's grown."

"I'm going to have to think about everything you've told me. And, I would like to see the cattle for myself."

"You're entitled to that, I think."

"Thank you." Ben turned to Miranda.

She felt his eyes on her lips. And damned if that didn't send a shot of heat right down to her knees. She didn't dare try to stand at that moment for fear she just might swoon herself.

It was a long night. Ben stared up at the angled roof above him as he lay on Jonathan's small bed. Thad had apologized for putting him in the cramped quarters, but Ben was pretty sure the big man took pleasure in thinking Ben would be uncomfortable all night. He had to admire the man's loyalty to his wife, and he was beginning to think Thad's affection extended to Jonathan, too. Both Thad and Mercy really cared for the boy, or they were the best actors Ben had ever seen outside a theater.

Ben curled onto his side. Little did Thad understand that the small bed and low ceiling were the least of Ben's worries. The knowledge that his bed was directly above Miranda contributed far more to his discomfort.

He cursed his impulsiveness once again. What the hell had driven him to seek her out, and what insanity had caused him to kiss her? He swallowed, remembering the delightful torture of holding her close, of indulging his desire only to the point where he needed her and wanted her more. If she'd played upon his thoughts before, now she would haunt him. He would not be satisfied until he joined with her. But that he could never do.

It wasn't only for her sake, though that should be enough to force him to take the gentleman's path. No, he must keep away from the young vixen for his own sake as well. Involvement with her would only complicate his investigation. Mercy and Thad were suspicious enough of him. If he were to prey on an innocent young girl in their family, they would be within their rights to demand that he stay away. So far away he might never find out the truth about what had happened to his brother's money. He had to find the answer to that question, for his nephew's sake as well as his own. If he found proof the Buchanans had stolen money or cattle from the boy, he would know that all of the tenderness they were showing him was an act. In time, they would no longer feel it necessary to pretend to care about Jonathan, and that would break the child's heart.

Ben had many good, logical reasons to forget about Miranda. Even as the thought entered his mind, a more persistent thought forced it out. Those eyes, those lips, and the tear that had drifted down her cheek when he'd kissed her. He couldn't be certain what she'd been thinking, of course, but he would wager that tear was not caused by unhappiness. In fact, he felt sure it was the opposite. He'd given her an unexpected pleasure.

All the more reason to keep his distance. If she'd enjoyed that and wanted more, hell, he wasn't gentleman enough to resist her twice.

Chapter 11

Ben dragged into town after a sleepless night in the loft above Miranda. He went directly to return Lightning to the livery. Once again, the young boy greeted him.

"Keep him for me, will you, George?" Ben said as he handed the reins over to the lad. "I may need him again tomorrow."

"Whatever you say, Mr. Lansing." George grinned up at him. Ben took the hint and gave the lad a coin.

He headed back to his room, his head churning through ideas for raising more money. Ben reached under his bed for the leather roll that held his canvases. If anyone in this town had the cash to pay for these, it would be the Wyatts. Or maybe they'd sell the paintings on his behalf.

He took a few moments to brush the trail dust from his coat and wash his face and hands. He pulled his jacket back on and checked his image in the mirror, making sure his collar and tie were straight. A day's growth of beard darkened his jaw, but he looked respectable enough. He examined the dull brown eyes looking back at him. It wasn't only the color—they had no life, no light sparking in them. He was twenty-seven years old with the eyes of an old man. Or perhaps simply a man with no idea of what to do with his life.

He knew only what he didn't want—a life working in his father's bank. He'd searched Europe, hoping to work with the art he loved. Even if he couldn't paint, he'd hoped to make a living trading art. He might have succeeded if he hadn't spent all his money on wine.

He ran a comb through his hair and judged himself to be presentable. Tucking the leather roll under his arm, he stepped quickly down the front stairs that led through the saloon. He'd failed as a businessman before he'd even begun. His only talent had been rendered useless when his hand was smashed. Luckily, he had only himself to support, and he could live simply. All he needed was enough for passage on a ship and a little cash to set himself up in a quiet life. If Arthur had lost the money, so be it. Ben would find another source of funds.

It was too early in the day for a large crowd, but the place never seemed to be empty. Rita leaned across the bar, serving a glass of beer to a customer and laughing. The proprietress had a delicate laugh that matched her lithe body. She was beautiful. There was a time when he would have wanted to paint her. If nothing else, that would have given him a chance to spend time alone with her, watching her body, studying each curve as only an artist is allowed to do without appearing indecent. He smiled as he went out the door. Knowing that he'd never paint again didn't keep him from looking, but he looked for different reasons.

A certain blonde with cornflower blue eyes came

to mind. He pictured her full pink lips and the way her tongue darted over them in innocent seduction. He most certainly wanted to paint her. Knowing it wasn't possible didn't seem to matter. He wanted to touch her. To kiss her again. To bury himself inside her womanly places.

But he also wanted to take her image with him, preserved in oils. Something to remember the look in her eyes after he'd kissed her—that expression of surprise and joy. He wondered if he could begin to depict all that life on a flat piece of canvas even if his hand were whole again.

Growing up in Boston, he'd admired the work of John Singleton Copley. As he traveled in Europe, he'd discovered a whole world of art, including the great masters of the past—Da Vinci and Michelangelo.

Painting technique had changed over the centuries, but one thing remained true—art was not simply a matter of reproducing an image. Many people had the talent to capture a likeness in a drawing or a painting, but few had the ability to capture the life, the being of the person.

It was perhaps vain for him to think he would have developed that ability. What did he have to show for his efforts? Only a few simple paintings he'd done when he was studying—landscapes and seascapes that captured the image well enough, but nothing more. They were beautiful, and he'd sold each of them for a good price to help him fund further studies. Then he'd done the paintings he carried now. They were his attempts to capture the pain and fury of war, as Goya had done so vividly in the work Ben had seen when he was in Spain.

During the war, Ben's memories of battles were alive and fresh. And if his own memory failed him, he merely had to look into the eyes of the men around him to bring the battle back to life.

He'd spent weeks working until he felt he had not only one instant of terror frozen in time, but rather the whole war—the broken countryside, the confusion, the noise. The curious strength that worked inside the soldiers to keep them at their task when good sense might tell them to run.

It was quite a lot to put on one small, flat canvas. He hadn't managed all of it, but he was proud of the attempt. There was substance to these paintings even if they were a poor imitation of the scene he had attempted to depict. Putting everything he could into the work had helped him to find some sense that there was life beyond the bounds of the battle, and he dared hope that one day he would capture those things with his paints as well. Beauty. Serenity. He saw things with a new eye—from the petals of a flower to the scarred jaw of a blond beauty.

It would take real talent to depict her hidden passion in paint. But he no longer possessed the primary tool he needed to try. Without control over his hand, it wasn't possible to wield a paintbrush.

He had made a few attempts in Paris. He had even tried painting with his undamaged hand, but he could barely scrawl his name, let alone make delicate strokes with a brush. Whatever gift he had for art had died when he lost the fingers from his left hand. No use in being sentimental over his losses. He needed cash, and the only way to get it was to sell these paintings. Just as well. It wasn't as though he needed reminders of his worst nightmares. Better to forget the battles along with the life he might have had if he'd survived with his hand and his talent.

Ben pushed open the door as he entered the mercantile.

"Good afternoon, Mr. Lansing," Clarisse greeted him. "I'll be with you in a moment."

She leaned over the counter, speaking quietly to a woman with golden hair a few shades darker than Miranda's. She was taller, too—a good two inches taller than Miranda. *Hell, Ben, that girl is not the measure of everything.* He moved toward the front of the store and feigned interest in some canned goods in order to get a look at the woman's face. It was fair and angular. He couldn't tell more looking from the side, except that her figure was pleasant enough.

"What do you think, Ingrid?"

"Ja," Ingrid said. "That is, yes. I think you're right. It will be goot to make these dresses."

Several sketches covered the broad wooden counter. Ben couldn't help himself; he moved in for a closer look. "Miranda's drawings?" Ben lifted the top one. "This one is new, isn't it?"

"You have an excellent memory, Mr. Lansing. Miranda has been busy and seems determined to keep us busy as well, doesn't she, Ingrid?" Clarisse's eyes twinkled with mirth.

"Ja." Ingrid straightened, and Ben concluded she was a good deal taller than Miranda, though not nearly as tall as Mercy. "We will be very busy this winter, sewing dresses." Ingrid's eyes seemed to measure him. "You know ladies' fashion?"

"No, I'm no fashion expert. I am . . . I was an artist though. I appreciate a skilled drawing."

"You were an artist?" Clarisse asked. "Do you mean, professionally?"

"Yes, I've sold a few of my works. In fact, that's what I've come to see you about." He glanced at the other woman. "When you're done here. I don't mean to interrupt."

"Pardon my poor manners, Mr. Lansing. Have you met Mrs. Hansen?"

"No, ma'am, I haven't." He bowed his head. "Pleased to meet you, ma'am."

"I am most pleased, too," Ingrid said. "I was so sorry for your brudder's death. A tragic loss for your nephew."

Ben inclined his head. "Yes, it's a terrible thing for a young boy to lose his father."

"My oldest was about the same age when her fadder died. She recovers with time."

"As I'm certain Jonathan will," Clarisse said. "Especially with a loving family taking care of him."

"Yes, this is certain." Ingrid smiled at Ben. "Now, I will go. Pleasant meeting you, Mr. Lansing. I hope you enjoy your stay in Fort Victory."

"With so many lovely ladies here, I can't imagine how my stay could be anything less than enjoyable." Ben was pleased his words elicited a bright pink blush from the widow. He was out of practice in flirting. What he needed was a new start, to consider all the women around him as possible partners in fun. Widows could be especially amenable. He'd met several who were not interested in another marriage, but did miss certain of the delights a man could bring to them.

"I hope I will see you again before you leave." Mrs. Hansen nodded at Ben, then turned and walked out the door.

Mrs. Hansen or the lovely Rita Diaz. Plenty of women who might satisfy his newly kindled desires. Yet, even as the thought came to him, he knew it was untrue. The only woman he desired was the one he must avoid at all cost. Best to take care of his business, get the hell out of Fort Victory, and forget about Miranda Chase. He'd find some exotic beauty on his island, and all memories of the pretty young blonde would soon be gone.

"How can I help you, Mr. Lansing?" Clarisse's words brought Ben back to the present.

"I've come to see whether you might be willing to purchase these paintings."

He unrolled the canvases over the counter so that Clarisse could view them. She gasped.

"Mr. Lansing, you *are* an artist."

"Not any longer," he said before he could stop himself.

"Why ever not?" Clarisse held the corners flat and bent to examine the top painting more carefully. "A man of your obvious talent—"

Ben laid the maimed hand on the counter for her to see. "It's useless."

Clarisse looked at his hand, then up to his face. "I'm sorry," she said. And he was certain she meant it. She looked back at the canvas, then lifted it to see the one underneath. "The horses remind me of . . . Your brother had a painting of a foxhunt."

"I gave that to him. It was a wedding present."

"That was your work?"

Ben smiled. It wasn't one of his better pieces, but he'd been proud of it at the time. And his sister-in-law had pronounced it lovely. "Yes, I did that when I was in school."

"I can see some similarity. The way the animals seem so real, as though they could run right off the canvas."

"Do you think you could sell them?"

Clarisse nodded. "I've no doubt of it. I'll give you fifty dollars for the pair of them."

Fifty dollars. It was more than he'd hoped to get here in the middle of nowhere. "They are yours, then."

Clarisse smiled at him. "If you have any others—"

"No," Ben said, "these are the last." He thought for a moment. "I guess my foxhunt was lost in the fire." That single blaze had taken everything he'd come to Fort Victory to find.

"Yes." Clarisse met his gaze. "Mercy and Thad told me it was all they could do to escape before the building collapsed. No time to salvage anything."

"I'm surprised the hired men didn't help."

"Hired men?"

"My brother's letters mentioned several men working for him."

Clarisse busied herself wrapping the paintings back into their leather cover. "He did have at one time. The last of them left more than a month before . . . the fire."

Ben scowled.

"The rumor was he hadn't paid them. As a matter of fact, he tried to borrow money from us to meet his payroll, but . . ." Clarisse looked up at Ben. "Thank you for these paintings. It's been a long while since I've seen art as fine as this."

"If you need help stretching and framing them—"

"Oh, no." Clarisse grinned up at him. "I have plans for these."

Ben concluded his business with Clarisse and strolled back to Rita's with money in his pocket. At least he had accomplished something. He considered stopping for a celebratory drink, but thought better of it and ran up the back stairs instead. He shrugged out of his jacket and pulled off his tie and collar before slipping out of his boots.

His sleepless night had left him exhausted. The white sheets of the bed looked inviting, but Ben had work to do. He pulled out his journal and a pencil to finish compiling the facts he'd gathered. The puzzle was beginning to look quite clear now, and it was becoming difficult to imagine his brother as an innocent victim.

A quarter of an hour later, he studied his list. *Damn.* Not that he was surprised. The moment he'd learned O'Reilly claimed to be Arthur's ally, he knew something was wrong. A light rap on the door startled Ben and he dropped the pencil. He bent to pick it up and set it next to the journal. There was another knock at the door.

He walked across the floor in his stockinged feet, hesitated for a moment, then opened the door. Miranda stood in the hall, looking up at him with her wide blue eyes. The sunlight streaming through the window behind her shone on her fair hair, making a glow over her like an angel in a Renaissance painting. Except that the view of an angel had never caused heat to radiate through Ben's groin as it did now. He was grateful the door was between them, because he was certain his physical response would be apparent right through his trousers.

"I come to talk, Mr. Lansing. Ben." She blinked, and he noticed her lashes, a golden color a shade darker than her hair. Her eyes opened wide again, pools of warm liquid.

"I'll meet you downstairs. We'll sit in the saloon. We could have some . . ." He couldn't very well offer the young lady whiskey. "Coffee?"

She shook her head and took a step forward. "I

think it'd be best if we talk privately." She leaned toward him, but he didn't move. "Could I come in?"

If he had any sense he would refuse. Didn't this sweet young thing realize how dangerous it was for a girl like her to be alone with a man like him? Once again, he studied her eyes and wondered whether they held innocence or knowledge. He stepped back, pulling the door open and allowing her to enter. She turned and pushed the door closed behind her.

"You can't take Jonathan." She glared up defiantly.

"Is that what this is about?"

Miranda stepped up to him, taking his large hand between her small ones. "Please, you need to understand how much he means to my sister. Even before Arthur died, Mercy always had time for Jonathan. She spent hours with him, played with him, taught him to play the piano and ride a horse, and she always had a story for him. His father never did those things for Jonathan, but Mercy did."

"I . . ." He studied her face, those wide eyes so full of worry. He was tempted to reassure her, but he had some unfinished business with O'Reilly. "I can't leave town just yet."

"Even if the money is gone as Mercy says?"

"There are some things I need to find out for myself."

"You want to count the cows? Jonathan will have his cattle, I promise you."

"Miranda . . ." Ben took a deep breath. "I don't believe your sister intends to cheat my nephew."

Miranda threw her arms around him and squeezed tight, though that wasn't the reason Ben found it difficult to breathe. "Thank you."

She stepped back and smiled up at him. It wasn't

the desire to drive himself into her that nearly over-
powered him—he could control that—it was the
need to taste the lip that she now held between her
teeth that had his mind wandering in circles so that
he had difficulty understanding what Miranda said,
let alone conceiving how he should reply.

"I haven't promised to leave," he managed to say,
though his voice cracked.

"They love him. My sister and her husband."
Though she no longer touched him, she didn't
back away either.

"Even with another baby coming, their own
blood?" he asked.

"Most parents have it in their hearts to love more
than one child."

Ben wondered. He'd never been certain his father
loved him. Though he wasn't sure his father had
really loved his brothers either.

"I don't know whether that's true."

Miranda smiled. "Course, I don't have a lot of
experience. But I know my pa loves me *and* my
sister. Don't think me coming changed the way he
felt about Mercy. Nor did I ever think he couldn't
love me 'cause he already cared for her."

Ben pondered her words. Hell, it made a lot of
sense. That was how things were in a family. "But your
mother was there to help—"

"If you mean to say that Mercy and I had the
same ma to love us both like Pa does—no, we didn't.
We had different mamas. They both died, leavin' Pa
to raise the two of us." Miranda shifted her weight
from one foot to the other. "Different as we are, we
both love our pa and each other. It's the one thing
I know for certain I can count on in my life. That and

the fact that my sister loves Jonathan like he's her own flesh and blood."

Ben only wished he knew how to recognize a parent's love as easily as he could identify the simple love of a child. "Jonathan loves them, I'm certain of that."

Miranda smiled. "You're right about that, Ben. There just might be some hope for you yet."

He couldn't help himself—he returned her smile. "I'm beginning to believe that's true, but I still have some questions."

She blinked up at him, and he ached at the thought that she might cry. "You're still worried . . . about the money," she said.

He turned away from her and glanced out the window to the dusty street below. "Yes, I want to know what happened to my money. I can't believe my brother . . . simply lost it all." He turned back to Miranda.

"My sister would not have taken it."

"No." Ben stared into the depths of Miranda's eyes. "No, I don't believe she did." O'Reilly was the more likely culprit. "I have some other suspicions, though. I'm not leaving here until I find out what happened."

She bit her lip, then looked up at him. "But you will be going?"

Ben nodded and took a step closer. "I want to be on my way before winter comes. You can stop worrying about Jonathan. I don't intend to take him."

She smiled, a slight, shy smile. "I just have one more thing to ask." She drew her tongue slowly across her lip. "Will you? Would you kiss me, again?"

Ben took another step toward her and leaned down until his lips brushed over hers. His hands settled on her hips and he pulled her close. Their lips met again, this time with more force, and he allowed one hand to roam slowly up her back until his fingers tangled into her hair. Her tongue teased its way inside of him, fanning flames already dangerously hot. His mind fought every part of his body, forcing him to pull away.

She smiled up at him, her lips trembling a little. He caressed her soft cheek, brushing his finger back over the ear he would have liked to nibble. He swallowed hard, reminding himself that he was a gentleman and Miranda was too young to understand what she was doing to him.

Ben's eyes went to her hands as she worked down the front of her shirt. "No one knows I'm here," she said.

"Wait." Ben stared at her. "Stop," he heard himself say, although it was the last thing he wanted her to do. "Miranda, what are you doing?"

"You want me, I think." She frowned up at him, intensely serious.

"No," he snapped, "I—" But he couldn't force the words from his lips, because the fact was she was right. He'd wanted her from the moment he'd first seen her swirling her spoon through her soup.

Her eyes dropped to the floor, and he reached a finger under her chin, lifting her face so that he could see tears pooling in her eyes. His resolve vanished like a cool mist under the heat of the morning sun. "You can't know how much I want you," he whispered.

She pulled her shirt away, revealing the curve of her breasts against the white cotton of her chemise; her nipples stood out like small pearls against the thin fabric. "Then, please . . ."

He forced himself back a step. "How . . . old are you?"

"I'm twenty years old. Did you think I was a child?"

"No." Ben's response was nearly a groan. "I can see that you're no child."

"Then show me." She lifted her chin and favored him with a timid smile. "Please. Show me what it feels like to be a woman."

It took one long stride before he had her in his arms, pulled tight against him; her supple breasts pressed against his ribs. He covered her mouth with his and drank of her soft, full lips. His hand found the hem of her chemise and skimmed up, under the fabric over her warm skin; he traced her ribs until he found her small, firm breast. He ached with pleasure at the weight of that gem against his palm. Fire burned through him with an unexpected fury.

He groaned with need and ripped her chemise up and over her head, bending to suckle her breast. He lifted her easily in his arms. She was weightless, lighter than air—this beautiful nymph of a girl, and he wanted her as he could not remember wanting anything.

He set her on his bed, naked from the waist up, her hair flying in every direction and her lips and cheeks rosy from his caresses. She sprawled out, opening to him, pulling her skirt up to ready herself for him. Her legs were bare from the top of her boots to the tangle of yellow curls that protected her womanly places.

He tugged at the buttons of his pants, pulling the first two out with so much force the buttons dropped to the floor.

"Damn," Ben muttered, feeling like an eager adolescent. Silently admonishing himself to slow down, he bent to unfasten the other buttons more carefully. Holding the waist of his pants up, he looked back to Miranda's beautiful face. Her bright eyes glowed with fear.

Ben sucked in a breath and turned his back to her, pulling his pants back up around him. He walked to the window and leaned out, breathing in the cool autumn air, desperately trying to gain control of himself. What in perdition was he doing? What had he nearly done to her?

"Get out!" His voice was harsh with anger. He pulled in another breath and forced his voice to quiet. "Please, leave."

He heard her behind him, gathering her clothing; perhaps she was dressing herself. He dared not look, but continued leaning out the window, breathing, forcing himself not to picture the small pink circles on the peaks of her breasts. How he wanted to kiss those breasts, to taste them and feel their tenderness.

"I'm sorry," she said in a hoarse whisper. "So sorry."

"Please, go." He fought to keep his voice calm, not wanting to frighten her any more than he already had. He heard her walk to the door and slip quietly into the hall before he turned around, leaned against the wall, and sank to the floor. He closed his eyes.

"Forgive me," he whispered, though he knew she was gone.

Miranda slipped out the back door of Rita's. She couldn't go through the saloon or the kitchen, for fear Rita, or someone else she knew, would see her and figure out she'd been up to the guest rooms. There wasn't a good reason for her to be up there.

Whatever they imagined she might have been doing, it would be no worse than what she'd actually done.

Her hands shook as she checked the buttons of her shirt. She had offered herself to a man thinking he wanted her. Thinking this was her chance to find that magical pleasure Mercy had described to her. After months of promising herself to keep away from men, to stay out of trouble, she'd jumped with both feet right into a kettle of hot water. *Stupid, stupid, stupid.*

She moved down the alley into the shadow of Rita's storage shed. Again, she checked her buttons and looked down to be sure her skirt was straight. Breathing in and out deliberately, she willed her hands to stop shaking. Nothing torn, no outward evidence of Ben's touch. She pulled the blue ribbon off her hair and rearranged it, binding her wild locks tight into the same ribbon. Her fingers brushed over her cheek, which was still tender from rubbing against the stubble on Ben's face. Likely her face would be pink, but riding in the sun usually left her rosy. No one would notice the difference, she hoped.

Her index finger moved over her raw lip, remembering his lips on hers. She felt tears pooling in her eyes again. No sense in crying. Miranda cleared her throat. He'd been warm against her—and hard—pressing with the force and fury of desperation. But not desperate enough for the likes of her, apparently. He had wanted her, then something changed. She'd done something to displease him.

She thought back; everything had been fine until she was on the bed. Lawrence had always urged her to be ready. He hated waiting and blamed her if he didn't get hard. Sometimes he seemed ready, hard and full of desire, but he'd go soft and that was always her fault, too.

Ben had still been wearing his trousers, but she could see he was ready to come inside her. She'd done her best to hurry. Had even lifted her skirt so that he didn't have to. One tear escaped, then another. There was only one explanation. It wasn't anything she'd done. When he'd looked at her face, he'd been so repulsed he couldn't even look at her as she left the room.

Chapter 12

It seemed strange to Miranda seeing cowboys rounding up cattle for branding without Mercy there bossing them. Her older sister had taken charge every spring and summer since their family had started this ranch. Working with the cattle could be dangerous, so Mercy had decided to stay home rather than risk hurting the baby she was carrying. Miranda was glad to be able to help with the roundup, but she envied her sister, too.

Miranda watched Thad work with Buck to cut a calf from the herd and head him over to the cowboys who were doing the branding. The roundup was for counting and sorting the beef stock from the breeders. The male animals chosen for meat would also need special treatment. Miranda shuddered thinking about what they would do to that poor calf once they got him down on the ground. At least it was quick. The men thought nothing of it; they even enjoyed eating the . . . male parts they'd removed.

The same coals that kept the branding irons red hot also served to fry up their special delicacy. As far back as Miranda could recall, roundup was the only time that Buck took charge of cooking. He used a big iron skillet over the coals to cook up the prairie oysters for the men.

Miranda had come along to do the real cooking, but she stayed away from this special ritual. She didn't want to watch; but more important, the men preferred for the women to stay away. Even Mercy had always managed to find something else to occupy herself with when Buck took out his skillet.

"O'Neill, you take the first one," Buck shouted as he stabbed a fork into a hot piece of meat.

Miranda glanced over at the cowboys. O'Neill had just turned sixteen, and the men had been teasing him all week about his lack of experience with the ladies. They all swore they would provide him with the cure. Once he'd eaten the magical prairie oyster, women would line up to be with him.

Miranda retreated about fifty yards away to the cook wagon, where she had the makings of a real supper. A hearty beef stew, corn bread, and apple cobbler. For some reason, eating a bull's private parts never seemed to diminish the cowboys' appetites. Miranda reckoned their increased manliness simply required more food. She chuckled at the thought.

What they did with the added masculinity they thought they'd acquired was another matter. *Manliness.* She'd had enough experience with it to be wary. Some men worked to prove their masculinity, for others it came naturally. A pair of broad shoulders on a lean body shoved into her mind. No question about it—Benjamin Lansing was all man. He didn't need any special food, or a magical elixir. If his kiss told the half of it, he could please a woman in the way Mercy had described—a shooting star ride. Hell, flying through the sky was pure fantasy—

the thrill of Ben's kisses was very real. Miranda could only imagine what it would be like to have all of him. If he hadn't found her repulsive, she might well know for certain.

It was for the best he'd rejected her. She'd given herself to two men. To Harold Pearson, she'd given her heart. He'd left her for another woman. Still reeling from Harold's rejection, she'd given her body to Lawrence Frimm. Their coupling had always felt awkward to her. She'd tried so damn hard to please him but had never quite managed it. And he'd found ways to punish her for her failings. If she hadn't felt obligated to marry him, she'd have left him the first time he hit her.

Her past failures with men should have been enough to warn her away from conjuring up ideas about her and Ben. Even if he'd wanted her, he was leaving Fort Victory as soon as he concluded his business. And then where would she be? Good sense aside, there was something arousing about the idea of a man's strength directed at pleasing her rather than hurting her.

She thought back to Ben's kisses. His probing touch, the strength of his long, solid body against hers, and something else—the warm and inviting way he held her. Tenderness. That was it. A gentle touch that told her all that strength was under control.

Restraint and power was a potent combination. Even the thought of Ben made her knees go weak. When he'd kissed her in the barn, she'd have landed on her seat if he hadn't been there holding her up. Despite all her misgivings, she'd wanted more. Had hoped for more. Hell, she'd gone into town and thrown herself into his arms. A sure sign she'd lost her mind entirely.

She turned back to the men. They'd finished their snack and were back to work. It was time to get the stew started. She pulled out a board and commenced chopping the carrots. Miranda could work the cattle as well as any of the men out there, but she could cook a far sight better than any of the cowboys. She'd had one helluva year away, when all was said and done. But one good thing had come of it. Everyone was glad to have her back in charge of the kitchen. It was mighty nice to be appreciated.

She glanced back over to the men. A movement coming out of the hills to the west caught her eye— horsemen riding like the devil was chasing them. She called out to Buck, but Thad and Buck were already positioning themselves between the cattle and the approaching horsemen.

Miranda climbed into the wagon and grabbed the old Sharps rifle a heartbeat before the shooting started. *Rustlers!* Only they weren't going after the unbranded cattle. What the hell were they trying to do?

Another pair of riders came thundering toward Miranda from the south. She turned, aimed, and fired.

Ben stopped to get his bearings. Mercy had told him it would take around an hour riding directly southwest from the house before he came to the herd. He pulled his watch from his vest pocket and verified that he'd been riding nearly an hour.

With the sun almost directly overhead, he might have lost his direction, though Mercy had told him to use the *C* mountain as a landmark. He looked at the mountains ahead and found the peak she'd pointed out to him. It looked almost as if someone had chiseled a *C* shape out of one side just below the peak.

He continued riding toward the mountain until he came to a stand of cottonwoods. He thought about going around when the sound of gunfire drew his attention. He rode into the trees, ducking his head to avoid the branches. The full array of autumn-colored leaves offered plenty of cover. Ben drew his pistol and bent low over his horse's neck, moving toward the popping sounds. It might be prudent to leave the area, but not until he could be certain he was avoiding trouble, rather than riding into it.

His heart raced as the cacophony of bellowing cows, shouting men, and more gunfire reached his ears. From the relative safety of the trees, he watched across the meadow as a group of riders stormed down the hill toward Thad Buchanan and his men. Before he could decide whether to assist Buchanan, a mass of wild blond hair drew his attention to his right.

Miranda knelt in a wagon bed, aiming a rifle toward the oncoming horsemen. She wisely held her fire; the attackers were within range, but it would be difficult to distinguish friend from foe in the confusion. Suddenly, another pair of men came charging at Miranda from Ben's left. Before Ben cleared the trees, Miranda fired off two rounds. She missed the riders, but at least she caused them to veer away from her.

"Good girl," Ben mumbled as he urged Lightning forward, intent on giving chase. As he burst into the open, another rider emerged from the trees to his right. The man raised his gun, aiming in Miranda's direction.

* * *

"Miranda, get down!" a man shouted from behind her.

A bullet splintered the side of the wagon inches from her head as Miranda dropped flat. Her racing heartbeat stopped for an instant before galloping on. She scrambled to reload the Sharps with shaking fingers as gunfire exploded around her.

Miranda gripped her weapon and peered above the side of wagon. A riderless horse galloped past her. A few yards away, a lifeless body was sprawled on the ground with a familiar figure leaning over him. *Ben?*

Men's voices carried over the bellowing of the frightened cows. She sucked in a breath as a tall man in a fine dark suit approached the wagon.

"Miranda?" Ben called. "Are you hurt?"

She let the rifle slip out of her sweaty hands and stared at Ben's face. He leaped up and knelt at her side, concern lining his brow. Miranda reminded herself to breathe.

"I'm all right." She rose to her knees, looking around at the men trying to calm the cows and horses. "When did you . . . how . . . ?" She looked at the body on the ground and back up at Ben. Her stomach lurched.

Ben turned away from her toward the body. "He was one of O'Reilly's men."

"Is he . . . ?"

Ben wrapped an arm around her shoulder and pulled her against his chest. "I had to shoot him. He had a gun aimed at your back."

Her eyes squeezed shut and in her mind's eye she saw men galloping toward her, firing guns, and a deep voice shouting for her to get down. "It was you who warned me?" She looked up at him.

He nodded and took her hand in his. "You're cold."

"Miranda!" Thad called to her.

She jerked her hand away from him. "I'm fine, Mr. Lansing!" she snapped.

She turned to see Thad bent over O'Neill; the young cowboy lay still on the ground.

"Damn!" Miranda's heart pounded as she jumped into the driver's seat and snapped the reins over the frightened mule. "Ya!" she shouted to get the reluctant beast moving.

Miranda drove the wagon up the hill as close to the fallen man as she dared. She jumped down and rushed over to him, carrying the bag of supplies she'd assembled in case anyone was injured.

She knelt next to Thad, who was pressing his kerchief against the cowboy's shoulder. The wounded man was as pale as a ghost. His eyes were wide with fear, his breath quick and shallow.

"I can do that." Miranda knelt next to O'Neill and bent to tend to his wound.

"Miranda's gonna take care of you, son." Thad spoke softly to the young man. "You're gonna be fine, understand?"

O'Neill nodded, and Thad walked over to join the other men.

"Whiskey first, I think." Ben was there next to her, looking through Miranda's bag.

She started to tell him to take his helpful suggestion on back to Boston, but she bit her lip. The man had just saved her life; she felt some obligation to be civil. Besides, another hand would be useful. "Give him a drink," she said. "Then we're gonna clean the wound and get this bleedin' stopped."

She kept pressure on the wound, while Ben helped O'Neill drink from the flask.

"Not too much, son." Ben's voice was quiet, but steady. "Won't help if we make you sick."

"Hurts like hell," the cowboy said through clenched teeth.

"It's going to be a lot worse when I use this to clean your wound," Ben said while Miranda ripped the man's shirt open to expose the wound. "I'll tell you what," he continued, "you keep your eyes on Miranda's pretty face. That'll keep your mind occupied."

Miranda's face heated at Ben's words. "O'Neill's wounded, he ain't blind!" she snapped.

Before Ben could cover his mistake with another lie, Miranda poured whiskey over O'Neill's wound. The curses the young man shouted made further conversation impossible.

Miranda clamped her jaw shut tight. When she was finished helping the wounded cowboy, she intended to give Ben a piece of her mind. *Pretty face, indeed!*

Ben watched Miranda glaring at Thad. In other circumstances, it might be funny to watch a small woman challenge a man twice her size. He smiled. It was amusing except that Miranda was deadly serious.

"I don't need a man guarding me!" She hefted the Sharps rifle. "I know how to use this."

Thad crossed his arms over his chest and looked as though he was ready to dig in for a long fight. "I used to think your sister was stubborn," he said.

Ben stepped closer. "It seems to me Miranda is right."

Thad and Miranda both turned to glare at him.

"She's perfectly capable of taking care of herself." Ben raised a hand to keep Thad from interrupting. "On the other hand, it seems to me that someone should ride along to watch out for young O'Neill." He pointed at the wagon and was pleased to see Miranda turn her head in that direction. "I could ride along behind and watch him while Miranda drives the wagon."

Miranda nodded, and Thad had sense enough to put a hand over his mouth to hide the victorious grin that appeared on his face.

"We'd best be moving," Miranda said as she stepped toward the wagon. "It's gonna be a bumpy ride. With luck we'll be there before O'Neill wakes up."

Thad followed Ben over to his horse. "I want to thank you, Mr. Lansing."

"Ben."

"Ben. I was too far away to help Miranda when those men came after her. I don't like to think what might have happened if you hadn't arrived when you did. . . ."

Ben glanced at the body of the man who'd been aiming at Miranda's back. "No need for thanks."

"I'm trustin' you to see her home safe, now."

Ben nodded. He watched Miranda bend over O'Neill in the back of the wagon. "You just get O'Reilly and the other bastards who were with him."

"Rest assured we will," Thad said.

"I'm leavin' now," Miranda shouted as she jumped into the driver's seat of the wagon. "If you're gonna come with me, you'd best stop jawin' and get on that ugly beast."

Thad grinned as Ben mounted Lightning and set off to follow the wagon.

"Seems like she'd be more grateful to the man who saved her life," Thad said.

Ben shrugged. He was glad he'd been of some help today, but he knew it didn't make up for his behavior when Miranda came to his room. After what he'd nearly done to her, he certainly didn't deserve her gratitude.

Ben watched Jonathan draw two parallel lines in the dirt with the edge of his boot. "Do you think you can shoot the marble from this line to the other line?" Jonathan asked as he dropped three glass marbles from his pocket onto the ground. "I bet I can. Do you want to go first?"

"You go first, Jonathan," Ben said. "Show me how it's done."

Ben had offered to watch the boy while Mercy and her father took care of O'Neill. He'd worried he wouldn't know what to do with a five-year-old child, but so far Jonathan hadn't run out of ideas. The boy launched the marble with his thumb, and it rolled nearly the entire distance between the lines.

"Well," Ben said, "I'm impressed. I doubt I can do so well."

"You have to try, Uncle Ben. You won't succeed if you don't try."

Ben grinned at the boy. Then he leaned over his marble. He tapped it, sending it skidding toward the line, but not nearly as far as Jonathan's had gone.

"Hmm." Jonathan leaned over the marbles, examining their positions carefully. "I reckon you'd better try again."

"I believe you're right."

At that moment, Miranda came out of the house and began pacing across the porch, back and forth, until Ben thought he'd grow dizzy watching her.

"It's your turn, Uncle Ben."

"Right." Ben made another feeble attempt at

shooting the marble, falling far shorter than he had on his first try. "I'll tell you what," Ben said, "you keep practicing. I need to talk with your aunt."

"I don't reckon I need as much practice as you do," the boy called after him as Ben strode toward Miranda.

"What's wrong?" he asked as he stepped up on the porch.

She glared at him, opened her mouth to speak, then shut it again.

"Is it the boy . . . O'Neill?"

Miranda shook her head. "Mercy reckons he'll recover."

"That's good news."

"I'm not needed here." Miranda resumed her pacing. "But Mercy don't want me goin' after O'Reilly."

"Thad and the others will find him."

"The more folks lookin' the better chance of findin' that old son of a . . . birch tree." She shoved her hair back away from her face. "He's been hidin' for a year. The sheriff stopped lookin', figurin' he must be long gone. We all figured he'd never get justice. Now here he turns up again. If we don't get the snake before he digs under his rock again, we might not find him at all."

"I'm sure you're right about that, but that doesn't mean you should—"

"I'm not afraid."

"Maybe you should be."

She stepped closer and pressed her palm against him, sending warmth through his chest. "You listen to me, Ben Lansing. I know damn well what you're up to. You promised Thad to look after me, didn't you?"

"I—"

"You think I'm slow-witted? I know you didn't come

along to watch O'Neill in the back of the wagon. I was just tired of arguing." She glared up at him. "I know you didn't want to be saddled with me." She looked down at the boards under her feet. "Sorry."

"Saddled?"

"You know what I mean."

"I'm glad to have a moment with you. It gives me a chance to apologize . . . for the other day."

Miranda walked away from the house, and Ben followed her until they stood near a pair of apple trees. "You ain't to blame. There's plenty of folks who find it hard to . . . look at me."

Ben squinted at her. "Hard to . . . ?"

She lifted her chin. Her lips curled up in a smile that held more pain than joy. She touched a finger to her scar. "I pretty much avoid mirrors myself, truth be told."

"Miranda." Ben reached for her, but she turned away.

"No." She stepped quickly toward the house. "I know you can't help the way you were raised. Talkin' fancy to ladies, sayin' her face is like a blushing pink rose, or a bright angel. Well, my face ain't so pretty, and it hurts to hear you lie about it!" She spun around and Ben flinched at the sharp look in her eyes. "I wanted nothin' so much as to have the earth open up and swallow me when you told O'Neill to look at my face!"

"Miranda—"

"No!" She raised a fist, then let it drop to her side. "No more talkin'. You should be out helpin' find O'Reilly, and so should I."

"All right, then, let's go find him."

"What?" She took a step back and stared.

"Let's join the hunt," Ben said. "I have an idea where he might have gone."

Miranda raised an eyebrow but didn't question him further. "I'll saddle my horse."

James Borwick

"I told them not to do anything illegal."

"You mean you knew they were going to try and take the cattle?"

"I didn't know they could prove that."

"You just said they were going to try something illegal."

He turned his head to the side and went back to his whittling. "I didn't believe them. They tried that before and couldn't do anything like this until I believe them now. But I said I'd pay them fifty dollars for the proof, and they couldn't do it."

Chapter 13

Miranda trailed behind Ben on the steep, narrow path. Her heart was pounding at the thought of finding O'Reilly. If they caught him red-handed with her sister's cows, the wise thing to do would be to mark their location and head back to find Thad and the others. But there was a part of her that really wanted to get the cows and take them home.

"Tell me again how you know about this place?" she asked.

"O'Reilly sent a message to me in town. I didn't know who he was, of course. But his message said he had information about what happened to my brother." Ben turned to speak over his shoulder. "He told me he could prove Thad and Mercy were cheating Jonathan."

"And you believed him? He's . . . he's an ass!"

"I know that!" Ben snapped. "I refused to get involved with his scheme unless he gave me real proof." He hesitated for a moment. "I promised to pay them fifty dollars for evidence that proved his accusations."

"And the cattle would be proof?"

"I told them not to do anything illegal."

"You mean you knew they were going to try and take the cattle?"

"I didn't! How could I know that?"

"You just said they were going to try something illegal."

He turned Lightning in a tight circle and went back to face Miranda. "You're not listening to me!" Ben glared at her. "I suspected they might try something like this, and I urged them not to do it. They don't work for me, and they certainly don't follow my orders."

"You could have warned us." Miranda pushed her hat back off her head so she could look Ben directly in the eye. "Someone might have been killed."

Ben let his eyes drop to Lightning's gray and white mane. A man *had* died. Ben's stomach had been churning for hours. Not that he regretted shooting the sorry bastard. It was the knowledge that the son of a bitch had nearly killed Miranda that had Ben's innards working themselves into knots.

"You're right. I . . . I should have said something to Thad. I . . ." He gazed into her eyes for a long moment. "If I'd known you would be in danger—"

Miranda turned away from his gaze. Then not wanting him to think she was hiding her scar, she looked back at him, letting him see her whole face again.

"I'm sorry," Ben said.

"Ain't no call for you to be apologizin'."

"If I did or said anything to cause O'Reilly to—"

"O'Reilly's a fool. Goin' after cattle while we're brandin'. Why not go after the cows we weren't watching?"

"My guess is that he planned to take some of the

freshly branded stock and show that they didn't have the Lansing brand."

Miranda laughed. "Did you see the brands they were usin'?"

Ben shook his head. With all the shooting he'd completely forgotten to check on the cattle at all.

"Thad helped Jonathan design his own brand—Circle J. The men were usin' the Circle J iron on half the cattle."

"So the brands wouldn't be proof of anything. . . . Then what did they hope to prove?"

"Who knows how O'Reilly's mind works. Maybe he thought if he did some shootin' you'd . . . take the boy. Get him away from this dangerous country."

"Maybe he just wanted to hurt you?" Ben turned again to look into Miranda's eyes. "Most of them were after the cattle, but it looked like . . ."

Miranda felt a chill creep up her spine. "O'Reilly has sworn to get even with Mercy. Killin' me would . . ."

"They weren't after the cattle. They were after you—"

"And Thad."

Ben nodded. "He couldn't convince me to take Jonathan away. Now he's found another way to attack her."

"He's not going to get away with it." Miranda spoke through gritted teeth.

Ben stared up the mountain. "It's not far now to the camp. Don't forget your promise. We're only observing."

Miranda pulled her Colt, then let it slip back into the holster at her side. "I'll be observing, but if they start the shootin', I'll be happy to be the one to finish O'Reilly."

"We're going to stay close to the tree line for

cover. We'll go in, see what we can, and get out. If they see us and if they start shooting—no heroics!" He pointed a finger at Miranda. "I want to see O'Reilly come to justice, but not at the cost of your life." When his words didn't seem to have much impact on her, he added, "Think about your family."

He could almost see Miranda thinking through his words before she nodded.

"I ain't afraid of dyin', but I don't reckon it's my time quite yet."

With those words they turned their horses and continued up the mountain in silence. A quarter of an hour later, Ben pulled Lightning to a stop. "The mining camp is beyond the next rise," Ben whispered.

They went over the rise. Ben pulled into the trees beside the road, and Miranda pulled up alongside him. She hadn't been to this particular mining camp, but she recognized the usual assembly of oil cloth tents and ramshackle wooden buildings. Everything that was needed to keep body and soul alive thrown together overnight as a gold or silver strike was found, or sometimes if a precious metal was merely suspected.

"Where's O'Reilly's tent?"

"Down this way." Ben turned where a road created by the pounding of hooves and feet meandered between two rows of tents. "But we're not getting close enough for them to see—" Ben pulled Lightning up short.

"What?" Miranda stopped next to Ben.

"Hellfire and damnation," Ben whispered. "Their tent was there." Ben pointed to an empty space in the middle of the crowded row. "Damn!"

Miranda saw the likely cause of Ben's cursing in an open space fifty yards down the road. Two small calves were roasting on a spit over an open fire, while men gathered around for a celebration. Miranda wondered what kind of price O'Reilly had gotten for the cows.

"They find any gold or silver here?" she asked.

"One of O'Reilly's men told me it was a rich silver strike."

Miranda took in a deep breath. "Most likely they got a good price for the calves, then."

A few drops of rain wet her cheek so she pulled her hat back up onto her head.

"Let's see if they're ours."

They rode through the camp, keeping an eye out for O'Reilly and his men. It didn't take them long to find out from one of the miners that O'Reilly had sold the calves before leaving.

"He made enough money selling his claim here to buy these cows and head to Texas," one miner said.

"Says he's gonna build up a cattle ranch," a toothless man added. "Tired of diggin', he was."

"Can't blame him for that!" the first miner said, and several men joined in laughing over the joke.

The rain was coming down in fat drops now, causing a general round of cursing from the gathered men.

"Come on," Miranda said, "let's get out of this rain."

Ben followed Miranda as the horses picked their way down the steep, rocky trail. The rain grew harder, pelting at his hat and soaking into his woolen jacket. They'd reached the main road before the driving rain turned to pounding hail.

Miranda led Ben into a copse of trees for a moment to escape the pummeling. She looked through the branches up to the sky. "Don't look like this is gonna let up any time soon."

"It's near an hour to the house, but I know a shelter close by."

Ben nodded. "Shelter sounds good to me," he shouted over the sound of hail pounding earth, rock, and trees.

Miranda led them out of the trees but kept to the edge of the road where there was some protection from the hail. After a few minutes, she turned Princess to follow a narrow trail back up the mountain. Ben could see the small cabin braced among the rocks on the hillside. They settled the horses on the downwind side of the cabin, working quickly to remove their saddles. Both Ben and Miranda were soaked by the time they made it inside and closed the door behind them.

Ben was impressed as he closed the tight-fitting door. The small cabin was sound and very dry inside. Miranda immediately went to work to start a fire in the stone fireplace on the back wall. There was a small pile of dry wood on the stone hearth. Ben tried to recall whether he'd seen any more wood outside.

There was sufficient light from the two glass windows, though Ben noticed a good supply of tallow candles on the shelf above the fireplace. The sparsely furnished room held a small table with three up-ended crates that served as chairs around it, a large wooden chest under one window, and a chest of drawers next to a narrow bed.

"Who lives here?"

"No one," Miranda said. "We built this cabin for shelter should anyone find themselves in a situation like this one. Cowboys'll sometimes stay here for a few days at a time when they come up to watch the cattle in the summer."

Ben wasn't sure whether that made him feel better.

Suddenly, the room seemed too small to share with her. There wasn't much he could do about it. It was a long way to the ranch house and even further to town. Even if he were willing to ride for hours through this hail, he wasn't going to leave Miranda alone here. Not when there was any chance O'Reilly could still be around.

Miranda looked over her shoulder at him. "There's a wood box outside. Would you bring firewood in before you take off your coat?"

Ben nodded and made his way back into the storm. He held his arm over his face to shield it from the hail, which was a goodly size and stung as the wind drove it at him. He gathered an armload of wood quickly and made his way back to the door. Miranda held the door open for him and closed it behind him. The small fire she'd set was blazing. Ben dropped the wood onto the pile and pulled off his soaked jacket, brushing hail from it. Miranda had already taken off her own jacket; it was hanging from a peg that protruded from the stone wall of the fireplace. Ben found another peg for his coat, then stood shivering a few feet away from her.

"This ain't no time to be shy, I reckon," Miranda said, though she made no move to remove any more of her clothing. "There's plenty of blankets in that chest." She pointed with her chin. "I reckon we both should take off our wet clothes and wrap up in blankets before we catch our death."

"Yes," Ben said, "that seems wise." Yet he couldn't help feeling terribly foolish for being in this enclosed space with that delicate body and his lusty thoughts.

They dug through the chest, releasing the spicy aroma of cedar that had woven its way into the blankets nestled inside. The scent reminded Miranda of walking through the woods on a fresh spring day. She opened her mouth to remark as much to Ben, but he had gathered his blankets and rushed away to the far corner of the room with his back to her.

The sight of him pulling his wet shirt over his head, baring those proud shoulders, rendered Miranda speechless. There was a small scar under his right shoulder blade; otherwise, his back was perfect—not smooth, but sleek and muscled. She swallowed hard and turned back to the blanket chest, closed the lid and walked away from the window to pull off her own clothes, careful to keep her eyes away from Ben.

"Tell me when it's safe to turn around," Ben said, with a slight tremor in his voice.

Miranda smiled, thinking of all that masculinity suffering as much as she was. At least they could share this misery—they dare not allow themselves closer contact. That would be a mistake. Stupid. If she was ever going to have a husband and family, she had better learn to control her impulses. She bent forward so that her hair fell in front of her and she wrung the moisture out of it, then combed her fingers through it, as though that would do any good. As soon as her hair was dry, it would curl every which way.

She pulled a small blanket around her waist, tying it to make a kind of skirt. She wrapped a second blanket around her shoulders, trying various methods of covering her chest until she finally found a way to wrap the blanket and tie it over one shoulder in an imitation of a Greek toga she'd seen pictured in one of Mercy's books. "I'm covered," she said, smoothing the blanket over her chest to be certain.

He was bending to retrieve his wet clothes off the floor and she caught a glimpse of his bare calves. More than a glimpse, since she couldn't seem to take

her eyes off them. Up until that moment Miranda
had not considered men's legs to be very different
from her own willowy limbs. Ben's, however, were
thicker, with a distinctive shape that tapered down
to his ankles. As he bent forward, the muscles rip-
pled, seeming to invite a woman's touch.

She managed to look away as he straightened
and turned to face her. As they worked together to
string a line across one corner of the room and
hang their clothes to dry, a little thought prickled
in the back of Miranda's mind. She'd come to think
of herself as an experienced woman. After all, she'd
shared kisses with several men and a bed with one
of those men. Yet, she had to admit, no kiss had ever
touched her as deeply as Ben's did. No man had ever
made her want him the way she wanted Ben at this
moment. The memory of his kisses stirred a wanting deep inside her. Miranda longed to persuade
Ben to kiss her now. Except that she couldn't bear
the thought of him rejecting her again.

Miranda threw her outer garments over the line
first, then felt her cheeks flame as she hung her
chemise and pantaloons. She stepped away from
the dripping clothing and straight into Ben's chest.
He caught her arms to keep her from tumbling but
lost his blanket in the process.

"Are you all right?" he asked as he pulled the
blanket back up in front of him.

For a few beats of her heart Miranda forgot to
breathe. She swallowed hard as Ben pulled the wool
covering around him, leaving those shoulders bare
and stunning for the whole world to see, or at least
for Miranda to examine in detail. She licked her lips,
but her tongue was so dry it made no difference.
Breathe. It's not like you've never seen a man's chest before.

Only the ones she'd seen had been fat and sloppy, or so thin the ribs had shown through. Ben's chest had a light layer of brown fur over amazing cords that called for her fingers to touch, though she managed to stop herself. Just above his right breast she observed a great gash that had been stitched together.

"Is that from the war, too?" The words slipped out before she could catch them.

Ben nodded. "And this." He showed her a scar on his right arm. "And that's as much as I'm willing to say about the war."

"I understand." She looked away. It wasn't so much that she was interested in the war, though she was curious about Ben's experiences; mostly she hoped for a distraction that would keep her mind away from the man's delicious body. Miranda sucked in a breath. "There might be the fixin's for coffee, or . . . tea."

"Something hot would be . . ." Ben smiled and she wondered whether any tea would warm her so much. He cleared his throat. "We need to get warm. I'll build up the fire."

Miranda found a pot, filled it with water from her canteen, and set it over the fire to heat while she searched the cupboard.

"No coffee, I'm afraid." She kept up a cheery commentary on her search, hoping to keep her mind occupied with trivialities. Anything rather than . . . *Oh my.* Her eyes wandered over to where he squatted in front of the fire with his seat stretched against the blanket, nice and round and, she suspected, as firm as his arms, legs, and chest. *Damn, the man is a distraction!*

She needed some air. Looking around, she found a bucket. "I'll set this outside to collect rain water.

In case we need it later." She set out the bucket, clear of the eaves, and dashed back inside the door before her blankets soaked through. For a moment, she stood in the doorway watching the sky. The storm clouds looked as fierce as ever.

Back inside, she set about taking an inventory of the supplies on hand. "There's tea and some canned beans. Oh, and corn flour, bakin' soda and there's some jerked meat and . . . "

"We're only here until the hail stops."

"It's turned to rain now, but still driving hard. Look out the window. I'm afraid we could be stuck here for hours." Maybe all night, Lord help them. "Likely it'll clear before dark," she said, though there was little hope of that occurring. She spooned some leaves into cups and poured hot water into them. "My sister makes this tea with herbs that grow wild hereabouts. One day I'm gonna have to find out what she puts in it. It always tastes good, not bitter . . . and it'll warm you for certain."

She handed Ben a hot mug.

"You're shivering." He put a hand over her shoulder and she felt heat radiate through her. "Here." He set his cup on the small table and pulled a huge pelt out of the chest. "What is this?" He held the pelt up in front of him. "Bear?"

"Looks like a black bear."

"Come." He spread the pelt on the floor in front of the hearth. "Sit close to the fire."

She stood on the thick fur, folded her legs under her, and sat, careful not to disrupt her blankets. He handed her a thick porcelain mug and she wrapped her icy fingers carefully around it, feeling the warmth soak through her hands. Then he draped a blanket over her shoulders. She looked up at his bare chest pink with cold, his nipples erect, and she felt the response in her own breasts. This was not a good idea.

He rummaged through the drawers and came back wearing a shirt that had been made for a smaller man. The sleeves ended three inches above his wrists, the buttons threatened to burst, and the shoulders looked as though they would rip with the slightest movement. She couldn't help herself— she laughed.

Miranda's giggle sounded a clear melody like a brook splashing over rocks under the summer sun. The light of the sun reflecting off the water added harmony to the song as the shine of her eyes danced with her laughter. Ben found himself smiling again in spite of himself. It seemed when he was with Miranda, all he wanted was to smile.

And touch her.

He fled to the table and sat on one of the crates. "You'll freeze over there."

"I'm fine," Ben lied.

"I didn't mean to make fun."

Ben peered over his cup at her, allowing the warmth of the steam to cover his face as he breathed in the pungent aroma of the herbs.

"You do look silly in that shirt, I'm afraid."

Ben looked down at the cotton plaid shirt. It kept him decently covered, but was otherwise not the sort of thing he'd be likely to wear. He shrugged as best he could within the tight confines of the garment.

Miranda laughed again. "Be careful, you're likely to rip right through those seams."

Her laughter was contagious and he chuckled, too. The sound was strange in his ears.

"Come on, then," Miranda said, "you'll warm more quickly near the fire."

Ben's better judgment told him to stay where he was, across the room from the beckoning finger. A safe distance from that fairy smile with the magical properties that seemed to control his lips. If he had any sense at all, he wouldn't be standing and walking to her side, and he certainly wouldn't fold his legs into a tight knot as he tried to fit onto the space she made for him on the great bear pelt.

He squeezed his tea mug and allowed the warmth to soak into his hands. His eyes caught on the stubs of his fingers, and he dropped his left hand out of Miranda's line of sight.

"Don't," she said. "There ain't no point in hidin' what these blankets can't cover."

She turned so that he could see the scar on her face. He lifted his hand and touched her jaw, smoothing over the ragged surface of the scar with his battered index finger. "How did you come to have this?"

She favored him with that half-smile again. He felt the raw pain deep in his gut and knew the story held more pain than the injury itself explained. "It was an accident. A buggy overturned."

"With you in it?"

She nodded, but her eyes dropped away, and he knew the story was designed to cover a truth she felt unable to reveal to him. He wanted to question her but couldn't bring himself to do it. He had his own secrets. Instead, he pulled the blanket back up around her shoulders.

"You're still shivering." Ben held his blanket around his waist as he rose to his knees to add wood so that the fire danced high and hot, warming the stones of the fireplace and radiating heat into the small cabin.

"Won't take long to run through all our wood using it like that," she said.

"I hope we won't be here much longer."

Miranda's chest rose as she took in a deep breath, and Ben's eyes were drawn to the mounds that pushed her blankets into tempting curves. He swallowed and looked back into the fire.

Her hand over his caught him by surprise. He turned to see her smiling, a new smile, one full of mischief. She knew damn well she was tempting him, and still she had no mercy. He watched her rise slowly to her knees and lean forward, her tongue darting out to moisten her lips as she drew close. A small voice told him to move. To run outside and jump on his horse, to hell with his clothing, the freezing rain, and everything else. If he stayed here, he was going to lose the battle for control he'd been fighting since they entered the cabin. Fortunately, he wasn't listening to that annoying little lecturer.

Her breath brushed warm against his cheek first, then her nose touched his, a light stroke that made him smile again. Her hands pressed against his shoulders and she pulled him closer as their lips met with a tingle of heat that made him feel light-headed. The blanket fell off her shoulders and his hands touched bare skin, smooth and soft as a rabbit pelt. He wanted to keep exploring—to slide his palms on down her backside—but the small voice inside him was shouting now, and he could no longer ignore the warning.

"I can't." Ben gasped for breath, hoping the air would help him regain his senses. Hoping he could get the creature that was sticking straight as a board between his legs to relax and stop demanding sat-

isfaction, because he was not going to let that un-
controlled lout touch this beauty if he could help it.
"I . . . won't take advantage of you."

He pushed away from her and tried to keep the blanket loose about him, to hide the evidence of his
arousal. Lord help him, he was having one hell of a
time convincing himself to be a gentleman right now.

"Why?" Miranda seemed almost hurt.

"You're innocent. . . . I'm a lot of things, but I won't
be the one to steal that from you."

"Innocent?" Miranda closed her eyes and smiled,
heaving a sigh that seemed too big for her petite
frame. "I'm not . . . Would it make a difference if I
told you I have slept with a man before. More than
once, in fact."

Ben stared.

"Now I've made you think I'm . . ." She licked her
lips, unable to say any of the words people used to
describe a woman who let men have their way with
her outside of marriage. She drew her lower lip between her teeth. "I shouldn't have . . . I made it
sound . . . There was only one man, though it was
more than once. . . . Aw, hell. There's no way to make
it sound right. It was a foolish thing to do."

"Are you feeling . . . foolish now?"

"No." One corner of her lips curled up in a half-
grin that spoke of pain too deep for him to contemplate. "He wanted to take what I had—you're
different."

"Don't be fooled, Miranda. I want to take from
you."

"I know." Her smile grew, a full bow that sparked
pain inside him, but this time it was the ache of
desire possessing him. "But I have a feelin' you'll be
givin', too. Fair trade, seems to me."

She looked directly at him, and he felt himself
tumbling helplessly into those great pools of blue. He
bent to kiss her, tasting her sweet lips and breathing
in lavender and spices. He'd forgotten how sweet a
woman could be, how soft and . . . He pulled away.

"You're certain you want this?" His voice was husky
with need and though he told himself he was only
doing what the lady wanted, he knew damn well it
was his own desire that drove him to her.

"I want you," she mumbled into his ear. "Please
show me."

She didn't have to ask twice. He stretched her out
on the pelt and opened the blanket she'd wrapped
around her small, perfect breasts. He bent to kiss
each of them twice before he settled his mouth
over one and rested his palm on the other. He'd
waited a long while for this pleasure, had dreamt of
it, and pausing now so near his goal was sweet torture. The kind of pain that would make his release
that much more triumphant when it came.

A blanket still covered her below the waist, and he
was well covered with shirt and blanket himself.
The small voice returned, telling him he could stop
now before it was too late—before the insanity of
desire put him beyond all sense. He laughed at the
small voice, though the sound he emitted was nearer
that of a man in agony. He could feel the pleasure
of conquest within his reach. Like a mountain
climber approaching the summit, he knew he would
have his goal. And he was a man suffering the worst
deprivation of all—layers of fabric separating him
from her soft skin. But she had wanted him to give
as well as take, and he intended to do some giving
before he rewarded himself. Hell, she didn't need
to know that each shiver of excitement she felt

echoed within him, that half of his delight came from hearing that delightful mew of pleasure she made when he touched her.

For a moment, he suckled, content merely to taste her. Before he could memorize the exquisite surface of her nipple, his impatient tongue began stroking, teasing her until she groaned a new sound that bubbled up from deep inside her.

"Ben—oh!" It was magical. He was a wizard who touched her breast so that she felt each stroke of his tongue through her body until she was throbbing between her thighs. It was heaven, and she wanted him never to stop. She gasped. His tongue continued its fantastic efforts, but his hand drew away from her breast. She felt a rush of cold to her bare breast, but before she could protest, she felt his hand wriggle under the blanket that stretched around her waist. He slid it down over her belly and between her thighs until his palm rested on the curls that covered her womb. Her eyes opened wide to see Ben smiling at her.

"Did I surprise you, love?" His fingers pressed against her, gently probing. "I promise, you'll like this."

She reminded herself to breathe, then she quickly moistened her lips. She wanted to say something, but she couldn't find words. Thought perhaps she'd lost her voice until— "Oh!" His fingers worked their way inside her, and some instinct made her rise to press against him.

"Patience, love," he murmured as he pressed his lips against her throat.

She rose off the ground. Surely she did, for she was definitely flying, soaring across the sky like an eagle on a fine summer's day.

Miranda cried his name and the sound went deep into his chest.

"Have I given you enough, love?"

"Yes. Yes." Miranda pulled at the blanket. "Please take me now. You've given me enough, I promise you."

"No, love. Not yet. I haven't given you nearly enough." Ben kissed her. He combed his fingers through her hair, pulling her close to him and demonstrating with his tongue what he was about to do to her womanly parts, driving deep inside of her. She was ready to let him in. Yet, he delayed. "Take my shirt off, love."

Her hands trembled as she worked the buttons, but it was well worth it to touch his bare chest. She relished the feel of his corded belly and his powerful shoulders, first with her palms, then with her tongue. The scar she'd glimpsed before was now fully revealed. It looked as though his breast had been shattered and stitched back together—one nipple was missing, and lines scattered up and away from it like the spokes of a broken wheel. She kissed him there and stroked the soft fur of his chest with her cheek.

"Look at my face, love." Ben lifted her chin so that she was looking into his eyes. "That's better. You don't have to look at the ugly scar."

"Only wondered how . . . how you lived."

"This is no time for telling stories, Miranda. We have business to take care of."

"Of course," she said and pulled the blanket away from her legs and her most private places.

"You're beautiful," Ben murmured against her belly before dipping lower.

Before she knew it, he was licking her knee and working his way up the inside of her thigh, slowly, driving her to distraction until she was certain she couldn't wait another moment. She noticed the blanket had dropped from his waist; he was fully aroused. He was so large she worried for a moment whether she'd be able to keep her part of the bargain. She promised herself not to flinch or do anything to show her fear. She didn't want to make him angry.

His kisses reached the apex between her thighs and he lifted his head. "I'm going to come inside you now, love."

Miranda nodded, not trusting her voice. His smile reassured her, but she closed her eyes, bracing herself.

He touched her. And she felt him solid against the moist opening. She spread her legs, opening to him, and he slipped inside slowly, pressing and pulling back again before he thrust deeper and filled her. She opened her eyes and let out a little breath. Somehow he fit inside her, and it was nice. He started to move slowly at first, then a little faster and faster until she was caught up and felt herself moving with him. Then it happened.

The pleasure that she'd felt, the soaring eagles in flight, swept her up again, and this time she flew beyond the sky and hurtled past the stars. She dug her fingers into his ribs, wanting to hold him there to continue on this flight forever. He surprised her by pulling out. He pressed against her chest and pulled her breasts together around his shaft until his seed spilled against her. He collapsed next to her and used the old shirt to wipe her clean before he pulled her close. Without letting her go, he pulled blankets over the two of them.

"Miranda," he whispered into her ear. "Miranda, love."

She examined his face—his eyes closed. He wore a contented smile such as she'd seldom seen before.

It was not an expression she'd ever hoped to see on grim Ben Lansing.

He bent to nuzzle her ear, and she curled up against him. As the wind howled and the freezing rain beat against the windows, Miranda fell asleep in Ben's warm arms.

When they awoke, the moon gleamed bright against a frozen hillside. Ben dashed outside for more wood, and they built the fire back up to warm themselves.

"I think our clothes may be dry," Miranda said. "We'd be warmer if we put them on."

Ben's grin shone in the firelight. "I think I know a better way to get warm."

Miranda grinned, too, then bent to kiss his nipple, teasing him with her tongue.

"Oooh. You, my dear, are a quick study," Ben whispered. "I think I shall teach you a few more tricks."

In fact, he taught her several tricks that pleased them both until they were, if not sated, at least exhausted. They slept skin to skin on the bear pelt with blankets piled upon them, and neither of them suffered any cold even when the fire died.

Chapter 14

Benjamin woke feeling a cold draft on his shoulder. He turned to Miranda and smiled, remembering their play of the night before. She'd fallen asleep curled into a tight ball and had pulled the blankets away from him. Although he remembered whispering only a few hours ago that he would need a week to recover, strong desire pounded through him as soon as he saw her. He glanced at the window. The sun would rise soon, but they had enough time if he acted quickly.

He rolled over onto his side and brushed a kiss against her naked back. She screamed and pulled away.

"I'm sorry!" He rose to his knees. "I didn't mean to frighten—"

"No!" She held a blanket tightly against her chest. "I ain't . . . I'm not . . ."

"I think I must have surprised you."

"No." Miranda inched away from him. "I . . . It wasn't because you . . . I was asleep."

"You're shivering." He wrapped a blanket around her. She leaned away. "I need to"—she looked around the room—"it's time I dressed and . . . I'll make us some breakfast."

He pulled the drooping blanket back over her shoulder. "I would never hurt you." He kept his voice low.

She stared at him, her eyes small points in the near darkness. "I know."

He placed a hand on each of her arms. "Someone has. Another man?"

"I told you, I was in a deep sleep and—" She choked on a sob.

He pulled her against his chest, careful to hold her loose enough that she could escape if she wanted. She leaned against his shoulder, until her tears streamed down his chest.

"Shh, shh." He combed his fingers through her hair.

"Please, I don't want to." She sobbed against him.

"Go ahead and cry, love. Do you mind if we get back under the covers before we both freeze?"

Miranda nodded and stretched out next to him on the bear pelt that still held their warmth and the musky sent of their lovemaking. He held her close with one arm and used his free arm to cover them both with blankets.

"Will you tell me?"

"I can't—" She sniffed. "I'm sorry about all these tears."

"What's wrong with crying, sweetheart?"

"Ain't nothin' wrong with cryin', it's showing weakness to a man that—"

"I know you're not weak. You cry all you want, love."

She sniffed and Ben reached for his jacket hanging from a peg in the stone wall of the fireplace. He managed to pull his handkerchief out of a pocket without letting go of her. The desire to keep her warm and safe was nearly as strong as other desires she gave him. He forced his mind not to dwell on those thoughts.

She blew her nose in the handkerchief he offered her.

"Now, tell me," Ben said. "Who did this to you?"

"Don't follow your meanin'."

"Who turned a brave girl like you into a frightened kitten? Was it the man who did this to you?" Ben traced the scar on her jaw.

"That was an accident—"

"Truth now."

"I can't tell."

"Yes, you can." Ben stroked her hair and held her close, keeping his own breathing calm, trying to soothe her until she told him everything. Until she identified the man Ben intended to hunt down and bring to justice—preferably with his bare hands. "I'll make a fair trade: You tell me your story, and I'll tell you about the scar on my chest."

"Promise you won't"—she choked on a sob—"won't tell anyone?"

"You have my word."

She sniffed and pulled the blanket across her eyes. "It was in Philadelphia. And it was my fault, you see. My family can't know about this. They wouldn't understand."

"Your story won't leave this room."

"I went to Philadelphia to get away. Thought I was going to die from a broken heart." She made a sound that might have been an attempt to laugh. "I realize now I was more embarrassed than heartbroken."

"Your beau found another girl?"

"How did you guess?"

Ben shrugged. "So you left. Why Philadelphia?"

"I had a good friend—Lydia. She was from Philadelphia and she wanted to go back. So we left together. I took a job in a dress shop."

"Where you learned something about fashion design."

"I wasn't doin' anything so special. Just stitching dresses together." She took a deep breath and let it out slowly. "He said he loved me. Lawrence was his name." She took another deep breath. "Promised to marry me." She swallowed and rested her head against Ben's chest. Luckily it was still dark, since she couldn't bear to look at him. "I was so foolish, to think a man like him would love the likes of me."

"Likes of—" Ben touched her cheek. "Miranda Chase, I will not have you talking as though you were anything less than—" Guilt stopped him from scolding her. "You're a beautiful and appealing young lady. Don't think any less of yourself on account of some lout who doesn't know his ass from a mule."

"I don't know that I'm much of a prize." She sighed and he thought she would argue with him. "But you're right, he wasn't either. He was a buyer for a mail order store. Bought women's dresses from the shop where I worked. And he started paying attention to me the first day I went to work there. Complimentin' my fine stitching and such. Soon it was comments about my eyes and my, well, lots of things. Damned foolishness. I know I'm pretty—or I was anyhow."

"You mustn't say 'was.' You *are* beautiful, Miranda." He drew the side of his finger along her jaw and pressed his lips to her head. "So the idiot wasn't blind. What happened next?"

"He said we would be married as soon as his

mother was better. She was ill, he said. I was so stupid I didn't even get suspicious when he wouldn't take me to meet her. Turned out his mother had died years before. It was his . . . his wife who was ill."

"Wife?"

"Yes, that's the true reason why he couldn't marry me, not that he would have. I mean, even if there hadn't been a wife, I don't imagine he'd really wanted to marry me. But at first, I had believed he cared about me. I . . . I let him . . . he said he needed a woman and he'd go pay a . . . a whore if I didn't allow him in my bed. It didn't seem right for me to make him wait until we were married, not when he was worryin' about his mother and all. He had a way of talkin' that made me feel guilty no matter what I did." She swallowed. "And so I let him come to my bed. I did everything he asked of me, but I could never please him. And he . . . when I did something wrong he would . . ."

"He hurt you?"

"Usually it was just a slap. But sometimes, when he was really angry, it was worse than that."

Ben stroked her hair, trying to comfort her, knowing that he couldn't.

"I had decided to leave him, to pack up and move somewhere he'd never find me. And then I . . . I found I was carrying his child. I thought if he knew about the baby he'd want to marry me, start treatin' me better." She swallowed, picturing the wild look Lawrence had in his eye when he came after her. "Instead, it made him ferocious mad. Worse than I'd ever seen him before. He shouted and then . . . then he started to beat me. While he was beatin' on me, he told me about his wife, his children. I don't remember what all he said. I was so scared. I tried to protect the baby, tried to run away. He had this walking stick and he used it over my head until it broke. I don't remember much after that, except that my friend Lydia found me half dead on the floor of my room. She got me a doctor. I don't know how." Miranda shivered, remembering those dark days. "Somehow Lydia convinced me I shouldn't die."

"You lost the child?"

Miranda closed her eyes, remembering the small flutter of life she'd felt only days before Lawrence had tried to kill her. "I remember crying with Lydia, telling her my baby had gone to heaven and I would never see him because I was going to hell."

Ben kissed her forehead. He tried to take away the pain but understood that he couldn't. It was too much pain. Too difficult to dull.

"I'm sorry," he said.

"Well, it's over and done. To tell the truth, I'm glad I told someone. Tellin' the story, it's almost like it happened to someone else."

"But it didn't."

"No."

"You should tell Mercy about—"

"No! And you promised you wouldn't tell either."

"I won't. But . . . won't it be difficult for you, helping with her baby?"

"I thought so, at first. But she's my sister and her havin' a baby doesn't add to my loss. I reckon when I see her holdin' her little one, I might feel an ache inside. But I think I'll feel more joy for seein' Mercy happy. And I've found with Jonathan that I enjoy bein' an aunt, too."

"You're a remarkable woman, Miranda Chase." He pressed a kiss to her head. "Will you . . . tell me one more thing?"

She turned, and he could see her features in the glimmer of dawn.

He took a breath to keep his voice calm. "What happened to him?"

"The accident. The one I've been telling about? It was real. He was driving his buggy and he was drunk. He ran into a farm wagon and his carriage overturned. He was killed."

"I'm glad." *Saves me the trouble of killing the bastard myself.*

"Don't seem right to be glad a man died," Miranda said. "But it is hard for me to be sorry."

Ben held her close as he watched the rain pelt against the window. "What do you say we make a fire and warm ourselves before we head out into that?"

"Good idea, then you can tell me about your scar."

He kissed her for good measure before he braved the cold outside of their warm nest. When the fire was blazing, he snuggled back under the blanket with her. "I suppose we should get dressed now."

"You're not gonna avoid keeping your promise, are you? I want to hear your story."

"There's not much to tell. I was shot in the back; I'm told the wound is small. You may have seen it."

Miranda nodded.

"I survived because the bullet came straight through without damaging anything important. The ugly scar in the front is where it came out." He took a breath.

"That wasn't a fair trade." Miranda pouted. "I told you the whole story."

"There isn't much more to it. There was a battle, lots of gunfire . . ."

"What were you doing? Why would someone shoot you in the back?"

"You have to stand up in the open to fire a cannon. We made a good target when they could get to us. That day they had riflemen out to try and stop us."

She rested her head against him, tracing a finger over the scar on his chest. "Your arm and your hand—did that happen at the same time?"

He closed his eyes and nuzzled the top of Miranda's head. "You don't really want to hear about this."

"You promised."

"The arm . . . was the same battle." He lifted his right arm and looked at the old wound. "It wasn't as bad as the scar makes it look; the bullet ripped through pretty cleanly. We had to keep the cannons firing. Our infantry troops were depending on us."

"You kept fighting even though you were hurt?"

"You make it sound heroic, but it wasn't really. You get caught up in a battle and you keep going until you can't go on."

"And so you were nearly killed by this bullet." She brushed a kiss to the scar on his chest.

"I didn't die. I was lucky. When I got my strength back, they sent me back to my company and I was able to finish out the war." He pulled her tight against him with his right arm. "Luck is a strange thing. I might have lost my right arm and been sent home a cripple."

"And you would still have your left hand." She took his battered hand in hers and stroked the remaining fingers. "You would still be able to paint." She kissed his left hand. "Ben." His name seemed almost a sigh escaping her lips.

"I've had more than one person tell me it makes no sense to prefer the loss of an arm to a few fingers, but . . ." He swallowed. "It's not as though wishing could change any of it."

"No, I reckon not." Her tears dripped onto his chest and she wiped them away. "I know it was hard for you to tell me. And to listen to me." She caressed his cheek, feeling the rough stubble of his beard. "Thank you." They held each other in silence as the room filled with the light of a gray dawn. "And thank you for showing me how nice a man's touch can be."

"That last was my pleasure. I only hope this night hasn't made things more difficult for you."

"One thing's certain: I'll remember Ben Lansing for the rest of my life."

Ben felt something squeezing his heart. "You'll remember me, but not for long. Soon you'll find an honest, hardworking man who will want you desperately. You'll marry, bear him children, and think of no one else but him. I only hope the man will realize what a treasure he has."

"You're a kind soul to imagine such a life for me."

"It isn't my imagination. It's what you deserve."

Miranda bit her tongue. She was afraid to think about what she deserved, but Ben had surely described the life she dreamt about. She traced a finger through the hair on his chest. "Can I ask you one more question that has nothing to do with the war?"

"Won't promise I can answer."

"When we get back to the house, will you tell Mercy and Thad you've decided Jonathan should stay with them?"

"I'll tell them." He touched her face. He didn't want to think about facing Mercy and Thad. Didn't want to think about closing his business here, because that meant he would no longer have an excuse to touch Miranda's unruly corn silk hair, to swim in her great blue eyes, or to bask in the glow of her smile.

"I don't suppose before we go you'd kiss me one more time?"

"One more kiss?" Ben asked. That was like asking a beggar at the feast to take one slice of bread and leave the roast pig, the fruit, the cheese, and the fine wine. "No, I don't think I'll settle for one small kiss."

Ben feasted from Miranda's lips to her toes and he relished her gentle touches. Surely, a village of island maidens could not give him the pleasure of Miranda's trim body.

They both knew it had to end; they could hardly stay in this shelter forever. As the sun peeked through the clouds outside they made a game of dressing each other. She helped him pull on his pants, spending far too long on fastening each button. He helped her pull her chemise over her head, covering her breasts and her waist and her hips; then he knelt before her, pulled the hem of the garment up, and found her navel with his tongue.

He had her giggling fiercely when the door flew open and Thad Buchanan stepped inside holding two pistols hip high and aimed straight at them.

Ben jumped to his feet, blocking Miranda from view.

"What the hell are you doing here, Lansing?"

Ben opened his mouth to speak, but Miranda shouted. "Put those guns away before you hurt someone." She pulled a blanket around herself and stepped in front of Ben. "What the hell are you doing barging in without knocking?"

Thad's face flushed and he looked away from her as he shoved his guns back into his holster. "We were out lookin' for O'Reilly, and when I saw the smoke—" He shoved his hat back on his head and mumbled something that might have been "damnation." He glared at Ben. "Lansing . . . This is a hell of a strange way to look after a girl!"

Ben and Thad each stepped around Miranda, driven by some mysterious male instinct, she supposed. Thad's fist connected with Ben's jaw, causing the smaller man to stumble back a step. Thad landed a second punch on Ben's chest; Miranda could hear the whoosh of air forced from Ben's lungs.

Hell, Thad was going to kill Ben if he didn't start defending himself. "You stop!" she shouted.

Neither man seemed to hear her. Ben came to life, and Thad grunted as Ben drove a fist into his gut. He tackled the larger man, and they rolled over the table and onto the floor in a tangle. Miranda could no longer tell who was dominating in the blur of fists and knees and elbows. She had to do something to get their attention and she remembered the bucket she'd set out to catch the rain. Her aim was true as she doused the pair of ruffians with icy water.

"Dammit, that's cold!" Thad bellowed as he rolled away.

Ben grinned up at her and winced as blood trickled from his lip.

"You boys about done with your antics?"

They sat like two chastised schoolboys and stared up at her. Ben was still grinning. Thad looked angrier than a bull locked away from the cows at breeding time.

Miranda stood wrapped in a blanket and glared at the pair of them. "Thad Buchanan, you're married to my sister. That gives you no rights over me. I'm a grown woman."

Thad touched the side of his face, where it

appeared a bruise was starting. "I know what Mercy would say if she'd walked in here and saw you." He glared at Ben.

"I didn't . . ." Ben started, then looked up at Miranda.

"He didn't do anything I didn't ask him to do." She pulled the blanket tighter around her shoulders. "I'm old enough to make my own decisions."

"I'm sorry, Miranda," Thad said. "You may be old enough, but Lansing is a good bit older, and he had no right to take advantage of you. A gentleman would offer marriage."

Miranda laughed.

"Of course I intend to marry her, Buchanan. You certainly didn't think she'd allow such liberties otherwise, did you?"

Miranda gaped at him, but she couldn't find her tongue to tell Ben that no such offer was necessary.

"I realize it's a bit of a surprise, Mister . . . Thad. We were on our way to tell you the good news last night when the storm drove us into this cabin. I'm afraid being alone here, we were carried away."

It was Thad's turn to gape. He stared at Ben, then turned to Miranda. "Is that right, Miranda? You intend to . . . to marry Lansing?"

Miranda swallowed. She watched Ben for some clue as to how she should respond, but he wasn't looking at her. She forced a smile. "Of course. We'll be married in the spring."

Thad looked from Miranda to Ben. He brushed dust from both of his knees, then stood, towering over Ben, who was still sitting on the floor. "The hell you will," he said in a voice so quiet it was frightening. "Preacher's in town this week—you'll be married on Saturday."

Ben looked up and Miranda expected him to say he'd been joking, he'd never intended to actually marry her. Instead, he smiled at Thad—that smile that made Miranda think he wanted to sell a used buggy without any wheels.

"Well, that's good news, isn't it, sweetheart?" He looked up at Miranda. "We won't have to wait, after all."

"Good news." Miranda couldn't think of anything else to say, at least not out loud in front of Thad. The moment she could get the madman posing as Ben Lansing alone, there was a hell of a lot she planned to say.

Miranda took a sip of coffee. It was cold and bitter. She glanced up at the clock over the mantel. They'd been sitting around the kitchen table going over plans for the wedding. The strange thing was that Pa seemed happy about it. Of course, he was the only one.

Mercy rubbed her temples and closed her eyes, then looked back at Ben. "There's one thing I want to ask you, Mr. Lansing."

"Ben." He smiled at Mercy. "Please."

"Very well, Ben. Is the purpose of this marriage so that you can provide a home for your nephew?"

"Jonathan?" Ben looked from Mercy to Thad. "No, of course not. I should have said earlier, only in the excitement about our plans it escaped my mind. Jonathan's place is here, with the two of you. I hope you'll forgive me for doubting you. I am most grateful for all you've done for my nephew. As for me, I've no desire for children—"

"Except for the children the good Lord may bless you and Miranda with," Thad said.

"Yes, exactly what I meant." Ben's Adam's apple bobbed. He smiled at Miranda. "I mean no children other than those we're lucky enough to have."

"Children are not a matter of luck." Thad leaned across the table and glared at Ben. "They are a blessing to be cherished. As I'm certain you will cherish your wife."

Ben put his hand over Miranda's and squeezed tight. She noticed his hand was damp, which meant his calm appearance was an act. "I'll do everything in my power to protect Miranda."

And I will do what I can to make certain that doesn't include marrying me against her will.

"What the hell are you doing?" Miranda asked when she was certain no one else was in the barn.

Ben kept his eyes on Lightning. "Checking on my horse."

Miranda reached up and clasped his shoulder. "That's not what I mean and you know it."

He smiled at her, then turned back to his horse. "Thad's right. I don't want my actions causing anyone to think less of you."

"It's not as though you forced me. If anyone is to blame, it's me."

Ben nodded. "That's exactly what people will think. Your family will believe that I took advantage of you. The rest of the world will believe this reflects on your character, not mine."

"You know damn well you weren't the first for me."

"I'm the only one in this town who knows about that, aren't I?"

Miranda turned away from him. She had done her best to keep the secret. She wet her lips. "I still can't ask this of you." Miranda shook her head. "I was willing to play along. No harm in pretendin' we're engaged. We could have a fight and it would all be over. But—they are in there now planning our wedding." She glanced back toward the house where she'd left Thad, Mercy, and Pa talking about the "good news."

He turned her and pulled her against his warm chest. His musky scent reminded her of their long night of passion. Lord how she wanted to believe there would be more nights like that, nights of tender kisses and long, slow lovemaking.

"It's no sacrifice, love."

Her heart stopped as he used the name he'd called her last night. She looked up at him and he smiled, a warm, tender smile that filled her heart and caused tears to pool in her eyes.

"You want me?"

He nodded. "How can you doubt it?" He brushed a kiss to her forehead. "Did I seem reluctant last night?"

"No, you didn't." She blinked back a tear and sniffed. "Only I thought . . . Ben." She pulled him down for a kiss and felt the same spark of passion that was always beneath the surface when he was near.

He held her close. In that moment everything became clear—the two of them belonged together. She hated the idea of Thad forcing Ben into this. His kiss convinced her that this wedding might be rushed, but the marriage was going to work.

Chapter 15

"Well, congratulations, Mr. Lansing." Clarisse surprised him when he walked into the store early the next morning. How she'd heard he couldn't imagine. Word traveled more quickly than his horse, apparently.

"Thank you. I can't tell you how pleased I am." Shocked would be a better adjective. Yet, he knew he was doing the right thing. A few months spent here playing husband to Miranda wasn't such a high price to pay for her future. All he was putting off was his retirement on that tropical island. And he still needed to find a way to fund that. "Miranda will make a beautiful bride."

"Miranda?" Clarisse walked right up to him and stared as though she were trying to decide how he'd managed to acquire a third eye. "Miranda is to be married?"

"Yes, of course, Miranda. Who else would I marry?"

"You're marrying Miranda?" Clarisse repeated.

"I . . . What else would you be congratulating me about?"

"Why, the sale of your paintings, of course."

"My . . ." It was Ben's turn to be puzzled. "The paintings you purchased from me?"

Clarisse nodded. "I didn't give you nearly enough, it turns out." She moved behind the counter, opened a drawer and removed a small package. "I gave you fifty dollars because I wasn't certain how much I'd get for them." She grinned and handed him the small rectangular package. "You'll find another fifty in there."

"Fifty." Ben felt the weight of the parcel. "Dollars?"

"I set this money aside for you when I received the wire from my friend in New York. He bought the paintings and wired the money to our account in Denver."

"New—" Ben stopped himself from echoing her again. "I don't understand. You bought the paintings."

"I sent them to an art dealer I happen to know, in New York." Clarisse smiled as though it were common for the proprietor of a small mercantile in the wilderness to be friends with New York art dealers. "I knew he'd be able to get more money for them there than what I could get here, or even in Denver. The only surprise was the speed of the post and well, I never thought he'd get over a hundred dollars." She wiped her hands on her apron. "I took out a small commission and the cost of shipping them, of course."

"Of course." Ben stuck the wrapped bills into his jacket pocket. He wondered if the money would be enough for passage to the Sandwich Islands. He'd heard that mail ships left from San Francisco regularly. Then he remembered the reason he'd come to the store. "I . . . I wondered if you had a wedding ring."

Clarisse winked. "You came to the right place." She waved him down to the end of the counter where she pulled out a drawer and set it on top of the display case. "Now, which one do you suppose Miranda would like?"

Ben had no idea. But the fact that his stomach twisted at the question struck him as a very bad sign.

"You don't have to do this."

Miranda scrubbed the old iron skillet. She did not want to have this conversation. Her sister was too good at knowing what was in Miranda's heart. Although perhaps this time it would be harder for Mercy to figure out since Miranda wasn't quite sure herself.

"I know I don't have to."

"Thad. I love him dearly, but he can be bull-headed about these things. He doesn't know Fort Victory like we do. Things are different here. Could be that in the East you'd become an outcast, I don't know. But that isn't the way it is here. There are a few folks, of course, who will gossip, but a little talk isn't as hard to live with as a man you don't love." Mercy sighed. "If you find yourself in a family way, you know we'd help you."

Miranda stopped her scrubbing to look up at her sister. "I know, Mercy. It isn't as though I feel I have to"—she stumbled over the words—"marry him." She took a deep breath. "I want to."

Mercy took a step closer and Miranda could feel her sister's eyes probing her. "You love him?"

Miranda hesitated. She hadn't thought of it that way until this moment. She wanted him and felt he needed her. That was enough. It was more than she'd ever expected to have from a man. "I do."

"I'm happy for you, little sister." Mercy grabbed her

then and hugged her close. "It's awfully quick, but Lord knows it happens that way sometimes."

Miranda wrapped her arms around her older sister and let her tears run freely. She sniffed into Mercy's shoulder. "I've got black grease on my hands; you're gonna be a mess."

Mercy stepped back, touched Miranda's cheek, and smiled. "Why didn't you tell me the two of you are in love? I was so worried with Thad ranting and all that he'd forced Ben to—"

Miranda turned away and wiped her hands on a towel. She glanced back at Mercy.

"Ben did ask you before Thad came barging in on you?"

Miranda wet her lips. That was Ben's story. They were already engaged before they'd slept together. "I thought we'd already explained all that," she said, though she knew her statement lost a good bit of credibility since she couldn't look her sister in the eye.

"Miranda." Her sister heaved a sigh and sat in one of the ladder-backed chairs their pa had made. "You're very sure about this?"

Miranda blinked back more tears. Her sister would think her tears were a sign of sadness or fear, but that wasn't the case. She was happy. Ben might not love her, but he did want her, and she was going to be a good wife to him. "I'm very sure."

Miranda had surprised everyone when she announced that she intended to move into the small cabin on the mountain. Come winter they might have to move into the main house. The narrow trail up to the cabin was steep and difficult enough in the summer. When the snow came to stay, it could be icy and treacherous and might even be impassable for days at a time. If she were honest, Miranda would have to admit that the prospect of long days and nights alone with Ben in the small cabin held a good deal of appeal. But that wasn't the main reason she'd chosen to make this place their home.

It wasn't fair to Ben to force him to live with Thad, Mercy, and Pa. Not yet, maybe not ever. He had grown up in a mansion with servants and extra rooms for houseguests. Miranda was certain she'd be lost in such a house, but she imagined Ben would find frontier life just as difficult to accept.

If Miranda was going to find a way to show Benjamin Lansing how much he really needed her, they were going to need some privacy.

She'd spent hours cleaning and making the simple cabin comfortable for her new husband. Pa had given her a sturdy table and two new chairs. If they had callers, they would still have to use the old crates for sitting. She laughed at the thought of entertaining guests in this little building. Like everyone else in these parts, if they had visitors, Miranda would offer them hospitality.

She glanced at the freshly painted bed frame. They'd thrown out the old straw tick, and Thad had spent all yesterday afternoon working on the frame. Ingrid Hansen had organized several women to make a quilt as a wedding gift, and Clarisse had promised a new featherbed and two pillows.

Miranda's heart sang with the idea of being a wife to Ben, a man who was handsome, intelligent, and strong enough to fight when he had to. She smiled at the memory of Ben tackling Thad. The man could take care of himself and protect his family. But he would never raise a hand to her in anger—she was certain of that.

Against all odds she'd found the man who was meant for her. All that remained was for Ben to understand the gift they'd been given. And he would, in time. He'd agreed to marry her to protect her from disgrace, which showed he was a man of honor. In time, she was certain he would come to really care for her. Perhaps not the way she loved him, but there were many different kinds of caring. For the moment, she'd settle for the knowledge that he truly desired her. He wanted to hold her and touch her and have her touching him.

He even thought she was beautiful—in spite of her scar. She brushed a finger along her jaw, feeling the ragged line the scar made. Ben wasn't blind to the flaw, but it didn't matter to him. She was sure there weren't many men who would feel that way. Surely that was a sign that he was the one for her.

She made him smile—not that pretend snake-oil-vendor grin, but a real smile that came from deep inside him. A smile of contentment that warmed her heart nearly as much as his kisses did.

One day they would have a real house and children. Ben would find joy then, Miranda was certain of it. Funny how easy it was for Miranda to see Ben's folly. He was a clever man, too smart perhaps. He had himself fooled into believing that a man could live alone. But living alone wasn't really living, and it didn't suit Ben at all. He needed her as much as she did him. It wasn't until she'd found Ben that she felt womanly and wanted. Almost whole again. Her love was starting to heal him inside, too, though it was bound to take some time.

She pulled his bag out from under the bed and put

his things into the drawers she'd cleared. He didn't have much, just two suits, three shirts, some stockings and undergarments, and three books. Miranda opened the first of the books and found it wasn't filled with printed words, but pictures. Pencil sketches. She turned through page after page and found horses, and women. Men too, as well as buildings, trees, and rocks. There were sketches of anything you could imagine, animals of all kinds and people of all ages.

The faces almost made her cry. Sadness and horror, terror and woe. She stared for a long while at a picture of a man sitting with a blanket wrapped around him. It was so real she could almost feel the cold.

The second book had pictures of seashore and river, trees and mountains. Almost all of the pictures were outdoor scenes, some with horses, cows, and sheep. One picture seemed to be looking up at a few clouds and a hawk dark against the sky.

"Miranda." Ben strode across the wooden floor, pulling the book out of her hand. "That's mine."

"I was putting the books away with your other things," she said. "I couldn't help looking. Your pictures—"

"I'd rather you didn't."

She let him take the books, which he returned to his bag and shoved back under the bed.

Ben spun back to her. "I appreciate your efforts, love, but my books are private."

"I'll do as you wish, Ben." She stretched up to the tips of her toes and kissed his cheek, then looked away.

He lifted her chin. "I don't want you feeling you must bow and scrape to my every wish."

She grinned. "No need to worry, I won't. I'll respect your wishes about your books, though."

"Thank you." Ben looked around the room. "I didn't expect to find you here. Thad made it clear you weren't to move in until after the wedding," Ben said. "You've cleaned up a bit."

"I wanted it to be nice for us—a home."

Ben shifted his weight from one foot to the other. "You're not changin' your mind about tomorrow, are you?"

He smiled then, his genuine smile, the one that always made her heart skip a beat.

"No fear of that, my dear." Ben pulled her close. "I intend to stand beside you in front of the preacher tomorrow and make my intentions clear to anyone who will listen."

Miranda pressed her lips to his, wove her fingers into his hair, and held him tight until they were both breathless.

She rested her head against his chest, feeling his heart pounding as hard and fast as her own. "I hope I can hold up my part of the bargain."

"You have nothing to fear," Ben said. "All you have to do is be a beautiful bride, and I have no doubt you will be that."

Chapter 16

Considering the haste with which the family had planned this wedding, Ben was amazed to see the entire community join in the celebration. There weren't enough seats in the small church for the assembled crowd. Even the preacher remarked he would like to see so many faithful for a regular Sunday service, though he wasn't willing to provide free whiskey as an incentive. This comment drew laughter from the congregation.

Ben wiped his palms on his jacket as he waited near the minister for the ceremony to begin. His stomach churned as he reminded himself he was doing this for Miranda. It was the right thing to do. Thad was correct. It wouldn't be fair for Ben to destroy Miranda's reputation in the community, then leave her to deal with the consequences alone.

All eyes focused on Miranda when she entered the room, and Ben gave up all effort to think sensibly. The usual bounce was missing from her step; instead, she seemed to float toward him. When she reached his side, she stood in a ray of afternoon sunshine coming through the window, glowing in her blue satin dress. It was unfair of her to wear something that so exactly followed and emphasized every one of her womanly curves, from her luscious, round hips to her narrow waist and on up to her delicate bosom. The cut of the bodice dipped low enough to show the rounded tops of the pair of firm breasts that had been created to fit precisely into a man's palm. His mouth went dry as he imagined dipping his tongue into the warm crevice between those breasts and around them and all over her smooth, creamy skin.

Yes, she was heartless to make him have such thoughts in church in front of a large crowd. It was no wonder he'd lost his mind and repeated whatever the minister suggested. He was helpless. Surely no one could be expected to live up to promises made under such conditions.

Ben was stunned as the crowd let out a whoop at the end of the ceremony and swept the couple up into the tide carrying the crowd from the church to Rita's. The saloon had been decorated and re-arranged for a double celebration—the wedding and Jonathan's long awaited adoption. Food and drink spread out along the long bar for the taking, provided by Rita, the Wyatts, the Buchanans, and many of the other families in attendance. Ben could hardly believe the quantity of food, or the speed with which it disappeared.

When some of the women teased Miranda about letting her man go hungry, she piled a plate high with food and brought it to him. Giggling, his bride sat on Ben's lap and fed him with a crowd of on-lookers cheering her on. He smiled and indulged her in the ritual, though it all seemed senseless to him. It had been a day of absurdity. He had stood in front of a room full of strangers and made promises to a woman he barely knew. A woman who intrigued him, puzzled him, and filled him with incredible desire. And that was the worst of it.

As much as he tried to convince himself that he was going through with this ritual for her, he could not escape the truth. He wanted the chance to make believe that she really was his, even if their marriage was to be short-lived.

The sounds of fiddles tuning drew Ben's attention. He looked up to watch the musicians assemble: Thad on guitar, Clarisse and a man Ben hadn't met on fiddle, and Mercy playing the piano. Several of the men moved the tables against one wall to create a dance floor in the middle of the large room. As there were three men for every woman, Ben relinquished his wife after the first dance. The men were lined up to partner her, but she sought out Jonathan. After all, she said, it was his party, too. Jock Meier swept in for the next dance. Then an officer from the nearby fort led her out for a reel, while Ben found a table in the corner to sit and watch.

He studied Miranda. Her smile never faltered as she was handed from one partner to the next. Occasionally, she looked at Ben and shrugged, which seemed to be her admission that she was perhaps a bit guilty for neglecting him. But there was no question that she was enjoying herself. That was it— Miranda could enjoy herself more thoroughly than anyone Ben had ever met.

He'd known men who, under the influence of spirits, could laugh and sing all night, but their pleasure never seemed real. Miranda's laugh was filled with pure joy. Perhaps that was why she seemed so . . . alive to him. And knowing the truth about the pain she had endured, Ben couldn't help but wonder how she managed to feel so much now.

That smile of hers nearly made him feel alive, too. It was natural—he was certain of that. She didn't have to stop and think to smile. When he smiled it was deliberate, something he did because he had to, or because he thought it would help him get something that he wanted. He could use a smile to persuade, to woo. But he didn't smile because joy compelled him to smile. At least he hadn't done so in a long, long time.

When he was very young, his mother had told him that his smile was her sunshine, and he had wanted to smile for Mother. Being with her made him feel content.

He looked back at Miranda, who was now dancing with her father. The old man hobbled around, not quite in rhythm with the music, but they were both laughing. He glanced at the gathered musicians and noticed Thad watching the dancers; he was smiling as well. Most of the folks in the room looked happy at that moment. The atmosphere of the celebration and the contribution of the liquor, too, no doubt, had everyone feeling something like joy.

Ben poked a fork into the plate in front of him. He wasn't going to indulge in whiskey to achieve that artificial joy. That was too fleeting. And real joy was beyond his reach.

Mercy sat down near Ben and he braced himself for a lecture.

"Been wanting to have a moment with you." She leaned toward him, her clear green eyes focused on his. "I don't need to tell you how much I care for my sister."

"I know what you're going to say. If I hurt your sister, you'll break my arm."

"You have me figured wrong, Ben." Mercy's eyes gleamed as she broke into a wide grin. "If you hurt my sister, your arm will not be my target. And, in case you're wondering, I do generally hit what I'm aimin' for."

Ben cleared his throat. "I assure you, I know how to treat a lady."

"Yes, Miranda did mention that." Mercy favored him with a more demure smile. "I'm not talkin' about that."

They both turned to where her sister was dancing with yet another soldier. Miranda was beaming one of her sunshine smiles at the man, and Ben felt a tug of jealousy—he hated sharing her. Though, since he wasn't planning on staying with her, he had no right to demand her sole attention.

"I expect . . ." Mercy still focused on her sister. "You intend to leave her soon. Thinkin' you've done your duty, marrying her so she'll be respectable."

Ben schooled his expression to hide his surprise that Mercy had guessed his plan.

"I want you to know—you'll be making a mistake." She turned and shot him a look that could burn through an iron plate. "You stumbled on a treasure when you found Miranda. Only a fool walks away from treasure." She stood and tugged at his hand. "Now, you best come dance with me. Your wife has danced with near every man in Fort Victory and here you sit in the corner alone. Folks'll think you aren't a happy bridegroom."

Ben followed Mercy across the floor, aware of Thad glaring at him. Mercy turned to her husband and his expression changed to a brilliant smile.

Hell, the whole damn family is always grinning like a pack of fools. Ben wasn't sure he could last through the winter with so much absurd happiness around him all the time.

It had been a long while since he'd danced, and he felt clumsy as he stepped to the music first with Mercy, then Clarisse. When it was time to partner Miranda at last, Ben's feet felt lighter than air. It was her laughter that went right through his heart and made him feel weightless. Before the dance was over, he was smiling a foolish smile himself at the wonder of her.

Mercy went back to the piano and started a waltz that brought Miranda into his arms. He liked the feel of her there, close. Step by step together they followed the dancers around the room until he was dizzy and wild with the desire to be alone with her, alone with his wife. Temporary though it might be, she was his and he wanted her.

A hundred dances and a thousand congratulatory slaps on the back later, they found their horses for the journey home. They rode slowly, following the wagon that carried Thad, Mercy, Pa and Jonathan. The party was still going at Rita's. Miranda told her the cowboys would likely be in town all night. The sun was sinking behind the mountains, and it was nearly dark when they reached the old cabin where they would set up housekeeping.

Ben was glad Miranda had chosen not to live in the small house with her sister's family. He was happy to have Miranda all to himself and grateful not to have to invent polite conversation with his new family. Every time he spoke to them, he was afraid they'd see him for the liar he was.

They called out good nights and promised to be

in church in the morning. Ben was certain he'd feel like a thief when he faced the preacher the next day.

"You'd better have meant all those promises," the old man would say, and he'd be forced to lie again.

Settling the horses seemed to take forever. When he entered the cabin, Miranda had it glowing with candles and a warm fire. She greeted him with a kiss that made him forget all his misgivings about the wedding. He'd treasure each night he had with her. Although he questioned whether marrying Miranda had been the right thing to do, he had no doubts about the pleasure of having her for a wife.

Once again, he felt the tug of guilt.

"Look, Mercy fixed the bed for us." Miranda led him to the bed and ran a hand lovingly over the cover.

In the dim light, Ben couldn't see much of the new quilt, but that didn't matter. He was only interested in getting Miranda under it.

"Seems a shame to make a mess of it." Miranda teased him as she opened the buttons on his vest. "I could pull the bear pelt out."

His mind seemed incapable of forming a word, and he had another use for his tongue in any case. He tasted her throat and made his way slowly down to her breasts. The sweet lavender scent she wore mixed with the salt on her skin and he breathed it in. He kissed the part of her breasts that her dress revealed, then probed his tongue down into the crevice between them until Miranda mewed with pleasure.

Her hands stopped the work they had done on his buttons and tangled into the hair at the back of his neck, pulling him tight against her. He wrapped his arms around her and fumbled with her buttons while his tongue continued its work. He took a little bite.

"Ugh," she groaned.

"What?" Ben lifted his head. "Did I hurt you?"

"No." Miranda's voice was husky. "Only I'm afraid someone will be hurt if we don't get this damned clothing off!"

Ben grinned. "You make a good point," he said. He stepped behind her and managed the buttons and laces quickly, pausing only briefly to nibble at her graceful neck.

Ben pulled the quilt back, revealing clean white sheets. The rest of their clothing fell into piles next to the bed. They fell together onto the soft featherbed.

Ben drew his hand along her naked body from her hip to her breast. "You're perfect, did you know that?"

Miranda surprised him by coming up to her knees and bending over him. She took him deep into her mouth, which only served to make him harder and more anxious to plunge into her. "Miranda," he gasped. "You're full of surpri—oh," he groaned. "I need to come inside you. Now!" The need was so urgent, in fact, that he nearly forgot the prize he'd managed to find in town after some discreet inquiries at Rita's.

"What's that?" she asked as he retrieved the small package.

He unwrapped the parcel and pulled out one of the sheaths. "It's made from a sheep's intestine. If I wear it, we won't make a baby."

"Oh." Miranda pulled him back into the bed, and it was all he could do to remember to cover himself with the damn thing before joining with his lovely bride at last. It was a bit clumsy, like working with gloves on, yet well worth it to stay inside her until they were both satisfied.

He rocked deep within her until she cried out his

name. He watched her face as he surged harder and faster inside her until his own pleasure matched hers.

They held each other close as their hearts slammed against their chests. Ben nuzzled Miranda's ear and held her small body tight against him. "Perfect, love. You are perfect," he mumbled.

Later, Miranda put out the candles, while Ben banked the fire for the night. When they slid back under the blankets, they pressed together for warmth.

"Why?" she murmured into his chest. "Why don't you want to make a baby?"

"I wouldn't want to leave you with a baby to care for," Ben mumbled as he nuzzled her shoulder.

Miranda felt like she'd swallowed a lead ball. Of course he hadn't meant to stay with her. He considered the marriage a sham. "I can take care of myself. Don't you fret about me."

"I'm a selfish cad, it's true; but I'm not that selfish. I'd worry about you and the child."

"If it should happen, my family would help me." Miranda blurted out before she had a chance to think. In her mind, she had settled back in Fort Victory to be close to her sister and father. Her dreams had grown to include Ben and their children.

She knew damn well she didn't want to let go of Ben. But she sure as hell wasn't going to hold him here against his will.

"I'm certain they would. But—" He turned Miranda so that they were face to face in the darkness of their bed. He brushed a kiss on her forehead. "You will make a wonderful mother one day, but I don't have it in me to be a father. I'm sorry. I know I'd feel obligated to stay here, and I'd end up making your life and mine a living hell. I won't treat you that way, and I damn sure won't treat my own blood that way. Do you understand?"

"I . . ." Miranda couldn't understand this man at all. The one thing she knew for certain was that she craved his touch like she needed water. Being without him would feel like being stranded on the desert. "I understand, Ben. I'll be careful."

"It's not your obligation, love." Ben pulled her close and kissed her with such tenderness she couldn't help the tear that trickled down her cheek. "What's this?" Ben brushed the tear away.

"Just . . . happy. Everything was so beautiful today, and you make me feel . . . almost like a real bride." She sighed.

"You are a real bride, love. I'm the charlatan here." Ben held her close and she felt him getting hard between her thighs. "I promise I'll be good to you while I'm here. And when I leave, I'll make our parting as easy as I can."

"Don't talk about parting, Ben. Not tonight."

"All right," he whispered. "Is there something else you'd rather be doing?"

She reached down and wrapped her fingers around him, touching the smooth tip of his erection. "Oh, no. I can't think of anything. We should get some sleep now, don't you think?"

"No." Ben rolled her onto her back and straddled her. "No sleep yet, love."

He bent to suckle her nipple. She was soon soaring high above the mountains that guarded her sister's ranch, free from every thought but one. She loved Ben Lansing.

* * *

The next morning, Ben opened one eye to watch Miranda bent over the fire preparing breakfast. The aroma of bacon and coffee tickled his nostrils. How she'd managed to leave the bed, build the fire, and dress without waking him was a wonder. His stomach growled and she turned to look at him.

"Sun will be up soon." She grinned. "You'd best get some breakfast; we have chores to do before church."

Ben stumbled out of bed, wondering what chores she had in mind. He pulled on his trousers, boots, and jacket and went outside to relieve himself. When he returned, he saw that Miranda had prepared a bowl of warm water for him to wash and shave.

"Breakfast!" She fairly sang the word as she plunked the skillet on the table and set about serving them.

Ben sank onto a chair and reached for the coffee cup. After he'd drunk his way through half the cup, he looked up at her. She was still grinning at him.

"How long have you been up?"

"About an hour, I reckon. There's lots to do, as I said."

"Hellfire and damnation," he mumbled into his coffee. "You didn't warn me you wake up cheerful."

Miranda laughed at that. "Eat your eggs. You'll feel better."

Ben was used to having breakfast at a civilized hour and didn't think he'd be able to eat anything. But the smells had increased his appetite, and he had no trouble with the three eggs, bacon, and biscuits that Miranda had made.

"You did all this in that fireplace?"

"You can cook about anything with some good hot coals, a Dutch oven, and a skillet." She added hot coffee to his cup. "Finish up and you'll have time to split some wood before we go to church."

He sipped his coffee and watched Miranda tidying their small house. She started with the bed, which they'd left in a tangle. "It was mighty thoughtful of the ladies to make us this quilt, don't you think?"

"Very nice. A practical gift."

She smoothed the quilt and fluffed the new pillows Clarisse had given them, placing them carefully and adjusting them until she was satisfied that everything was exactly where it should be. Again, she ran her hand over the colorful quilt, pausing on a square of familiar blue satin.

"That matches your wedding dress," Ben said as he stepped up behind her.

Miranda walked over to the fire and lifted out the kettle. "All the ladies in town contributed cloth from their wedding dresses. That green is Mercy's." She nodded her head toward the quilt. "Ingrid Hansen made a point of saying she wouldn't put hers in. Didn't want to jinx our marriage."

Miranda was making a valiant effort to keep her voice light, but Ben detected the pain there.

"Of course"—Miranda winked at him—"they had no way of knowing this is all make-believe." She sighed.

"It was a nice thought anyway," Ben said. He stood and retrieved the ax from the corner. "Sun's up. I'd better get some work done."

She didn't look up from scrubbing the skillet. He walked outside and dragged the cold morning air into his lungs. Instead of helping her, he'd hurt her. His chest ached with the knowledge. She'd have been better off if he'd walked away.

He hated the thought of joining the list of men who had betrayed her. He took his frustrations out on the wood and soon had a substantial pile. *Dammit!* Hurting Miranda was the last thing he wanted to do.

He pulled out his handkerchief and wiped the sweat from his brow. As much as he'd like to stay and live up to his wedding promises, he couldn't. He was not a family man, and that is what she deserved—a man who could truly love her and their children. Staying with her would only make things worse.

A week passed, then two. Miranda woke each morning cheerful, even without any coffee at all. Ben was almost getting used to it, though he didn't think he'd ever be able to emulate all that energy without the benefit of a strong cup or two of coffee to fortify him. He was more useful later in the day, though. He'd filled their wood bin, hauled water from the creek, and helped Thad repair the roof and build a rain gutter, which would direct water into a barrel they placed against one corner of the cabin.

And he did try to give her something to remember every night. That part of the marriage, at least, had been satisfying for both of them.

They'd settled into a domestic routine by the time the last leaves had dropped from the cottonwoods. November was mostly cold on the mountain. This afternoon the sunshine stayed warm throughout the day. Miranda decided it was a good day for an art lesson, so she dragged Ben outside. She made a quick sketch of the trees that grew beside the creek.

"Seems like the pencil makes bare trees look bleaker on paper than they are in life." She handed the book to Ben and looked at him, anxious for his opinion.

"You've made a fine likeness of the trees. You have a real gift for drawing."

"Now that sounds like you're keepin' somethin'

from me. A good likeness is not the same thing as a good picture, is it?"

Ben sighed. He was staring up at the mountains behind her as he so often did, and she had the sense he was choosing his words carefully.

"A good likeness is . . . It would satisfy Mrs. Wick. Do you remember her?"

"The woman in Denver who thought she knew more about art than you did."

Ben smiled. He loved Miranda's loyalty. "That's the lady I mean."

"She wanted pretty pictures of flowers. Nice colors that would look good on the wall of her parlor."

"And perhaps something that wouldn't require any thought from the viewer." Ben sat next to Miranda on the stiff, dry grass and looked up at the tree she'd drawn. "You can make a likeness of the tree, or you can . . . make a new living tree on your paper." He ran a finger over her drawing. "I saw some pictures in Europe where the artists captured the feeling of flowers, the calm of a lake. Not just the image, but the heart of the thing and something more."

Miranda stared at Ben for a moment. "More than the original tree you mean?"

"Yes." Ben took the book from her. "Suppose I tried drawing the same tree." He made a few quick lines. "I can't really draw anymore, but that doesn't matter for this exercise. You see?"

She looked at the picture. "It's the same tree. But it isn't."

"Exactly." Ben smiled. "Your tree has a bit of you and my tree has a bit of me."

"That's what I saw in your work."

Ben pulled his eyes back up to the mountain. "Did you?"

"When I looked at your pictures of the war—not just your paintings, but your drawings in the book, too. I could see courage and fear."

Ben swallowed. He walked away and followed the creek up the mountain. Miranda came up behind him and pulled on his arm. "I'm sorry—Did I offend you?"

Ben stopped. He shrugged out of her grip and shoved his hands into his pockets. "No." He glanced at her, then looked back up the slope. "No, you haven't offended me. You've given me the greatest praise."

"I've also reminded you that you might not be able to do that again."

He turned and looked deep into her moist eyes, knowing he'd caused the tears that were pooling there. "Don't cry for me, Miranda."

She took his injured hand and brushed a kiss over the stubs of his lost fingers. "I can't help feelin' your hurt."

"You shouldn't." He tried to look away from her, but his eyes were drawn to hers. "You have your life ahead of you without worrying about me." He smiled, his salesman grin. "I have plans. I'll be living in a tropical paradise without any cares. Fruit grows everywhere for the taking. Fish in abundance from the sea. And until I save enough money for that trip, I have you."

"Ben." Miranda wanted to tell him how much she loved him—how he was a part of her body and soul and there was nothing he could do to stop her loving him. But she knew the words would only make him hurt more, so she bit her tongue. "Let me help you forget the pain."

He bent to kiss her. She felt an urgency that would

have frightened her a few months ago. Now it swept her along until she felt a growing need for his skin against hers. He swept her into his arms and carried her inside, shutting the door against the pains of the world.

"Miranda!" Clarisse greeted her with a hug. "We're in business."

"They bought the dresses?"

"Bought them and agreed to buy as many as we can send them. Ingrid will move into town and work here every day. With the money I'm paying her, she's hired a man to run the farm. Her girls can play with my boys, and we'll both get a good deal more work done."

"Don't forget me. I can help, too." Miranda figured it was best to spend some time away from Ben. She was feeling more and more attached to him, and he needed to have some time to decide what he wanted to do.

"I haven't forgotten. In fact, I bought this for you." She went into the storage room and came out with a rectangular wooden case, like a small suitcase.

"What's that for?" Miranda wondered if Clarisse expected her to travel to Denver with the dresses. But the case was too thin to be a traveling bag.

"This holds your new paints."

"I don't understand."

"Hiram wants color pictures to hang in the store. That way ladies can choose not only a dress design, but the colors they want. You can mix the paints and match pretty well to the fabrics we have."

"I'm no painter."

"Don't worry; Ben can show you."

Ben. Miranda wasn't sure he would want to have anything to do with paints. He didn't even like to talk about painting. On the other hand, maybe it was time he made peace with that part of his life.

She was afraid Ben wasn't coming back. His note said he'd gone to see Thad. What on earth could those men be doing that was taking all day long?

She'd set out the paints, hoping to start on the project today, but they might lose the daylight before Ben returned. She counted the tubes of paint again and ran her fingers over the soft brushes. The case contained everything a painter needed, Clarisse had told her. A palette, brushes, a small knife, and tubes of paint, fourteen of them in all, including blue, yellow, red, white, black. These colors she understood, but not vermilion, indigo, cerulean blue. She was tempted to squeeze them out onto the palette to see what they looked like. But she didn't know what to do after that and was afraid of spoiling something. So she waited.

Clarisse had given her several smooth boards to paint on. Miranda had made a pencil sketch of two dresses on one of the boards so she'd have something to start painting as soon as Ben returned. If he ever came home. Her heart thumped heavily in her chest. He had said he'd make their parting easy. Perhaps this is what he had in mind—leaving without a word.

Princess neighed a greeting sound, prompting Miranda to peer out the window. Ben was riding Lightning up the hill. He'd purchased the old nag from Jock Meier for twenty-five dollars. That was twice what the animal was worth, in Miranda's opinion, but the beast did seem to have a few good years left in him.

Miranda ran out the door and flew into Ben's arms the moment he dismounted.

"I thought you'd still be in town," Ben said.

Miranda could barely catch her breath. She was so pleased to see him. "I came right home. I needed your help with something."

"Happy to oblige, ma'am." Ben kissed her, pulling her tight against him until she'd clean forgotten what it was she was going to ask him.

"Will that be enough help, or would you like to go inside?"

"That's not the sort of help I mean," she said. "Though come to think of it . . ." She sighed. "Later. First there's something for Clarisse."

"Oh, well, you'll have to tell her I'm a married man."

"That's very funny." The word *married* pricked at Miranda's heart like a pin. "I have some signs to make. Clarisse gave me some paint to make colored pictures of my dresses." She looked behind Ben. "What are you hauling?"

"Wood." Ben stepped back, revealing a mule hitched to a small cart. "Thought we could use a privy. Thad and Pa are going to come up tomorrow and help me with the digging and building."

Miranda smiled at Ben's use of "Pa."

"I'll be glad for that convenience." Miranda had ten questions at once, but they all boiled down to one: Did Ben mean to stay? And that question she couldn't ask. "I'll help you with these beasts, and then you can help me."

"Fair enough," Ben agreed.

It was pleasant working side by side with her husband

as he removed his horse's saddle and she took the harness off the mule. She could almost imagine they were really married and making a life together. Even though she knew such thoughts were likely to lead to heartbreak, she allowed herself to imagine a future with this man. And one day perhaps a child.

They went inside and she showed him the paints. "We don't have enough light to work in here," Ben said. "Let's take the table and chairs outside and I'll show you what to do."

They moved the furniture outside where the sun shone full force on her board. "The sketch is a good one, but you'll want to paint a base first." He squeezed some paint onto the palette. "Now we'll mix a bit of blue in with the white—don't generally want pure white." He handed her the brush. "Just mix them together." He watched her. "Good. Now take that white and paint the board. It will give you practice working with the paint. We'll let it dry overnight, then tomorrow you can paint a dress over the background."

Miranda daubed at the board with the brush. Ben leaned over her. "May I?"

She looked up at him. "Please, show me."

He put his right hand over hers and helped her make short strokes over the board, then longer strokes. "Experiment with it now. Do what you want with the brush and watch carefully how the strokes show up on the board." He let go of her hand and watched for a moment. "There. You see? The brush gives it texture; it isn't just a color."

Ben watched for a moment, then sat on the other chair and took up the second brush. "I don't think I can do any harm just painting the background. Do you mind?"

"I'd appreciate the help."

Miranda watched him out of the corner of her eye as she continued playing with her brush. It was only a white board that he was painting, but you wouldn't know it from the look of intense concentration on his face.

They worked on the painting until the sun grew dim, then carried everything inside their small house. Ben wrote in his journal, and Miranda made a simple supper of cornbread and the sausages she'd purchased in town. Together they cleaned up before going to bed. They explored each other in the darkness until they were both sated and fell asleep tangled together, neither of them willing to break the connection they found in their lovemaking.

Two days later, Ben took a short break from splitting wood to watch Miranda hanging laundry in the sun. The mountains made a lovely backdrop, but Miranda was the true beauty in the scene. Ben pulled his handkerchief from his pocket and wiped his brow. He stepped into the cabin and found the jug he'd filled with cool water from the creek that morning and took a deep swig.

Again, his eyes drifted to Miranda, who was now framed in the window, as she reached high to throw a sheet over the line. For a moment, Ben thought to go out and help her, but his wife managed it even though the line was above her head.

His wife. Ben shook his head. Six weeks of marriage and he'd grown used to thinking of her that way. Leaving was going to be damn difficult. The fact was he'd enjoyed their time together. He'd even enjoyed the domestic routine they'd created in their small home.

He dug out his journal from the bag he kept under the bed. Slowly, with Miranda's urging, he'd unpacked his bag. The journal, however, was too personal to keep in the same chest of drawers where Miranda kept her things.

He found a pencil and pulled the chair up to the window. His right hand trembled as he made the first stroke, which represented the tree that held one end of the line. One stroke followed another until the picture included Miranda, her arms outstretched as she reached up to the line.

He held the book up to the light of the window and examined the sketch. The pencil marks lacked the confidence that had once marked his drawings. Yet the picture was true to the image in his mind. He closed the book and put it back into his bag with the pencil on top. He wiped his palms over his trousers and walked outside to help Miranda dump the wash water from the tub, his heart pounding as though he'd just run up the mountain.

His eyes caught on the boards Miranda had painted with his help. He ran a finger over the lines of the elegant dresses and thought of old Mrs. Wick, the Denver woman who had purchased his last landscape. She would love to wear such elegant gowns. He had no doubt that the women of Denver would buy Miranda's work.

The paint kit sat on the table ready for the next project. Ben ran his hands over it. After guiding Miranda's strokes, he had managed to wield the brush himself well enough to paint the board white. That hadn't taken a great deal of skill, but his right hand hadn't been nearly as clumsy as he remembered it.

In fact, the drawings he made in his sketchbook were getting better almost daily.

"Real art comes from the artist's soul—not his hand." Miranda's voice startled him.

He spun around to see her striding toward him.

"Ain't that what you told me?" She smiled. "It's about time you considered the possibility that you might use those paints."

"I wasn't . . . I can't!" He couldn't bear the thought that his work might look like a child's scribbles.

"Why not? Ain't nothin' wrong with your soul." Miranda picked up a paintbrush from the table and pressed it into his hand. "No one else has to see it."

"I don't have any control over my left hand, and my right hand is clumsy."

Miranda took his right hand in hers. "Now, I know some of what this hand can do. You have a real delicate touch, seems to me. Why not see what you can do with a paintbrush?"

He was getting excited. "We have some good light now." He looked through the window into the house. "I wonder."

"Of course, you can. What will you paint? The mountains? That cottonwood down by the creek? The one that's still got a few leaves on it, so you can use some colors?"

"You," Ben said. "There"—he pointed to the fireplace—"I want a picture of you on the bearskin in front of the fireplace."

"There's better light outside."

"I don't want to chance a neighbor passing by and seeing you."

Miranda grinned. "Why, Mr. Lansing, don't you think these Colorado folks understand art?"

"They may understand art just fine. I still don't want them seeing my wife's naked body."

She was beautiful, and that was a hell of a lot of inspiration. His hands shook and his palms were moist as he prepared to make the first strokes on his board. If he failed, it would be easy enough to paint the board white again.

And if this picture showed promise, he'd have to get canvas and stretch it properly. No doubt, Clarisse could help. She seemed able to find anything and bring it here to the wilderness.

Getting ahead of yourself, Benjamin. He drew a deep breath and faced the board Miranda had prepared with a bluish white background. He'd mixed the paint to the color of Miranda's fair skin. This time he would focus on Miranda stretched against the dark rug. It wouldn't be a complete picture—no fireplace, no pine floor, just dark bearskin and creamy complexion.

He made a stroke and another until the picture began to take shape. As the sun dropped behind the mountain, the room grew dark, forcing Ben to stop. Miranda pulled her nightgown over her head and came to stand next to him.

"It don't look like me."

"No, not yet," Ben said as he gathered the brushes, wiping the excess paint from them with a rag before placing them in the turpentine.

"It doesn't, and yet it does." Miranda tilted her head one way, then the other. "Yes, I see how it will be me."

"Not you exactly. Not as though I can duplicate you, or would want to—"

"One of me is more than enough, Pa always said."

Ben brushed a kiss on her forehead. "One is exactly right." He took the painted board to the window where he could see it in better light. "What I want to do here is to capture something of your life and preserve it."

"A bit of my soul, you mean?"

"In a way, yes."

"I like that." Miranda looked carefully at the board. "My soul and your soul—together on that board forever."

The cabin had one window, the light from it falling on the floor. Only two. There was one bunk. He wiped his forehead, sank to the floor. He tried to sit up, to reach over and . . . He slid his arm across the floor.

Chapter 17

Ben walked into their small cabin and spied Miranda, head bent, studying the corner of the window frame. He watched her for a moment, her hair and skin glowing in the sunlight. She was chewing on her lower lip, so intent in her thoughts that she didn't respond to the sound of his footsteps on the rough plank floor. On the other hand, his response was unmistakable and urgent. *Control yourself, Ben. You'll frighten her.*

"What is it, love?" He managed to make his voice sound calm.

"Hmm?" Miranda turned her intense scrutiny on him. "What do you mean?"

"You have that look you get when you're trying to solve a puzzle."

"No, not a puzzle." The brightness of her smile made the sunlight around her seem dim. "Look."

Ben forced his eyes away from her face to follow the direction her finger was pointing. Nothing there. He stepped closer to get a better view. "Miranda!" He pulled her back away from the spider. "Good

Lord, that's a big one." He searched for something to crush it and found one of Miranda's shoes.

"No!" She grabbed his arm. "Don't kill it."

"It might be poisonous."

"Let's take it outside then." Miranda bent over the web again. "I can't bear to kill anything that weaves so beautifully."

Ben stared at her, then back to the ugly black creature perched upon the intricate web.

"It seems a shame to destroy it." She sighed, then scooped the critter into the palm of her hand.

"Miranda Chase! If that thing is poisonous . . ."

But she wasn't listening. She ran out the door and into the woods near the creek; she bent to place the spider on the trunk of a cottonwood. "You can build a new home here, little spider." Miranda watched it scamper away, then stood up and beamed another smile at Ben.

"Do you think I'm very silly?"

Ben pulled her up against him. "No, love. I'm the silly one." He turned her and looked into her eyes, feeling the pull of the deep, warm pools. That smile of hers could warm him on the coldest day of winter. He felt so hot now he had trouble breathing.

"And may I remind you my name is Lansing now."

"You're so very beautiful, Miranda . . . Lansing."

"You don't have to say that."

"You who sees the beauty in a spider's web must surely understand the beauty in your own face. Not perfection, but real beauty." His voice was husky and deeper than usual.

"I know my scar ruins it. An artist like you can't help but notice how it makes my face . . ."

He took her hand and pulled her back up the hill

toward the house. Then he turned around to face the woods. "Look."

"What is it?"

"You tell me. What do you see?"

"Trees and the mountains beyond."

"Look at the trees—where do your eyes go?"

"There"—Miranda lifted a hand to point—"the tree in the center."

"The one with the broken branch?"

"Yes, what is your point?"

"That isn't the center, not really."

"No, not exactly center. A bit left of center."

"Yet your eye goes there."

"Because of the flaw—the broken branch. I know people can't help but look at my scar, if that's what you mean. Often they can hardly take their eyes from it."

"Look at the trees again, Miranda. Are they beautiful?"

"The trees are . . . peaceful right now, sleeping. Come spring they'll be pretty, and next fall when they turn their colors—"

"I think they're beautiful right now, bare and stark against the December sky. Do you disagree?"

"Can't disagree about how beautiful you think—"

"Exactly my point, love." He brushed a kiss to her jaw. "I'm the only one who knows what is beautiful to me. You're beautiful, love. Your face. Your eyes such a deep blue I could take off my clothes and swim in them. Your hair so wild—"

"Now, I can't help my hair."

Ben chuckled. "I wouldn't have it any other way." He kissed the top of her head and pulled his fingers through her curls. "I like the fact that your hair is always out of your control; it suits you perfectly. You are not one to keep things inside."

"You make me sound like a ninny."

"You're hardly that."

"Damn right, I'm not." She grinned at him. "I get things done and work hard. I'm as reliable as the sunrise."

"I can rely on you to be late. You were nearly late for our wedding."

"I was trying to look perfect. When have you ever had to work to look perfect?"

"Gentlemen don't spend time on their appearance."

"I don't believe that for a minute. You are always well groomed—clean clothes, hair combed and tidy, chin shaved and smooth." She brushed her fingers over his jaw. "Don't tell me you wake up with a smooth chin, because I know better."

"I have to be careful with that—I could slit my throat, after all."

"Heaven forbid you might look in the mirror to judge your appearance. A gentleman merely uses a mirror to keep his throat safe."

"Exactly." He bent to kiss her, fooling himself into believing that one kiss would satisfy him. As their lips met he found he couldn't help wanting more.

She wove her fingers through the hair that hung over his collar and pressed her tongue deep into his mouth. Her breasts rubbed against his belly, causing a part of his anatomy that resided lower to come to life—hard, demanding, and ready.

Fortunately, his wife was easily persuaded. She'd already begun working the buttons on his shirt and had his chest bare before he could decide whether to change the venue for this activity.

"Bed?" he mumbled into her neck.

"No, here."

They tumbled to the ground in a tangle. Miranda managed to release the buttons on his pants. He found his way under her skirt and thrust inside her. The earth felt cold under his palms while all of his and Miranda's heat concentrated where their bodies joined together. The murmuring of the creek two hundred yards away echoed through the stillness around them.

She laced her fingers behind his neck and pulled him down until their lips met. Her tongue played with his, gently, as though they weren't both desperate to find their release. He lifted his head to watch her face as he settled deeper inside her and began rocking his hips. The joy that sparked in her eyes was a treasure he would keep locked away until he needed it one lonely day. When he felt her throbbing around him, he drove deeper still. She kneaded his buttocks with her hands until they found the pulse together.

"Ben!" She shouted.

He laughed, for the sheer joy of hearing her call his name. They soared together far above the mountains that towered above their home into the sky and past the sun.

When their ride was finished, he rested over her for a moment, feeling her heart pounding against his chest, listening to her ragged breath in his ear. He rolled next to her, but they remained twined together. He withdrew from her and remembered too late that he'd been careless again.

Hellfire and damnation, you are a self-centered bastard, Ben Lansing. You promised you weren't going to leave

Miranda with a child. The one promise he had really meant to keep.

"We need to be more cautious." He gasped for breath.

"Why?" Miranda caressed his cheek. "Are you afraid someone will catch us behaving like a couple of newlyweds?"

He pulled her hand away and bent to fasten his buttons.

"That is what we're supposed to be doin'. *Pretending.* It is all part of our deception, isn't it, Ben?" Miranda sat up. "Appearances. All the neighbors are to think we're in love. Have you even thought about what they'll think when you leave me?"

"That I'm a cad to abandon a pretty young wife."

"If you imagine they won't all believe that I'm . . . a failure—"

He took her hand and squeezed it. "They won't, love—"

"Don't!" She pulled her hand away from him. "Don't use that name."

"I'm sorry. I don't want to hurt you."

"Then stay. We can be happy together, I know we can."

"If you're worried about appearances, come with me as far as San Francisco. You can return the grieving widow—"

"That's your brilliant plan? You with all your education and refinement, you couldn't think of something better? Something with a bit of imagination, maybe? You run off to some tropical island and leave me here *pretending* to be a widow just as I've pretended to be your wife? All this deception just so that I can have the respect of the community?" She stood up and shook her skirt. "Damn you, Ben Lansing! I don't care about that kind of respect. I want you. *I love you!*" She brushed at the grass that clung to her wool skirt. "As far as I'm concerned, you can leave now! And you can tell the whole damn town that this marriage was a sham—all you ever wanted was an excuse to . . . to . . ." She ran toward the creek.

He took one step to follow her. If she wanted him to leave now, that is what he should do. He'd done her enough harm. He spun around and marched into the house ready to pack his bags. He had to get away from her. The woman was convinced she loved him. Benjamin Lansing, the most selfish man on earth. True, he would never beat her. That hardly mattered; there were plenty of other ways to do her harm.

The longer he stayed with Miranda, the more difficult the leaving would be. He pulled open his drawer and caught sight of the remaining sheaths he'd purchased. *Dammit!* He couldn't leave without knowing whether she carried his child.

He heard her soft footfalls behind him and turned to face her. "I promised Jonathan I'd be here for Christmas," he said. "I won't go back on that promise."

She opened her mouth and he was certain she would chastise him for keeping a promise to a little boy when he'd broken so many promises he'd made to her. Instead, she bit her lip and nodded. "I haven't seen Mercy in three days. I'm going to ride over and check on her." She pulled her saddlebag out from under the bed. "I may be gone a few days."

As he watched her pack, Ben pretended he'd be able to leave her when the time came. He even imagined he'd be happy to be free of the marriage vows he'd made under duress. He used to be a better liar.

Chapter 18

The idea that Benjamin Lansing could be a cowboy was a joke. And yet, here he was riding with his new brother-in-law. The man was the most irritating, stubborn creature he'd had the displeasure of knowing. Buchanan was correct when he'd said Ben would need some means of making a living if he intended to support his wife. Not that Ben was going to be here long, but he did have to keep up pretenses. He didn't mind work; in fact, he was glad to have something to keep him busy. He only wished it was something he found more interesting than watching cows and keeping them moving in the desired direction.

Ben watched Thad work. He seemed to enjoy yelling at the cows and bossing the cowboys. Thad liked to be in charge, and this was his way of controlling Ben. No doubt, Thad feared Ben would leave Miranda, likely with a few children. Miranda complained that her older sister still watched over her as though she were a child. But Mercy's meddling didn't compare with her husband's. Thad wouldn't be satisfied until he'd made Ben over in his own image as a husband and a father.

Well, Thad could try. Ben knew he didn't have it in him to raise children. There wasn't a good father in his family. Something in the Lansing blood must make it impossible for men to care about their children. The thought that his recklessness might have made a child ate at him. He watched Miranda carefully for any sign that she was in a family way. That task would be considerably easier if his wife weren't avoiding him. Not that he could blame her. She'd been hurt enough to be wary of men, and yet she'd allowed him to become a part of her life. He'd rewarded her by scoffing at the idea that they should be together. There was nothing he could do to convince her that he was entirely to blame. She would make a wonderful wife and mother when she found the right man.

He thought again about his plan for leaving her. He'd make it quick when the time came. He'd leave for San Francisco at the first sign of spring. It wouldn't be difficult to fabricate his own death before boarding a mail ship to the Sandwich Islands. He had no other family to concern himself with except for Jonathan. Mercy and Thad would look after the boy. As for the rest of Ben's family, they probably wouldn't notice he was gone. His mother, God rest her soul, was at peace. His brothers didn't care about him. His father wouldn't shed a single tear—he would be more upset if his bank profits went down this year. Ben wouldn't lose any sleep worrying about the old son of a bitch.

A simple message to Miranda from a fictional doctor and she would be free. Bless her heart, Miranda would grieve him. Her grief would be short-lived, though. A beautiful young widow would have no problem finding a husband in Colorado—a man who could love her properly, take care of her, and give her a real family. In the meantime, Ben was counting on Thad and Mercy to take care of Miranda.

He watched the man ahead of him, Buck, urging the steers forward and wondered how he did it. Somehow the cows seemed to understand him.

"They ain't all that bright." Cochrane rode up beside him.

"Who isn't?"

"Them cows." Cochrane slapped a straggler with the end of his rope as if to prove his point. "Get 'em moving in one direction and they keep movin' that way. It don't generally occur to 'em to wander off, unless they see a patch of grass that strikes their fancy. You see one wander off, give him a shout or a slap, and he'll catch up with the herd."

Ben noticed a straggler and positioned Lightning behind him. "Ya!" he yelled at the dawdling steer. The animal moved along, falling in line with the others.

Cochrane pulled up next to Ben. "See, cows ain't thinkers. They follow whoever seems to be in charge. You want them to believe that's you."

"I appreciate your advice," Ben said.

Cochrane grinned. "Oughta be Miranda here teachin' you. She grew up here—knows a hell of a lot more about it than that Buchanan fella."

Ben had sense enough to keep his mouth shut. He didn't much care for Buchanan, either, but he was certain the man would take care of Jonathan and he'd never allow Miranda to go hungry, either. Ben would be grateful to him for those things—he didn't have to like him.

A dust cloud on the horizon signaled a horse

approaching, carrying a man in a hurry. Ben checked
the pistol in his holster, making certain it was loose
and ready to draw if he needed it. He glanced at
Cochrane, judging the cowboy's response to the approaching man.

"Morgan!" Cochrane shouted. Thad turned his big
black gelding to face the oncoming rider.

"Wonder what's got him riding like the devil himself is chasing him?" Cochrane asked.

"I'm gonna find out." Thad shoved his hat down
on his head. He looked over his shoulder at Buck.
"Keep 'em movin'!"

"Will do, boss." Buck whistled at some dawdlers as
Thad pulled away from the group.

Ben turned his horse to follow Thad toward the
approaching rider. The men galloped to within a few
yards of each other, then pulled the three horses to
a stop. They approached slowly, the excited horses
snorting greetings to each other.

"Sheriff Bradford sent word they found O'Reilly,"
Morgan managed between breaths.

"O'Reilly?" Thad's eyes narrowed.

"Yes, sir."

Thad looked at Ben. "You comin'?"

"Damn right I am," Ben said.

Thad nodded. "Morgan can help Buck and
Cochrane move the herd." He turned to Morgan.
"Where is the bastard, and how many men with him?"

"Holed up in the caves near the south end of the
old Lansing place. Not sure how many. The sheriff
sent word for any man who wants to help to meet at
the old Lansing place."

Ben glanced at Thad. "Let's go."

As the men rode side by side, one simple fact meandered through Ben's mind. O'Reilly had tried

to kill Miranda. Ben would make certain O'Reilly faced justice. If he had to do it with his bare hands, so much the better.

Within an hour a dozen men had gathered at the old Lansing place. They approached the caves cautiously, making their way up through thick woods, rather than following the narrow path that would have exposed them to view from the cave openings.

Halfway up the hill, they tethered their horses and continued on foot, keeping eyes and ears open for any sign of O'Reilly or his men. As they approached the clearing in front of the caves, they all bent low, fanning out as the sheriff directed them. Ben crept silently to the edge of the trees, his Colt ready for action. His pulse raced as it seldom had since the war. He glanced around him and saw a dozen men all with guns drawn, ready for whatever might be waiting in the caves. Unfortunately, no one knew what that might be.

Ben peered through the brush at the remains of an open fire. There was no movement or sign of life. He glanced at Thad a few yards away, leaning to look around the tree in front of him. The sheriff came up to Thad's shoulder and whispered something, then crept over to Ben.

"Do you see anything?" the lawman whispered.

Ben shook his head.

"Damn!" Sheriff Bradford spit a wad of tobacco onto the ground. "I'm afraid we missed 'em!"

"They could be holed up in the back of the cave." Thad came and knelt next to Ben. "There's another way in." He pointed through the trees. "I'll take Ben around to the back of the cave. There's a small entrance there, hidden in the rocks. We won't be able to get through it, but we should be able to flush them out if anyone is inside."

The sheriff nodded, and Ben followed Thad through the trees and up onto the rocks that formed the roof of the cave. They moved silently, Thad in front and Ben following about two yards behind him. The ground was littered with old cans, bottles, and garbage. They found part of a butchered cow. The carcass appeared to be a few days old. Thad bent to look for a brand and pointed to the Circle J.

"Guess they don't mind wasting a cow that's been stolen," Ben whispered.

"Reckon you're right about that," Thad said.

They continued on over the cave, and Thad suddenly disappeared. Ben crept forward until he found the place where Thad had dropped between the rocks. Thad put a finger over his lips. Ben kept silent as he squeezed in next to his brother-in-law.

Thad pointed to a small opening and Ben peered into the dark cave. There was no sign of life inside. "I think I can squeeze through," Ben mouthed.

Thad shook his head, but Ben slipped off his gun belt and jacket. He wasn't going to let O'Reilly slip away from them this easily. If the son of a bitch was cowering in a dark corner, Ben would find him. He turned sideways and squeezed through the narrow opening. Once inside, he kept his back against the wall and looked around. As his eyes slowly adjusted, he found the cave was not completely dark. Besides the opening he'd come through, there was light coming from the front entrance and several small cracks in the ceiling of the cave. From what he could see, someone had been living in this cave. The stench of tobacco and liquor remained. Bottles, cans, and food waste were piled in corners.

There was no sign of any living creature. Ben touched the remains of a fire and found it cold. He made his way cautiously toward the front entrance and emerged into the bright sunlight.

Thad jumped down from the rocks behind him.

"They're gone," Ben said.

"Damnation," Thad mumbled.

Ben kicked at a loose rock. "That bastard is a slippery devil. Hellfire . . . Miranda." Ben glanced at Thad. "She went into town today—alone."

"I'll come with you," Thad clapped a hand on Ben's shoulder.

"No need for that," Ben said. "I'm sure you're anxious to check on Mercy and Jonathan. I may not be much of a husband, but I can protect my own wife."

Chapter 19

Miranda sat near the stove in Clarisse's kitchen. The days had grown cold, and she was still frozen from the ride into town. Clarisse and Ingrid had made a good bit of progress since the last time Miranda had been here. Now the three of them sat quietly finishing the garments. Ingrid added the buttons. Clarisse and Miranda added ribbons and lace, all the pretty niceties that would ensure these gowns were special. Not everyday dresses, but something a lady would wear to church, or to a fancy tea.

Ingrid hummed softly as she worked.

"How are your little girls, Ingrid?" Miranda asked.

The question brought a smile to the young widow's face. "Full of mischief. I am glad of a chance to rest here."

"Shh," Clarisse said. "I told the boys they had to watch the little ones while we work. Don't want them hearin' this is rest."

Ingrid and Clarisse laughed in a bit of shared maternal understanding. Miranda smiled. It was possible she would have the same worries someday.

Too bad Ben wouldn't be around to share the worries and the joys with her.

"Mrs. Hansen." Robert, the oldest Wyatt boy, came running into the kitchen. "I'm afraid your babe is cryin' so's we can't seem to stop her."

Ingrid mumbled something in Swedish under her breath. "Ja, thank you, Robert. I'm coming." She stood and shook her head at Clarisse. "We had a few moments of peace, no?"

"A few moments more than yesterday when one of the babies was fussing the entire time we tried to work."

"Ja, that is true. Today was better." She followed Robert out of the room.

Clarisse looked up from her sewing, catching Miranda's eye. "I'm glad we're alone for a bit. I've wanted to ask you how you've been feeling."

"I'm just fine, Clarisse. How about you?"

"I mean, you haven't been feeling sick at all?"

"No." Miranda wrinkled her brow. "Why do you ask?"

"Oh, no special reason." Clarisse bent back to her work. "I was only thinking, maybe you should take more fabric home with you this time, so you don't have to come to town so often."

"Why? You worried about the weather? It's early yet. Seems to me the roads are usually clear until after Christmas. I'll bet we have two or three weeks left of good roads."

"I wasn't so worried about the road as I was the risk of you ridin' back and forth so much." Clarisse set her work down and stared intently at Miranda until the younger woman returned her gaze. "I thought perhaps you might be expectin'."

"Oh." Miranda blushed. She had thought it was

possible. Had hoped and worried at the same time. If she was pregnant and Ben found out, she wasn't sure how he'd feel. He'd been so certain that a baby would ruin things for them both. And yet, she still hoped. "Do I look like I'm gainin' weight?" Miranda tried to joke.

"No, honey. I just had a feelin'." Clarisse made no pretense of sewing. "You are, aren't you?"

"I . . . it's too soon to be sure."

"You've missed your monthly?"

Miranda hesitated, and then nodded. "Near two weeks past." She'd managed to keep that fact from Ben's notice, she hoped. She'd spent a week with Mercy getting her kitchen root cellar ready for winter. When she returned, she had lied to Ben, telling him she'd been "indisposed" during her time away.

"Not too soon to be certain, then. Seems very likely. Have you been sick at all?"

"I feel fine. I'm probably just imaginin' . . ."

"Well, there's no rule that says you must feel bad. Many women don't."

Miranda knew, she'd simply been afraid to admit it to herself for fear Ben would guess. "I . . . I haven't said anything to Ben yet." *And truthfully, I'm not certain I should.* "I think I should wait—be sure."

"Well, I don't know what it's gonna take to make you sure!" Clarisse smiled at her. "I won't say anything, I promise." Clarisse squeezed her hand. "Mercy is goin' to be so pleased."

"Don't tell her!" Miranda snapped. "I mean, not until after I let Ben know. Thank you for understandin'." Miranda didn't think Clarisse could possibly understand her situation. But she sure wasn't going to try and explain it. The important thing was for Clarisse not to say anything.

"You can count on me." Clarisse grinned. "But I hope you'll make an announcement soon 'cause it's gonna be a hard secret for me to keep."

Miranda smiled. A hard secret indeed; she bent to her sewing and let her mind wander. She imagined sitting in the old rocker her father had made and holding her baby to her breast. It would be August or September. She could sit out on the porch and watch the sunset over the mountains. Ben would bring her a shawl. He always worried about her being cold. Except that Ben would be gone by then.

"I reckon the money from his paintings will be a help to you," Clarisse said.

"Yes," Miranda said. She was so pleased that Ben was painting again. The money wasn't necessarily a good thing, though. Once he had enough money, there would be nothing stopping him from leaving her.

"There's a great demand in the East for paintings of our mountains and rivers," Clarisse said. "And they loved the small one he did of the men with the cattle. He can make a fine livin' without ever leaving Fort Victory."

"Miranda!" Ben's deep voice startled her and she pricked the needle into her finger.

"Ouch!"

"Sorry." Ben knelt next to her chair. "Didn't mean to startle you." He pulled her injured finger into his hand and inspected it.

She drew her hand away. "It's nothing," she said, inserting the bleeding finger into her mouth.

He looked up at her, his dark eyes melting her heart. She pulled herself upright and tried to ignore the heat that spread through her body.

"I'm just glad I found you before you left town."

"What is it?" Miranda caught the concern in his eyes. "Has something happened? Mercy? Pa?"

"No." Ben put a hand over hers. "Don't worry. Your family is fine. I just wanted to make sure you were safe. O'Reilly has been seen near town."

Miranda jumped up. "Where is he?" She set the dress she was sewing on the table. "We have to go after—"

"Calm yourself, love," Ben said. "We've already visited his camp. He's disappeared. I don't want you riding alone until we find him."

Miranda bit back the retort that came to her lips. *Why protect me now when you plan on leaving me?*

The rest of December turned out to be mild. In fact, most of January passed before they had a real heavy snow. Although everyone in town and the surrounding ranches was watching for him, O'Reilly hadn't been seen again. There were rumors about him everywhere. He'd left for California, Mexico, or back to Kansas. The sheriff was certain O'Reilly and his men had left town and started the rumors in part to cover their trail. It didn't matter what the sheriff thought, Ben was certain O'Reilly was still close. Her husband didn't want to let Miranda out of his sight.

Somehow, she had managed to keep her secret through those weeks. But she wasn't sure how much longer she'd be able to fool Ben—not while she was living in one room with him and sharing a bed every night. She used her sister for an excuse. It made sense for her to be near her sister as Mercy's time grew close. And now that the road between their small cabin and the house was often treacherous with ice and snow, Miranda announced she would go stay in the house.

"You could move in, too," she said, knowing he wouldn't.

"I'm set here. Look at the place. My paints take up the entire room, and I've got my lights set so that I can paint no matter the weather or time of day." He shook his head. "You go, help your sister. I'll be fine here. I'll finish another painting, maybe two before I need to go into town for supplies."

"Then you'll come to the house and visit?"

"I'll come visit." He wiped his hands on a rag before stretching his arms around Miranda and pulling her close. "It won't be long, will it?" He brushed a light kiss on her lips.

"Mercy's baby could come any time now, or it could be weeks away."

"I will be visiting, then." He bent to kiss her; this time the kiss went deeper. Soon Miranda was wondering whether she was doing the right thing. It was going to be damned hard sleeping alone in a bed tonight. She hoped Mercy had this baby soon so she could come home where she belonged. Except that Ben wasn't staying, and this was only a temporary home. It was time for her to get used to the idea of sleeping alone.

A loud knock at the door startled them out of their kiss. Thad came bursting into the room immediately after the sound of the knock.

"Jonathan?" He looked around the room and settled on Miranda. "He'd been talking about seeing Aunt Miranda and I hoped . . ."

"He's missing?" Ben squeezed Miranda's hand as he spoke.

Thad nodded. "We've searched the house and the barn. I came straight here, hoping . . ."

"I'll saddle my horse and help look," Ben said.

"I'm with you, too," Miranda said.

"I'd like for you to stay with Mercy," Thad said. "She's terribly upset, and you know her. She wants to climb on a horse and head out to look for him. All we need is for her to start laboring on horseback."

Miranda smiled thinking of her sister giving birth on the back of a horse. She would do it, too. "I'll search from here to the house, then."

"You're not going to the house alone," Ben said. He looked at Thad. "I'll ride with Miranda as far as the house, then where will you be?"

"I've been thinking where he might have gone," Thad said.

"The caves?" Ben asked.

Thad nodded. "I hate the idea of him going up there, but he is fascinated with those caves."

"I'll look up there. We'll cover more ground if we split up. Where else would he go?"

"Might head out to his old house. I think sometimes he figures he might find his . . . father there. I'll look there."

Miranda squeezed Thad's shoulder. "Don't fret; we'll find him."

Chapter 20

Miranda and Ben looked behind every rock and fallen log from the cabin to the house—a good mile. All the while she imagined places Jonathan might go. The boy was curious about everything. He could have tried to follow the creek to see where it ended, or decided to go to town for some candy from the store. The ranch house came into view and Miranda gasped.

"Mercy! What the hell do you think you're doing?" Miranda couldn't believe her sister was standing on the roof of the barn. Hell, as big as her belly was, Miranda couldn't imagine how the woman had managed to get up there.

"I'm looking for Jonathan."

Miranda felt like her stomach had fallen down to her toes as she watched Ben climb the ladder and help Mercy down.

Miranda couldn't bear to watch her sister maneuvering over the slanted roof. She knew damn good and well that the weight of the baby could easily make Mercy lose her balance. Lord help her, after her sister made it safely back to the ground Miranda was going to kill her.

She hurried to steady the ladder as Ben led her older sister slowly down. When Mercy reached the ground Miranda threw her arms around her. "Have you taken leave of your senses altogether?"

Her sister's heart was pounding and a tear streaked down her cheek. "I feel so damned helpless." She smoothed her hair back with both hands, then pulled Miranda to her again. "Thanks for coming."

"Oh, Mercy. Jonathan will be all right, you'll see. No point in getting yourself killed. Ben and Thad will find him."

"Where's Buck? Or Pa?" Ben asked.

"Went to town, in case Jonathan decided to go that way. I thought maybe if I came up here, I'd see him." Mercy choked back a sob. "It's not like him to up and wander off." Mercy pressed a hand to her belly and pulled in a deep breath.

"I don't know if I should leave you two women alone," Ben said.

"Of course you must," Miranda said. "We'll be fine here, and you need to look for Jonathan."

"Please?" Mercy said.

Ben looked from his wife to his sister-in-law, then nodded. "Yes, you're right. I'll look for him. But you promise me you will both stay in the house."

"We can take care of ourselves," Miranda said.

"I know you can," Ben said. "I just can't help worrying."

"Come back quickly, then—with our nephew," Miranda said.

She watched Ben mount his horse and ride away, then she turned to Mercy.

"I'll get Princess settled, then help with dinner."

Mercy rubbed at her belly.

"You all right?" Miranda asked.

"Don't start frettin' over me. It's only a little twinge. They pass."

"You're awful close to your time to be prancin' up and down ladders and promenadin' on the barn roof."

"I know it was foolish, but I thought . . ." She chewed on her lip. "I reckon it wasn't so much a matter of thinking, more feeling like I had to do something." She rubbed her belly as she looked around. Miranda wondered again whether climbing on the roof had scared her sister more than she let on. "Looks like a storm coming."

Miranda looked up at the gray sky, which was rapidly growing darker. It did look like a storm. She shivered thinking of Jonathan out there somewhere alone.

"I can't believe he'd run off like this. He didn't want to take a nap, but I thought he'd finally fallen asleep. When I went to call him to help bring the cows in, he wasn't in his bed. Then we found his horse gone. I should have kept a closer watch on him."

Miranda pulled on Mercy's arm. "Let's get inside and have some tea. You're shivering."

"We should be out looking for him."

"Mercy Buchanan, I know you don't have any concern for yourself, but you could spare a thought for your baby. You want him born outside in the snow?"

"You think it'll snow?" Mercy looked around.

"Yes." Miranda pulled her sister into the house. "Let's get a fire going and some water heated. When Thad or Ben bring Jonathan back we'll get him warm and make sure he's fine before you give him a lickin' he won't forget."

"I've never . . . maybe I should have used a strap on him. But I thought he'd suffered enough at Arthur's hands."

Miranda sat Mercy down and went to fill the kettle. Mercy sat, rubbing a hand over her belly, as Miranda pushed back out the door and marched over to the well. Thad was right to be worried about his wife; Miranda had never seen her so upset.

She filled the kettle at the well, took it inside, and set it on the stove. Grabbing a bucket, she went outside for more water. If the men were caught in the storm, they'd be awfully cold when they made it back.

The clouds were gathering in a hurry now, blown along by a sharp wind out of the northeast. The air smelled of snow to come. She pulled her coat tight around her and spilled water from the well into the bucket. Plenty of hot water would be needed when the men brought Jonathan back. Besides, preparing the water gave her something to do.

She lugged the bucket into the house and filled a pot to set on the stove. Mercy went outside and returned with an armload of wood.

"I could do that." Miranda tried to keep her voice light and cheerful.

Her sister stared at her for a moment. "I need to do something."

Miranda nodded, understanding exactly how her sister felt. She was worried, too, and doing something, anything, helped a bit. "Just don't carry too much at once."

The women worked together to bring in more water and build the fire until the whole house was warm.

"I'll get some soup started," Miranda said, finding potatoes and carrots. "Any leavings I can put in it?"

Mercy hardly paid attention as Miranda searched the kitchen for any food left from dinner that she might add to the soup. Instead, Mercy occupied herself with knitting a blanket for the baby in between pacing to the window to look out for the men.

"I wonder . . ." Miranda came up behind Mercy and looked out the window. "You don't suppose Jonathan would head for the shelter in the winter range?"

"Thad took him there last week. They were stocking wood and checking the roof." Mercy looked at Miranda. "Surely Thad will look there."

"Likely he will," Miranda said. The sky was nearly black now, though sunset was two hours away. "He might not get there before the storm hits. He was headed in the opposite direction—to the old Lansing place. He thought Jonathan went there sometimes to visit his father."

"Thad is Jonathan's father now, more surely than Arthur ever was." Mercy touched the glass windowpane. "But Thad's right, sometimes Jonathan still thinks about Arthur. I suppose that's only natural."

"Of course it is." Miranda took off her apron and hung it from the peg next to the sink. "I'm going to go look for him."

"Would you?" Mercy smiled at her sister. "I'd be so grateful."

Miranda nodded. "It won't take me long to go out to the winter shelter and back. If Jonathan's there, I'll bring him home, and if he isn't, I'll come right back and let you know."

"Thank you."

Miranda pulled on her coat and hat and half ran out to the barn. She could be out there and back in an hour or a bit more. The snow would start before then, but that shouldn't slow her much. She hoped.

* * *

Miranda was barely out of the yard when the snow started. Big wet flakes of snow stuck to Princess' mane and gathered on Miranda's shoulders. The coat and layers of clothing she had on would keep her warm and dry, at least until she made it to the shelter where she hoped to find Jonathan.

Her sister needed to see her son, and Miranda would do her best to bring the boy home tonight, if the storm allowed it. If visibility grew worse and they were forced to wait out the storm in the shelter, at least Jonathan wouldn't be alone. She lifted a glove to wipe snow from her eyes. It was growing thick already, making it hard to see. She thought of the small life growing inside of her.

Even if Jonathan wasn't there, she would stay in the shelter for her own safety, if need be. She remembered the advice she'd given her sister. There was no point in risking the life of one child for that of another, especially when she knew Ben and Thad would do everything in their power to find the boy. One of them would find him, if she didn't.

She prayed her sister would have sense enough to stay in the house and take care of herself. Merc could be stubborn, which sometimes caused her to make foolish decisions. Miranda's ears and fingers were quite numb by the time the small shelter came into view. It was a dark shadow in the gray void of the falling snow. Princess sensed the approaching shelter and turned toward it, picking up her pace as Miranda bent forward, ducking away from the driving wind that whipped the snow into her face.

Her heart raced as she noted the smoke coming out of the chimney. She wanted to rush in and warm herself, but she had to be cautious—O'Reilly was still on the loose, after all. And she wasn't certain little Jonathan could have started a fire on his own. She hoped Thad had found the boy first and brought him here.

A wave of relief swept over her when she saw Zeus next to Jonathan's horse, Pegasus. Miranda tethered her own animal next to theirs and moved quickly inside to seek warmth.

"Hell!" she gasped and ducked back outside, fumbling her heavy Colt with her numb fingers. Before she could retrieve the weapon, two guns were aimed at her head. "Damn!"

"*Tsk, tsk,* my dear. Such language. What would your fine husband say?" O'Reilly's brogue was thick enough to gag her. "Don't worry about the gun. Jed will retrieve it for you."

In case she had any ideas of fighting them, Jed's rough hands grabbed her and pushed her through the door. Warmth washed over her, but it no longer held the welcome she'd hoped for.

"Miranda!" Thad's voice came from the corner of the room. His hands and legs were bound. Jonathan sat huddled behind his father.

"That ain't any way to treat a lady, Jed." O'Reilly seized her and tore her coat off.

"Keep your hands off her, O'Reilly." Thad sounded menacing.

"Or you'll do what to me?" O'Reilly laughed. Jed and another man Miranda didn't recognize aimed their guns at Thad. The big man was no threat to them, bound as he was. Miranda also noticed his shirtsleeve was torn and bloody. Thad was injured. That didn't keep him from kicking in O'Reilly's direction, which caused the two henchmen to cock their pistols and made O'Reilly laugh again.

"Don't shoot, boys," O'Reilly said. "I want him alive when Mercy gets here."

He turned back to Miranda. "Having little sister here is an unexpected bonus." He turned and covered her mouth with his own. The taste of stale cigar and whiskey made Miranda's stomach churn. When he shoved his tongue into her mouth, she bit down hard.

"Argh!" O'Reilly shoved her away, holding a hand over his mouth. "Damn you!" He brought the palm of his hand across her face, knocking her back into the wall. Before she could recover her balance, O'Reilly hit her again with the back of his hand, sending her sprawling to the floor. She saw O'Reilly lift a foot to kick her middle and curled herself into a ball to protect her baby. His boot struck her knee, and she felt the pain clear into her belly.

"Enough, O'Reilly!" Thad shouted. "You want to beat someone, come on, try me. I have only one useful arm at the moment. Untie me and let's see how brave you are against a man."

O'Reilly spun around and kicked at Thad, but the big man kicked his legs up and knocked the Irishman on his ass. O'Reilly pulled his gun back out and cocked it. Miranda closed her eyes, expecting to hear the explosion that would end her brother-in-law's life. Instead, she heard O'Reilly laugh again.

"Very good, Buchanan." O'Reilly struggled to his feet where he stood swaying for a full minute, his gun aimed at Thad's head. "Now, I could kill you quickly. Or maybe I'll kill the boy here."

Thad sat up and Jonathan curled into a ball behind him.

"Or"—O'Reilly twisted so he was waving the pistol more or less in Miranda's direction—"I could put a bullet in little sister's pretty head."

Miranda stared into the dangling barrel of O'Reilly's pistol. She kept her knees drawn up over her belly in case he decided to start kicking again. And she prayed God wouldn't let O'Reilly pull that trigger.

A few months ago, she hadn't cared whether she lived or died. She had been certain that her life made no difference. Everything was different now. Ben needed her, and she wanted to be with him for every moment he'd allow it. And there was the small life that would die with her.

"Shoot if you like, O'Reilly." The quaver in her voice betrayed her fear.

"No." O'Reilly holstered his gun. "No, ma'am. I want the pleasure of watching Mercy see you die. Each of you. Her sister, her husband, and her precious little boy. I'll kill each of you slowly while she watches, and then I'll kill her."

Chapter 21

Ben was on the porch shaking the snow from his hat when Mercy opened the door and rushed out of the house.

"Jonathan?" She looked around.

Ben blew out a breath. "Sorry," he said, "I was hoping I'd find him here."

"Thad hasn't been back yet."

He noticed Mercy shivering under the light shawl she had wrapped around her shoulders and guided her back into the house. The heat was nearly overwhelming after the biting wind outside. He pulled the door closed behind them.

"I won't stay long." Ben hung his hat and coat on one of the pegs near the door. "I'll take a lantern if you have one; it's near dark out there already." Ben looked around. "Where's Miranda?"

"She should be back any time." Mercy pulled a large mug off the shelf. "Some coffee to warm you, before you go out?"

"Miranda left?"

"She had an idea of where Jonathan might have gone." Mercy glanced out the window before handing

Ben the cup. It felt so hot against his numb fingers that he nearly dropped it. He set the cup on the table.

"How long has she been gone?"

"An hour." Mercy glanced at the clock on the shelf. "No, a bit more."

Ben's stomach pulled into a knot. The storm was building fast. If Miranda was out there, she could easily be lost. "Which way is it to—"

Mercy sucked in a quick breath and closed her eyes for a moment as she rubbed a hand over her middle. "Coming closer together," she mumbled.

"What's coming closer?" Ben searched her face, but he had a feeling he knew what she was going to say.

"Birthing pains." Mercy kept one hand across her middle while she rubbed her back. "I don't think it will be long now."

"I'll . . . I'll get your pa." Ben headed for the door.

"Gone to town."

Damn!

"Don't worry." Mercy attempted to smile, but he could see she was worried herself. "Miranda was going to make a quick check of the small cabin out on the winter range. She'll look for Jonathan and come right back—should be here soon."

"I'll go find her. It's getting hard to see out there."

Mercy grabbed the back of a chair and leaned against it as another pain gripped her. She nodded, but Ben wasn't certain he should leave her.

"Will you be all right, alone?" Ben realized he'd shouted at her. *Calm yourself, man. Women give birth every day.* It was likely much easier than he imagined.

She paced back to the window and peered out, holding the shawl wrapped tightly against her. Then she paced over to the stove, opened the door, and added fuel.

"Should you be walking around?" Ben asked.

"I'm fine, Ben." She gave him another quick smile that disappeared almost as fast as it came. "Don't you fret over me." She walked back to the window and stared out into the darkness again.

Ben started to grab his coat but stopped short when he heard Mercy grunt in pain. He turned back to where she stood leaning against the wall, looking pale and fragile as she fought the pain.

"It's against my back," Mercy said, rubbing her back. "The baby needs to turn."

Ben wondered what the hell that meant. He'd heard of breech births and knew they were dangerous. *Hellfire and damnation.* Surely Miranda would be back in a moment, and she'd know what to do.

"Should you sit down?" Ben led Mercy over to a chair.

"I . . ." Mercy sucked in another breath and shook her head. "Better to be up and walking as long as I can."

He swallowed hard as she leaned on him this time. He could feel her tense with pain.

"It isn't bad." She gave him another quick smile. "Truly." She licked her lips. "I could use some water, though."

He brought it for her and she took a sip, then resumed her pacing about the room. Ben didn't know what he should do. He wanted to go out and search for Miranda, wanted to assure himself that she was fine. But he couldn't leave Mercy alone.

"She will have made it to the shelter by now." Mercy read his thoughts. "I'll wager she's decided to stay there, especially if Jonathan is with her. Too dangerous to be out there now." Mercy grunted. "Too hard to see."

"I'll be of more use here, then."

Mercy gave him a quick nod and closed her eyes. She leaned on his arm and seemed to concentrate on something for a minute, perhaps two minutes. Then she relaxed her grip. "Sorry," she said, "I'll try not to squeeze your arm."

"Don't worry." He attempted a reassuring smile. "You won't hurt me."

Mercy looked into his eyes. "I know." She licked her lips and looked around the room. "Could be with the storm that you'll be the only one here when the baby comes."

Ben nodded. The same thought had occurred to him. "I don't have a lot of experience in these matters." For a moment, he worried that Mercy didn't either. After all, she'd never given birth before.

"Don't worry." Mercy sank onto a chair. "It isn't difficult. I could use some help, though."

"Tell me what to do. How can I help?"

"I have everything ready, I think," Mercy said. "Could be a long wait." She rubbed her hand over her belly and leaned back in the chair. "First babies are usually slow. But there's no telling for certain. They have their own timing."

Ben nodded. He tried to appear confident, as though he weren't terrified. Women died giving birth. He knew that much. And babies died sometimes. His mind flitted to Miranda out alone in the cold. No, she was safe, as Mercy suggested. Safe and warm in the shelter. "There's a stove—where Miranda is?"

"A fireplace. Thad just stocked it with wood. Don't you worry about your wife. She knows how to take care of herself."

"I know she does." Ben swallowed. Lord help him, he wished he had talked to her before she'd gone. There was so much he needed to tell her. He looked at Mercy. "I worry about her is all."

"It's natural to worry about our loved ones."

Mercy was caught up in another wave of pain, which saved Ben from having to respond. He hadn't yet said out loud that he loved Miranda. It was true, though. He did. It was only right that the first time he said it would be to his wife. To the woman he loved and hoped to spend a lifetime with, if she would have him.

Mercy changed out of her dress and showed Ben the preparations she'd made in the bedroom. They put some blankets near the stove to warm them and opened the bedroom door to allow the heat into the room.

"I wish we had a stove in here," Mercy said. "The baby needs to be kept warm. I reckon if we leave the door open the bedroom will warm some, and we can take the baby into the kitchen after." She paced back out to the kitchen and busied herself. "Miranda made some soup before she left. Would you like something to eat?"

"I . . . What if I'm eating and you need me?"

"You have time. Don't worry, you'll know when it's getting close."

Ben watched Mercy pace as he ate the soup and cold biscuits. "Shouldn't you eat something? Keep your strength up?"

Mercy shook her head. "I'll be fine." She resumed pacing, back and forth, and kept her eye on the door. After a while she walked up to the window, wiped the frost, and looked out.

Neither of them said aloud what they were both

thinking: Miranda wasn't going to make it home before this storm ended. Ben closed his eyes and mumbled a brief prayer for her safety. The thought crossed his mind that the Almighty probably found it strange hearing from him. *It's for Miranda, Lord. Don't blame her for my failings. Protect her in this storm.*

Assisting a woman in labor was a test of patience. The entire exercise was about waiting and feeling helpless. There was little Ben could do for Mercy as she struggled with each pain. After he'd begged her to give him something to do, she suggested he press against the small of her back as the pains came, and he found that this provided her with some comfort.

He imagined how it would be to see Miranda going through this. And worse, how it would be to imagine her going through this without him by her side. As the night went on, the latter prospect became an impossibility. He knew that no force on earth was going to keep him away from his wife as she gave birth to their child.

He still couldn't imagine himself as a father. He was terrified at the thought of holding the new life that Mercy was fighting to bring into the world, let alone his own son. But that dread could not compare with the fear that he would do something to make the child's life miserable. That somehow his child would grow to resent him. That his own flesh and blood would wish Ben had gone to that tropical island and never met Miranda, or fathered her child.

But what he most dreaded was to think of life without Miranda. He might be completely selfish in thinking that it was right for him to stay with her. He had little doubt she'd be better off without him. The child certainly would be, yet Ben did not have the courage to leave her.

"I think I have . . . to yell." And then Mercy let out a sound that scared the hell out of Ben even after her warning. He reminded himself how tough his sister-in-law was as he watched her take in another deep breath and blow it out between clenched teeth. She was red in the face and obviously tired, but he was certain she would soldier on. As she'd told him hours ago, there was no turning back now.

"We're making . . . good progress," she told him between quick breaths. "Won't be much longer."

"Good. I'm not sure men are meant to go through this."

Mercy started to laugh, but another pain took her and she screamed again.

"Just as well Jonathan isn't in the house," she joked. But he knew from her worried expression that her son and husband were not far from her mind.

He'd long ago given up looking at the clock and wondering how bloody long this laboring could last. Babies, Mercy kept reminding him, came in their own time, and there wasn't much anyone could do to hurry them along. He'd spent the first hour or two asking her to slow things down, to wait until Miranda or Thad or anyone else could be here to help. Now, he just wanted it to be done.

"The mirror," she snapped.

The birthing room was no place for polite formalities. She'd given up "please" and "thank you." He'd stripped down to his shirtsleeves. He wore no collar and his top button was open so that he could breathe. He held the mirror so that Mercy could see what was going on between her legs. It was impossible to avoid looking himself. Strangely, his sister-in-law seemed to have no modesty. And Ben didn't really feel as though he was looking at a woman's body. The changes brought about by the impending birth were that dramatic.

Thad, on the other hand, might well disapprove of Ben looking. He'd felt Thad's fist on his jaw once and didn't look forward to having that experience again. Yet Mercy needed someone, and Ben was the only one available.

"I see the head. Do you see it?" Mercy asked.

Ben looked and saw something, though he had no idea whether that bulge could be an infant's head. "I . . . um . . ."

"I'm going to push . . . now!" Mercy strained with effort, and the bulge did increase.

"Could that be a human head?"

"It is a head!" Mercy shouted at him. Or at least he thought she tried to shout. She sounded tired.

"I'm sorry." Ben set down the mirror. "What can I do?"

Mercy caught her breath. "We're getting close. I'll push and you watch—"

"Your husband—"

"Will be most grateful to you for helping his child into the world." Mercy stopped for several breaths. "I need to push. You're going to need to support the baby's head when it comes out. I should be able to feel it, but it will help if you tell me what you see."

It happened as she said it would but not on the next push. In fact, Ben lost count of the pushes; he lost track of time altogether. He'd seen a lot of courage in the war. Had seen men go on when they were wounded and in pain. This was different and yet the same. She'd been past exhaustion hours before, and now raw determination gave her the strength to press forward. By contrast, Ben felt more and more helpless. Or perhaps a better word was useless.

He heard her sigh as she collapsed back onto her pillow. His pulse started racing. He moved to her side and squeezed her hand. "No turning back, remember?"

She nodded. "It can't be much longer now."

"It won't be." He gave her hand another squeeze and she squeezed back as she began pushing again. He helped her sit more upright as she bore down with all her strength.

"Almost," Ben croaked. "One more will do it," he blurted out before he could stop himself. He could see tears streaming down her cheek and knew she was nearly spent. If he was wrong, his words might prove more discouraging than helpful.

But he wasn't wrong. The baby's head emerged on the next push. "It's out." Ben touched the small head, bracing it gently in the palm of his right hand. "The head is out." It occurred to him that the body would be larger, and he wondered how it would fit through the narrow opening that was barely wide enough for the head.

"Do you have the blanket ready?"

"Yes." Ben draped the clean blanket under her, fearful he would drop the tiny newborn. Mercy had warned him that it would be slippery, and he could see that it would be covered in fluids. He didn't have much time to worry, for the baby emerged whole and perfect in the next moments. After all the waiting, suddenly things were moving swiftly.

"It's a girl!" He wanted to shout, but something caught in his throat. "A tiny, perfect little girl." The infant squirmed and he wrapped the blanket around her, fearing she'd wiggle out of his hands. "There's a cord that, um, she seems to be still attached."

Mercy laughed. "Don't worry about that. Hand her to me, will you?"

He placed the miraculous bundle in her mother's arms and she checked the infant from head to toe. "She is perfect," Mercy announced as the little one let out a yell to rival anything Ben had heard from her mother.

"She sounds healthy." He spoke loudly over the infant's piercing cries. "Though she seems small."

Mercy glared at him, then laughed. "The one who gave birth never thinks the child is too small."

The baby continued squalling as Ben helped Mercy cut the cord and clean her with wet cloths. He brought the warm linens Mercy had set out next to the stove, and the baby seemed to calm as soon as she was swaddled. Once she was clean and wrapped, Mercy held her close and cooed nonsense words until the baby dozed in her arms.

"Will you take her near the fire and keep her warm?" Mercy held the infant out to him.

Ben feared the baby would start crying again if he took her.

"I need a moment of privacy," Mercy said, blushing a deep red, "to take care of myself."

"Oh," Ben said, though he wasn't certain exactly what she meant. He almost offered assistance but thought better of it, as Mercy's sense of modesty had obviously returned and he didn't wish to embarrass her. He held the newborn close to his chest as he carried her into the next room.

"Call out if you need me," he said as he closed the bedroom door behind him.

The rocking chair stood close to the stove and Ben

settled there, cradling the tiny infant so that he could study her face.

"Well . . ." Ben searched for something to call her. Mercy hadn't mentioned a name. "My little niece, I'm your Uncle Benjamin. You can call me Ben." The baby seemed to watch him with interest. He wondered whether that could be the case.

"What do you think of this great, wide world?"

He examined her features—eyes a dark blue color, a tiny button nose, small pink lips that she was now puckering in a most appealing way.

"Are you flirting already?" Ben couldn't help smiling. "I don't suppose your father will like that. He's liable to lock you up to keep the men away."

He stroked her soft cheek.

"You are a lucky little girl—do you know that? You have a remarkable family. Your mother and father to start. And then there is your Aunt Miranda. You'll like her, I think. She's very pretty and full of life. Her smile could rival sunshine." He watched the little mouth stretch into a huge yawn before her eyes drifted shut. "I seem to have bored you to sleep with my rambling." He brushed a kiss on the tiny girl's forehead. "I have a secret to tell you. I think you're going to have a little cousin soon."

Ben imagined holding his own precious bundle and watching Miranda's smile light up the room when she held their newborn infant in her arms for the first time. He would be there for certain. Only death would keep him away from that moment.

Chapter 22

The sun rose clear and bright, reflecting off the snow as though the ground were covered with diamonds. Mercy and the baby were sleeping and Ben did not want to wake them, but he was growing worried. Miranda would expect Mercy to be anxious—she would ride home as soon as possible.

Yet more than an hour after sunrise, Miranda had not arrived. Mercy had said it would take less than an hour to ride from the small cabin to the big house, even allowing for heavy snow drifts that could slow the horses. If she hadn't found Jonathan in the cabin, Miranda might have continued searching; but that seemed unlikely. It would have made more sense for Miranda to return to make certain that someone else hadn't already brought Jonathan home, to learn where others had already searched, and to let everyone know that he wasn't in the cabin.

Whether she found him or not, she should be here by now.

A familiar sound drew Ben's attention. Baby was starting to fuss. Mercy refused to give the child a name until Thad and Jonathan returned. Ben called her "Baby." He lifted the little one from her cradle.

"Oh!" Ben said. "You little devil—you've wet all your blankets."

"That's a good sign. A healthy baby will wet herself," Mercy said through a yawn. She pulled off her own blankets and stood next to the cradle. "I'll take her."

Ben handed the child to her mother gratefully since he had no idea what to do. Mercy took her, cleaned her, and wrapped her in fresh linens. She made her way into the main room of the house and lowered herself gingerly onto the rocker that sat near the stove. Ben brought Mercy's shawl from the bed and placed it around her shoulders. She smiled up at him.

"I'm worried about Miranda," he said.

Mercy looked up at the clock and frowned. "I'd have thought they would be back by now." Baby made little fussing sounds and Ben turned his back as Mercy reached for the buttons on the front of her gown.

"I hate to leave you alone." He glanced over his shoulder, making sure that Mercy had the baby settled under the shawl before he pulled a chair next to her.

"You should go." She favored him with a weak smile. "We'll be fine." She reached a hand out to him and he squeezed it. "Don't worry about us."

"I've no doubt by the time I get back you'll be splitting wood or plowing fields."

Mercy laughed. "I would, naturally, except that cattle ranchers don't plow." Mercy grew serious. "I'll never find a way to thank you for all you've done for us."

Ben nodded. "You did the hard work. All I did was watch."

Mercy smiled. "I'm very grateful to you, yet here I am asking another favor. Bring the rest of my family home to me?"

"I'll probably run across Miranda and Jonathan on their way here."

"Do you mind a word of advice?" She gripped his hand. "Don't let her out of your sight again without letting her know how you really feel about her."

"I don't deserve her."

"I'd have agreed with you had you made that statement on your wedding day. I can't be right all the time." Mercy sighed. "I'm sorry I . . . shouldn't have let her go off alone."

"You make it sound as though you could have stopped her. I know my wife better than that."

"I reckon you're right, but I should have tried to keep her here."

"It isn't as though either of you expected her to be out in that storm all night."

Mercy frowned. "Don't worry too much about Miranda. She's strong, and the child she's carryin' will be fine."

"You know about the baby?"

"Suspected. How long has she known?"

"She hasn't actually told me. I . . ."

"An observant husband couldn't fail to notice."

Ben smiled. He hadn't been any kind of a husband to her, but he hoped to have the chance to change that.

"Please bring her home."

"I will. I'll bring all of them home."

* * *

Ben wanted to urge Lightning into a gallop, but that would be dangerous on the thick snow, so he allowed the horse to set the pace as he found his footing. All the while Ben scanned the horizon for some sign of Miranda, or Thad, or Jonathan. Or the last man on earth he wanted to see—O'Reilly.

When he sighted the cabin, he first felt relief to see smoke emerging from the chimney, but that was short lived. If it had been Miranda who had made that fire, she would now be on her way to the house. He could only conclude that it wasn't Miranda in the cabin. Or if she was in there, something was wrong.

It was the latter thought that made Ben circle wide away from the cabin and into the cottonwoods along the creek to the southeast. He tethered his horse deep in the trees and peered out at the cabin.

Miranda's horse, Princess, was there along with Thad's and Jonathan's horses. He shook his head. Something did not feel right. Then he heard them. Following the sounds through the trees, he found three horses. He recognized a squat sorrel gelding—O'Reilly's ride. *Damn!*

He made his way back to the edge of the trees and tried to remember everything he could about the cabin. Unlike the place he shared with Miranda, this one had only two small windows flanking the door on the south side of the building. The other walls were solid to help keep out the bitter cold winds that often swept across the high plains.

It was perhaps 150 yards from the woods to the house, and there was no cover in any direction. Ben was fairly certain that the northernmost part of the woods was out of the line of vision from either window. If he left the woods there and aimed for the northern side of the cabin, he would not be seen. Once he was close, he could decide how to get inside.

He made an arcing path from the woods to the cabin, running as swiftly as possible through the snow. If someone happened outside while he was in the open, he'd be seen and would lose all chance of surprise.

Once he stood outside the cabin, he leaned against the thick wall, listening. It was damn hard to hear with his heart pounding in his ears. He fought to calm his breath and slow his heartbeat. Miranda's life might well depend on his actions now. He did not allow himself to dwell on the thought that O'Reilly and his lot might have already ended her life. Then he heard it—Miranda's voice.

Chapter 23

"He's just a boy!" Miranda shouted. Ben would recognize her angry voice anywhere.

His heart skipped a beat. She was still alive and likely so was Jonathan. Ben aimed to keep it that way. His mind raced. A part of him wanted nothing more than to burst into the room with his Colt blazing. Good sense stopped him.

Surprise would likely get him a shot or two before O'Reilly and his men started shooting; but there were three horses, which meant there were probably three men. He couldn't count on being quick and accurate enough to kill all three of them before they could shoot him. And he'd be taking a huge risk that Miranda and Jonathan would be hit by a stray bullet.

He didn't dare risk going for help. His best chance was to wait until someone came outside. If he was lucky, one or two men would come out to relieve themselves, or check on the horses. He'd be ready for them.

Almost before he could complete the thought, the door opened. Ben flattened himself against the rough wall just as Miranda led Jonathan around the corner and within feet of where Ben hid. Jed followed right behind them, his gun aimed at Miranda's back. *Damn!*

"You might give us some privacy!" Miranda snapped.

"I ain't lettin' you outta my sight." Jed motioned with his gun. "Go on, right here."

Miranda stooped to help the boy with his pants.

"I can't," Jonathan sobbed.

Miranda turned and glared at Jed, revealing an ugly purple bruise on one side of her face. Ben ground his teeth together and forced himself to be silent. Her eyes flicked to Ben for an instant, but she returned to glaring at Jed.

"Really, Jed. Are you afraid of a woman and a little boy? Where are we going to go? There's nothing around but wide, open country. You can shoot us easy if we start to run."

"O'Reilly give me orders."

"I suppose you let that drunken Irishman do your thinkin' for you?"

"Hell no."

"Then holster the gun, Jed. You're scaring the boy half to death. He can't relieve himself with a gun pointed at him."

Good girl. Keep talking now. Ben crept silently forward.

"Fine." Jed let the barrel of his gun drop. "One minute now. Get on with it—it's colder'n blazes out here."

As the scrawny cowboy inserted his pistol into his holster, Ben knocked the man cold with a blow to the head.

Miranda wisely clamped a hand over Jonathan's

mouth. "Stay quiet, you hear?" she whispered in the boy's ear. He nodded.

"How many inside?" Ben whispered as he grabbed Jed's gun.

"O'Reilly and another man they call Dally. Thad's in there, too. He was shot in the arm, but it's not too bad. He'll be fine if we can get him home. They've got him tied up in the corner."

Ben handed her Jed's pistol. "Take the boy and run for those trees."

Miranda started to protest.

Ben cut her off. "I want the boy clear of here in case there's any shooting." He took her hand and squeezed it. "Please?"

Miranda nodded.

"Good." He bent to talk to Jonathan. "Go with Aunt Miranda. Run that way"—he pointed—"so they won't see you from the window."

Miranda shot Ben a grim look, but she took Jonathan's hand and tugged him along behind her as she moved quickly toward the trees. Ben waited until they were out of sight before creeping around to the front corner of the house. He sucked in a deep breath, then let it out slowly as he took a step toward the door.

A soft creak sent him flying back to the side of the cabin. The door was opening again.

"Jed?" The gravelly voice must belong to Dally. "What the hell's keeping you out there? You playing with the girl, or the little boy?" The man laughed.

Ben forced himself to stay back, though he wanted to tear Dally limb from limb. "Come look." He tried to imitate Jed's high, nasally voice and muffled the sound by speaking into his hand.

"It's cold as Hades out here, Jed." Dally came

around the corner directly into Ben's fist. Before he could cry out, Ben shoved him face-first into the snow and straddled him. He pressed a gun against the side of the man's head with his left hand. Ben wasn't certain he could pull the trigger with his damaged hand, but Dally didn't need to know that.

Ben glanced over to where Jed remained motionless. That wouldn't last much longer. He fished out his own kerchief and shoved it into Dally's mouth. He holstered his gun long enough to tie the gag in place with Dally's bandanna. The numb fingers of his right hand were nearly as useless as the stubs on his left, but he managed a knot that would hold. Ben used Dally's belt to tie the man's wrists behind his back. He removed his own belt and used it around Dally's ankles. When he was certain Dally was no further threat, he hurried over to Jed. What he needed was some good rope, but there wasn't any at hand. He pulled off his tie and bound the unconscious man's hands, cursing the lack of dexterity in his numb fingers. The clumsy knot would have to do—he didn't dare take any more time.

Ben slid back along the wall of the cabin and peeked around the corner. No sign of O'Reilly. He crept under the window and knelt beside the door, flung it open, then plastered himself against the outside wall.

"What the hell?" O'Reilly bellowed. "It's cold enough in here without leaving the door wide open."

O'Reilly stomped across the floor. Ben greeted him with a pistol leveled at his gut. "You're going to be a hell of a lot colder before we get to the sheriff's office, O'Reilly."

Ben grabbed the man and shoved him back through the door.

"Glad to see you, Ben," Thad drawled from the floor.

"Face down on the floor!" Ben ordered, shoving O'Reilly down. He took the guns out of O'Reilly's holster and checked him thoroughly for other weapons.

"You all right, Buchanan?" Ben asked.

"Just tell me my son is unharmed."

"Miranda has him safe outside." Ben found some twine and tied O'Reilly's hands. "Your wife and daughter are also doing well."

"Daughter?" Thad struggled to sit up; his hands and legs were still bound.

"A beautiful baby girl." Ben pulled his watch from his vest pocket. "About six hours old now." He found a knife and cut Thad loose. "How bad is it?" He nodded toward Thad's bloody arm.

"It's nothing. O'Reilly's a lousy shot."

"I should have killed you when I had the chance, Buchanan."

Ben glared at the Irishman's back. "I'm going to need to gag him." He handed O'Reilly's gun to Thad. "Keep an eye on him, will you?"

Ben dashed out the door. Finding Jed struggling to his feet, Ben slammed his fist to the man's jaw, knocking him back down. "I should put a bullet through your head, you son of a bitch." He rolled Jed on his face and pulled his arms behind his back. "I saw the bruises on my wife's face."

"It wasn't me."

"I don't give a damn which one of you hit her!"

He pulled the lanky man to his feet and dragged him inside, then went back out for Dally.

"Thad's anxious to use that pistol on you boys," Ben said. "Don't get any ideas about running for the door," he said before dashing off to find Miranda and Jonathan.

They met him at the edge of the trees. He pulled his wife and nephew close to him and kissed Miranda gently, careful not to touch the bruises on her face.

"You're safe now, love," he whispered to Miranda before lifting Jonathan up onto his shoulders. "Come on, lad, we're going to collect your father and take you home. Your mother has someone she wants you to meet."

"Someone?" Miranda asked. "The baby?"

He winked at her. "A girl."

"Leave it to Mercy to give birth on her own."

"You mean my brother's a girl?" Jonathan asked.

Ben grinned. "She's a sister, I'm afraid."

"There's nothing wrong with girls, Jonathan," Miranda said.

"Nothing wrong at all." Ben took Miranda's hand in his and led her back to the cabin. He leaned toward her and pitched his voice low. "I have to ask—who hit you?"

"It was O'Reilly. Don't worry, I made him regret it." She gave Ben what he supposed was intended to be a victorious smile.

He draped an arm over her shoulder, wishing there was a way to hold her close forever and keep her in the shelter of his arm. "I'm quite certain he'll rue the day he faced you." He pulled her close.

When they reached the cabin, Ben directed Miranda to wait with Jonathan on the side. "I want to be sure it's safe before you come in."

Miranda nodded and held Jonathan close. She heard Ben stomp across the wooden floor of the cabin.

"O'Reilly!" Ben shouted. Miranda heard a grunt and a crash.

"Stay right here," she whispered to Jonathan as she stepped around to the front of the cabin, cocking the gun Ben had given her before peeking in the window.

"That's enough!" Thad shouted as Ben landed a punch to O'Reilly's jaw.

"The man needs to learn a gentleman doesn't hit a lady." Ben punctuated this statement with a fist to O'Reilly's gut, knocking him against the wall.

"I believe he's learned his lesson. Haven't you, O'Reilly?"

"Shut up . . . Buchanan." The Irishman sank to his knees.

Ben pulled him up. "Come outside, O'Reilly. A bit of fresh air will revive you." He pushed the man out the door, marched him to a snowdrift, and shoved him into it face-first. "Refreshing, isn't it?" Ben asked as he grabbed a handful of hair and used it to pull O'Reilly's head out of the snow. "Just once more, now." He shoved O'Reilly's face back into the snow.

Miranda carefully released the hammer on Jed's pistol. *Men!* She marched back to where Jonathan was waiting. Ben wanted to protect her. He had a lot of silly notions about how to do that. Marrying her. Beating O'Reilly to a pulp. Leaving her.

Miranda wrapped two blankets over Jonathan's shoulders and tied them under his chin. It would be a cold ride home, and the boy hadn't worn his warm coat.

"I wish you'd change your mind," Ben said.

"I'm going with you." Miranda lifted her chin

and glared at Ben, a sure sign he'd better stop arguing with her.

She helped Jonathan mount Pegasus and tied another blanket around the boy's waist.

Thad rode Zeus up next to his son. "Bury the boy in blankets and he won't be able to ride."

"He'll be better able to ride if he isn't freezing," Miranda snapped.

Thad had sense enough not to respond. Ben smiled. His wife might be petite, but she knew how to take charge of a situation.

"You should go home with Thad and Jonathan." Ben held Lightning's reins in one hand and Princess's in the other.

"I'm going with you," she said. "Thad, you tell him."

"She's right, Ben. It's too dangerous for you to take those three alone. I'd come with you myself, but—"

"Someone has to get Jonathan home," Miranda interrupted. She figured it was useless to mention the fact that her brother-in-law was injured and had no business making the two-hour ride into town. The bullet had torn through the fleshy part of Thad's arm and didn't appear to have damaged the bone. He was lucky. Still, the man should be resting, not riding across slippery, frozen ground. Miranda had fashioned a sling to hold Thad's wounded arm steady. But it would surely be a painful ride.

Miranda said the only thing she knew would persuade Thad: "Mercy will be anxious to see for herself that you're all right." She turned back to Ben. "I'm going with you."

Ben and Thad had tethered O'Reilly's, Jed's, and Dally's horses together and tied each man to his saddle. They were all gagged and unarmed. Miranda would lead the way into town, and Ben would ride in the rear with one gun aimed directly at O'Reilly's back and two more fully loaded pistols in his belt.

"Thad needs—"

"Don't worry about me, I have Jonathan to help me. Right, buddy?"

"Right, Papa."

"You just get O'Reilly and his lot to the sheriff." Thad nodded in the direction of O'Reilly, Jed and Dally. "And don't forget to collect that reward."

"Reward?"

Miranda's heart sank.

"It's not the five thousand you came for, but five hundred dollars is a lot of money."

More than enough for passage to the Sandwich Islands where Ben could start a new life. Without her.

Ben and Miranda watched Thad and Jonathan ride away before they mounted.

"Please give me an excuse to shoot you, O'Reilly," Ben said as they set off.

Miranda was going to scream. She was exhausted and starving and everything was taking three times longer than it needed to. The ride into town had been so lonely. Three men behind her mostly silent for fear Ben would shoot them. He would have, too. She'd never seen him so angry.

When they finally made it to town, the sheriff had to hear her story at least five times. The worst was when he insisted on giving Ben the damn reward—the money that would take him away from her forever. She had to smile and pretend she was happy to see her husband receive such a large amount of money, and make believe that the money would be theirs, not his.

They spent another eternity signing papers. Ben silently followed all the sheriff's instructions, hardly speaking a word. If Ben would only say something, talk about his plans, maybe it would be bearable. Once he told her he was leaving, she could find a way to let him go. But announcing he intended to leave would go against everything he'd promised her. He would act the good husband until he disappeared and left her a widow in the minds of the good people of Fort Victory. Miranda was certain of one thing—when the day came, she'd have no trouble playing her part. She would grieve the loss of Ben Lansing.

By the time the lawman was done with them, Clarisse and Buck and Pa had found them at the sheriff's office.

After quick greetings, Clarisse got to the point. "You must be starving." She looked directly at Miranda. "I fixed some dinner for my boys and Fenton and Buck here. There's plenty of stew left."

"We need to be goin' if we're goin' to make it home before dark," Miranda said. "Do you have something we could carry with us? Maybe some apples, or—"

"Miranda!" Clarisse frowned. "You need to be takin' care of yourself."

"Don't be silly, Clarisse. I'm fine."

"Would you like me to list *all* of the reasons you should have some food and rest?"

Miranda glanced from Ben to Pa. If she wasn't careful, Clarisse was going to tell her secret right now in front of everyone. Miranda opened her mouth to respond.

"I'd be happy for a hot meal," Ben said.

Miranda was relieved. "I reckon we could stay long enough for some stew, since you said it was ready and all."

"Don't be silly." Clarisse looked at Miranda. "You've had enough riding today. It would be best for your whole *family* if you rest in town tonight."

Miranda was going to have to kick Clarisse if she said another word.

"Food and a warm bed." Ben seemed to brighten for the first time in hours. "That sounds inviting. You don't mind, do you, love?"

Miranda stared at Ben. He was using his snake-oil-salesman grin. "But Mercy will be worried about us."

"We're on our way back to the ranch, Miranda." Buck slapped Pa on the back. "Grandpa here can't wait to see that new baby."

"You laugh now, bachelor," Pa said, "but one day you'll know what it's like to worry about your children."

Buck laughed. "Fenton, if you think for a minute some woman is gonna lasso and hog-tie me, you're mistaken."

Ben pulled Miranda close. She knew it was all part of his loving husband act, but she couldn't help herself: she enjoyed having his arm around her. Hell, she was not going to turn weak now. She had her baby to think about. Let Ben leave. She was going to get along fine without him.

Miranda shrugged out of Ben's embrace and threw her arms around Pa. "Give the baby a kiss for me. And tell Mercy I'll come see her tomorrow."

Pa kissed his daughter's forehead. "I'll tell her." He

looked over at Ben. "You two go on and have some hot food. Make this one rest, will you? She looks terrible."

"I'll have to take issue with you there, sir." Ben took hold of her hand. "Miranda's the most beautiful woman in the Territory."

Pa smiled. "As I have two daughters, you'll forgive me if I say Miranda has one equal."

"You've both gone mad," Miranda said. She gave her father another kiss. "Take care of yourself, Pa. I'll see you tomorrow."

"Bye, now." Pa nodded and turned to follow Buck. As they watched the old man walk toward the stable, Miranda's stomach growled. "We'd better get you fed, love," Ben said.

She scowled at him, then strolled slowly across the street so as not to appear too anxious to eat the stew that Clarisse had promised.

Miranda knew Ben was going to say good-bye to her as soon as he had a chance. He had his money now. There was no reason to stay any longer. As they sat around Clarisse's kitchen table and she told the story of her captivity one last time, he hardly looked at her. And though he must have been as hungry as she was, he spent more time moving the stew around in his bowl than he did eating.

Rita came bursting in through the back door. "Miranda, *Dios mío!*" She came and squeezed Miranda's shoulders. "I just heard what happened. Look at your face. The *son of a beech*, he hit you. I will be happy to see that man hang."

"The important thing is that everyone is going to be fine," Clarisse said. "Miranda could have been much more seriously injured."

Miranda felt Ben's eyes on her. He wasn't her true husband in any way that mattered, but that didn't keep him from feeling protective of her. It was a small crust of bread, and she relished it as any beggar would.

"Clarisse is right," Miranda said. "O'Reilly and his lot are in jail, and none of us was badly injured. It's over." She shot Ben a look that caused his stomach to plummet. "And there's good news, too. Rita, did you hear that Mercy had her baby?"

"It's a girl." Ben grinned. "She's tiny and . . . perfect."

Miranda looked over at him. "Ben was there to help, thank the Lord."

Ben looked around at the curious faces. "I went to the house hoping maybe Thad or one of the others had found Jonathan. Expected Miranda to be there, but Mercy was alone. I didn't dare leave her. Then the blizzard hit and—"

"I'm glad you were there, Ben." Miranda reached over and squeezed his hand. "Everything worked out for the best."

"It was Wendell who helped when our Robert was born," Clarisse said. "We were hauling a wagon with all our worldly goods from San Francisco to Fort Victory. Don't let anyone tell you a man can't be helpful with a birth."

"Well, Mercy did all the real work." Ben flushed as all the women in the room laughed.

"Miranda, I expect you're tired," Clarisse said. "I'll take you upstairs where you can lie down."

"No, no!" Rita said. "Come with me. I have a room with a bed and a hot bath."

"We can't afford—" Miranda started.

"*Gratis, gratis.* No charge for you. Consider it my thanks for your part in bringing O'Reilly to justice, *si*?"

And so they were swept away again. More helpfulness. At least this time it seemed as though the Good Samaritan intended to leave them alone. Ben followed behind as Miranda pranced next to Rita. The meal had revived his wife, and that walk was arousing some desires he intended to ignore. He'd talk to Miranda, then let her rest.

As he followed the ladies into the saloon, he wondered how long he'd be able to let his wife sleep. They passed the stairs and went to a back hallway and through a plush sitting room. The fine carpeting and furniture were different from anything Ben had seen in Fort Victory and a good deal more luxurious than the room Ben had stayed in upstairs.

Rita opened the door at the end of the hall and stepped ahead of them into a large bedroom. She opened the drapes and the winter sunlight revealed a sitting area at one end of the room, with upholstered chairs around a tea table. At the other end sat a large wardrobe and a huge four-poster bed, with a canopy of red velvet curtains hanging over it. In the middle of the room sat a large iron stove and a polished brass bathtub.

"The stove, she is hot." Rita opened the iron door and added more wood. "The water tank is full. Open the tap for hot water when you like a bath. There is cold water in the bucket if you need." Rita beamed a smile at them. "Only enough water for one bath. You will improvise, I think." She strolled over to the door, then turned with the knob in her hand. "I bring you supper later, if you like." Rita smiled at Ben. "You will find me in the kitchen."

Rita disappeared out the door and Miranda walked over to the tub. "Damn, that's big."

Her voice expressed such awe that Ben couldn't help but laugh.

"I've seen bathtubs before," Miranda said. "Don't want you to think I'm that ignorant. But, damn!"

"I'm not laughing at you," Ben said, pulling her into his arms. "I'm so glad to have you safe with me again."

He held her close, breathing her in. It was almost too perfect. Too good to be true. Here he was with a chance to finally talk and he couldn't find the words for fear he'd say the wrong thing and she'd send him packing.

"Miranda." He brushed a kiss to her forehead. "I wish I'd gone after you last night."

"It would have been plumb foolish to go out in that storm. Mercy knew where I was heading, that I would have been in the shelter before the worst of the storm. There was no reason for you to risk—"

"There was a reason, dammit." Ben touched her bruised jaw. "I worried about you. Mercy did reassure me, but . . ." Ben pulled away from her. "Miranda, I was worried something would happen to the . . . our baby."

Miranda looked up at him then, her eyes unreadable. "You knew?"

Ben took her hand in his. "I've been waiting for you to tell me. I . . . you're not . . . sorry about the baby, are you?"

"Sorry?" Miranda wet her lips as she searched for words to explain. "I want this baby more than anything." She looked into his dark eyes, asking silent forgiveness for the little lie she was telling. There was one thing she wanted more, but she'd settle for what was possible. "Please don't . . . I don't want you to feel any obligation. This . . . this gift is so much

nore than I—" She sniffed and wiped at a tear that
rolled down her cheek.

"Don't." Ben pressed his warm palm against her
cheek. "Don't cry, love."

There it was again. That name that meant so
much to her and so little to him. She hated him calling her that. He pulled her into his arms and she let
him. She allowed herself to feel warm and shel-
tered. A few more months. At least now she didn't
have to worry about keeping the baby a secret any
longer. She could have Ben with her until spring.
After all her brave planning, she was too damn selfish to let him go one minute before.

For a heartbeat she imagined that he might even
want to stay long enough to see his child born into the
world. He seemed genuinely moved by the birth he'd
witnessed last night. But she couldn't ask him to stay.

"You don't have to . . ." Miranda drew in a deep
breath. "I don't want you to feel obligated because
of the baby. The reward money will get you to your
tropical island." Miranda walked over to the window
and stared out at the alley that ran behind Rita's all
the way to the Wyatts' store. "You might not be able
to get to San Francisco before spring. The roads over
the mountains can be . . ."

"Miranda?" Ben stepped over to her. "Do you
want me to leave?"

"The truth?" Miranda worried her lip. It was so
damn hard to look at him. "You've asked a complicated question." Miranda walked over to the stove and
held her hands over the radiant heat. She rubbed
them together and stretched them out again.

Ben shoved a hand in his pocket. "It wasn't a fair
question . . ."

"No, I want to answer." She looked over at him.

"This isn't easy for me. But I may as well say my piece." She brushed a loose curl away from her eye. "I don't want you to leave."

Ben let out a breath.

"I do understand, though, why you have to go." Miranda crossed her arms as though she were hugging herself. Another tear trickled down one cheek.

"Don't cry, Miranda. I don't . . . have to go." Ben wiped the tear away with his thumb. "I don't want to go."

"No." She stepped back. "Ben, please don't make this any harder than it has to be. Last night, I had a lot of time to think about . . . us. How you were forced into this marriage. I . . . Can you forgive me?"

"Forgive you?" He had to touch her. "Miranda." He squeezed her shoulder. "I am a man who has been struck by lightning and survived it. Whether it was luck, or fate, or the grace of God, I don't know. But I am not forgiving you—I am grateful to you."

She tilted her head and wrinkled her forehead as though puzzling through his words.

"I won't leave you, not ever. If you'll have me for your true husband, with all the promises honest between us this time. Loving and cherishing and all—until death."

"Ben." Miranda gulped back her tears. She couldn't allow him to make this sacrifice. "I'll be fine here with my family. They'll help me with the baby. There's no need for you—"

Ben dropped to his knees in front of her, then gave her a pleading look that was almost too much for her to bear. "This child we created is . . . well, it's something I never expected." He placed a hand over her belly. "I promise to try and be a good father. I'm not certain I know how, and I don't want to make a promise that I can't keep. But if effort counts for anything, our children will know that I love them. That's all I can do."

Miranda stared at him. He'd said *children*. "You . . . Is this because of Mercy and seeing her baby?"

"No." He looked up at her. "I won't forget the miracle I witnessed last night and, yes, it made me think of you and our baby." He drew in a deep breath. He held Miranda's beautiful, graceful hand with his maimed one. They were meant to be together. Perfection and imperfection joining to make a life together. He kissed her palm. "I want you to know that I'm not staying for the child's sake, or for your sake. The honest truth is, I need you. I need your smile." He swallowed the lump that was forming in his throat. "And your way of seeing so much life around you—the smell of the earth after a rain, the miracle of a spider's web. All the things that I never noticed before you showed them to me. Even more than that, I need the way you make me feel—that I'm a man who has a right to be alive. I . . ."

She dropped to her knees then, kissing him and sending jolts of desire through him. He managed to get control over himself, to keep from pressing her back to the floor and driving himself inside of her. He was determined to take care of this precious woman and the tiny bit of life they'd made inside of her, and right now that meant getting her a nice hot bath and a good night's rest. "I love you, Miranda."

"I love you, Ben," she whispered into his neck. "I'll always love you."

"Let me fill the tub for you. I'm sure a nice hot bath—"

"Plenty of time for a hot bath later." She bent to open the buttons of his trousers. "Right now, there's something else I need. And months to go before I'm too big for you to want me."

There it was—the spark of sunlight in her eyes that could make him forget everything but her. "There won't ever be a time I don't want you." He scooped her into his arms and carried her over to the big bed. "You're certain it's safe?"

"Safe?"

"The baby." He set her gently on the bed. "I don't want to do anything that—"

But she'd found her way inside his pants and his last good sense left him.

"The only danger now is you may drive me to distraction if you don't come inside me soon." She pulled him down onto the bed, straddled him and bent to kiss him.

"Patience, my love," Ben mumbled through wet kisses.

She pulled back and smiled. "Say that again?"

Her smile was like sunshine peeking through clouds, and it warmed him in places the sun couldn't begin to reach.

"Patience." He pulled her back down to him. "Patience." He nibbled on her ear.

"Oh, Ben," she sighed. "Not the patience part. What you called me a minute ago."

He thought for a moment, then smiled. "Oh, my love." He brushed a kiss to her soft lips. "My love. My Miranda. Now and forever."

About the Author

Teresa Bodwell grew up in the West writing stories
in spiral notebooks, journals, and the odd scrap of
paper. After serving in the U.S. Army where she
helped make the world safe for John Philip Sousa
music, she read her first romance novel and knew
she had found her niche. Teresa lives in western
Montana where she practices law, marriage, raising children, and leading Girl Scout troops. She
hopes to get all of these things right one day. Visit
her website at *www.tbodwell.com*.